D0629957

A Journal to Read and Write

Sharon M. Draper

Scholastic Inc.   New York

Library of Congress Cataloging-in-Publication Data

Draper, Sharon M. (Sharon Mills)
Jazzimagination : a journal to read and write / Sharon M. Draper.
p. cm.
Summary: Thirteen-year-old Jazzy keeps a journal in which she records her thoughts about family, friends, boys, school, dreams, nature, and colors. Provides space for readers to record their own thoughts and feelings.
ISBN 0-439-06130-X (hardcover)
[1. Diaries Fiction.   2. Afro-Americans Fiction.]   I. Title.
PZ7.D78325Jaz   1999
[Fic]—dc21   99-20040
CIP

12 11 10 9 8 7 6 5 4 3 2 1   0 1 2 3 4 5/0

Printed in the U.S.A.   37
First Scholastic printing, November 1999

To Crystal, Kelsey, and Ebonne —
who helped me remember
what I'll never forget

A Note From Jazzy

Dear Friend,

I write in my journal every day - not boring stuff, like what color sweater I wore to school today, but thoughts that have been floating in my mind. I grab the thoughts and toss them into this book, where they wait for me to read again when I want to.

I'm going to let you read my journal because maybe you've had some of the same kinds of thoughts, and maybe it will help you to know that you're not the only one who feels that way.

I left blank pages after each chapter and lots of extra pages in the back, in case you want to write your own thoughts. Feel free to share your ideas with mine.

Love, Jazzy

Who Am I?

My name is Jasmine Joy Jeffries and I'm thirteen years old. All my friends call me Jazzy, but I really don't like jazz music much. Mama says I'll like it when I'm older. If that's what I have to listen to when I'm old, I can wait. I hate waiting. Waiting for Devin, my older brother, to get out of the bathroom is the worst. How can anyone stay in the bathroom so long and still smell awful when he comes out? I think most boys smell like walking armpits anyway. They put deodorant on to cover it up, but it's hard to hide.

The only boy I know who is not totally obnoxious is a boy at school named Mandela. He's tall and quiet, and when he smiles at me in study hall,

I feel nervous and sweaty. On top of that, he smells good! I sat next to him in an assembly one day and he smelled like fresh soap and new leather. I could hardly breathe. It was wonderful! Of course, I don't <u>like</u> this boy or anything, but he's nice to think about just before I go to sleep, when the sheets on my bed are fresh and clean and my pillow is just right.

I like to sleep. I take my sleeping very seriously. I need three pillows, lots of covers, my dog at the foot of my bed, and my favorite stuffed animals close by. I'm too old to sleep with them officially, but I allow myself to keep them nearby. I like the shades pulled down, the door closed, and the lights off. Good dreams come only in the black darkness of a cozy bed. I don't even wake up for thunderstorms or alarm clocks.

I live in Ohio, which I think is pretty boring. I live with my pets and my brother and my parents - in that order - in a big, old, ordinary-looking house that you'd never even notice if you drove past it. I go to school, I have a sloppy room, and I dream about places I've never seen and possibilities I can only imagine. My dreams are like soft whispers in my mind - I'm afraid to say them out loud, even to myself.

I guess I'm pretty much like every other girl my age, yet it occurred to me the other day that of all the humans on the face of the earth, there is no one else exactly like me. I'm all alone. That's scary. But that's also special. I'm unique in the universe. No duplications. Just me.

Now I'm scared again.

Yesterday I looked at myself in the mirror. Up close. I'm not sure if I liked what I saw or not. My eyebrows are too bushy, my mouth is too wide, and my nose is crooked. I counted seventeen potential zits and I think I'm getting wrinkles. Am I too young to get wrinkles? I wonder what I'd look like with green contact lenses.

I do like my face - from a distance. People say I have a friendly smile, and I guess I look okay. At least no one runs screaming into the night when they first see me. I wonder if I'm pretty. My mother says I look just fine. What does that mean? My father says I'm cute, but he also says that puppies, goldfish, and little, tiny finger sandwiches are cute. So where does that leave me?

My eyelashes are curly. I heard that pretty girls have curly lashes - or was that long lashes? I don't remember. What will I do if the hair in my nose starts to grow too long? Are teeth supposed to be bright white like in TV commercials or pale yellowish like mine? Did I brush today? Do I have bad breath?

When I put on lipstick, I look older, sophisticated, and a little scary, like I'm getting ready for a costume party. How will I ever learn to put on makeup? And if I do, will it help?

What if I have to get glasses? Or braces? Nobody will want to kiss me with braces on my teeth. It might take three years to get them off. That's a long time to wait to be kissed. I don't think I want to be kissed anyway, but I wonder what a boy's lips feel like. Probably like kissing a goldfish. Maybe not. There's got to be something good about it, or nobody would do it. There's so much I can't figure out.

I don't really know what I look like. Everybody else has seen the real me, but I've only seen myself in the mirror. Maybe I look different to myself than I do to other people. When I look at a photograph of myself, it doesn't look like what I see in the mirror. I've seen my hands and my body, but I've never really seen my face. Do mirrors tell the truth? Do pictures? Or do I look completely different than I think I do, and I'm the only one who doesn't know?

My Body

I used to like my body. It was always the same - strong and dependable and ready to take me where I needed to go. I could run faster and jump rope longer than most of the kids on my street. Lately, though, my body seems like it has a mind of its own. It gets strange pains that I never had before, and on days when I need to run fast, I feel like my legs are made of jelly. Maybe I'm catching a disease. I'm sore all over and it even hurts when I get hugged too hard. My body is all uneven and it's doing things that I can't control. It's like my body has been taken over by an alien. Maybe <u>that's</u> the explanation. Maybe while I slept, Martian invaders landed on Earth, took over my

9

body, and decided to see just how miserable they could make me feel.

Sometimes I get really moody, and I cry for no reason at all. Then Mama asks me what's wrong. I tell her nothing because there really is nothing wrong - nothing I can explain, anyway. She tells me I'm just tired or hungry and to have an apple and go lay down. I hate when she says that. I'm not tired or hungry. I'm just full of stuff that has control of me and won't let go.

At school the other day, the teacher asked my friend Stephanie what was the capital of Argentina. She said, "Bismarck," burst into tears, and ran out of the room. The teacher looked at her like she was crazy, but I understood, and so did every other girl in class. It just <u>happens</u>.

Every girl in my class, even the skinny ones, thinks she's fat. All the girls with short hair want it long, and the girls with curly hair want it straight. We moan over new zits and worry about new bulges. We worry about smelling funny and doing something stupid. We worry about not being allowed to go to the bathroom when we have a man teacher and we're too embarrassed to explain why we really, <u>really</u>, have to go. We cry for no reason. We sweat and leave big stains on our blouses even though we used a gallon of deodorant that morning. Sometimes we feel like skunks with book bags - sometimes we just feel like dead meat.

Once I wrote a poem for English class on how I feel about who I am. I couldn't put it into the right words, so I compared my feelings to food. The teacher liked it. She said I had used good similes and metaphors. I was just glad I didn't have to really say how I felt, because sometimes I just don't know how. But I saved the poem because every once in a while, it explains me.

> Sometimes I feel like scrambled eggs
> all runny in the pan.
> My life's the yolk
> and I'm the joke
> and served with cheese or bran.
>
> Sometimes I feel like broken chips
> all crunchy in the bag.

My brain is fried
and raw inside
and forced to choke or gag.

Sometimes I feel like pizza sauce
all thick with garlic spice.
My mind is oil
that will not boil
and baked like rancid rice.

Sometimes I feel like chunky soup
all green with lumpy peas.
My thoughts are tossed
not worth the cost
and cooked for none to please.

My mother tells me my body will be my best friend when I'm twenty-one. I don't know if I can wait that long.

Parents are strange animals. They want you to do your best, make good grades, be happy and cheerful all the time, and eat all your vegetables. They want you to agree with them yet think for yourself. They want you to grow up but stay a kid. They want you to be everything that they never were or never could be. And they don't want to accept that maybe you won't be it, either.

Sometimes my mother really gets on my nerves. She'll decide that my room is a mess or I've been on the phone too long and start yelling at me for no reason at all. And just because I'm the kid around here, I have to get off the phone right away - even if I'm in the middle of a really important call with this boy from the bus stop who finally called me - and do something stupid, like clean my room. Why do I have to make my bed in the morning? Nobody is going to see it all day. And when I get home from school the first thing I want to do is get back in bed and rest a few minutes before starting my homework.

So why do I have to make my bed? Must be for the dog, I guess. We've got a cocker spaniel that I love to pieces. She sleeps on my bed while we're gone. She doesn't think I know, but I came home early once and her spot by my pillow was still warm. She looked at me with those big eyes as if she felt guilty. She knows Mama would never allow it. When I'm sick, I let her get up on the bed with me anyway. Mama doesn't like it, but she lets it slide because I'm feeling bad. I guess she really is okay as a mom, but I wish she wouldn't yell so much.

Daddy is tall and skinny and laughs all the time. He likes to tell funny stories and make armpit noises. Mama hates when he does that. He works at an office downtown. I don't think

he likes his job much. He'd much rather be outside in the woods, collecting bugs and leaves. I
like to walk in the woods with him. The leaves
are crunchy under our feet and the sun seems
to shine brighter because he's whistling and
happy.

Mama went with us a couple of times, but
she's happier in the house or the mall than in
the woods. She's a social worker. She helps
people who have no jobs or money or homes.
She sees lots of abused kids and families that
are really hurting. It really bothers her. Sometimes she comes home in tears. Those are days
she gets real quiet and never yells.

I'm glad there's just the four of us. There's
a girl at school who has eleven brothers and
sisters. How do they manage? It must be awful when it comes to buying shoes or groceries.
What about sharing the bathroom in the morning? I just can't imagine having that many
people in one house. At least there's always
someone to talk to. That's good. But you'd
never have a chance to be alone. That's not
so good.

In my family, if I want to find a quiet spot

to think my own private thoughts, I can do it. My brother, Devin, is a pain sometimes, but he loves me. He'll tease me until I cry, but then he'll hug me and tickle me until I'm laughing again. He's going away to college next year. It scares me to think he won't be around. Who will answer my silly questions? Who will drive me to the mall?

Mama and Daddy are there, of course, but parents have to tell you to be careful and don't waste your money on foolishness. Big brothers are there to give you five dollars and tell you to go ahead and buy that mood ring that Mama thinks is silly. Big brothers are there to cover for you when you forget to bring home your report card or you spill a whole box of bird seed down the garbage disposal. A big brother is like a parent who remembers what it's like to be a kid, because he still is one.

I guess I'll be a parent one day. But I'll never yell, because I'm never going to forget what it feels like to be thirteen. I don't think my mother was ever my age. I think she was thirty when she was born! Daddy winks at me sometimes just to remind me that he remembers what it was like. At least my parents are still married. Most of my friends' parents are divorced. They go to their dad's house on weekends or in the summer. I would hate that. Sometimes my parents fight and I get scared. I'm so afraid that I'll have to figure out how to split my love in half.

Names

I love my name. <u>Jasmine</u> rolls off my tongue like music. Jasmine is a flower that grows wild and beautiful. Jasmine is not a smell but a scent that whispers in the memory. My name is like a poem to me - I can sing it, sigh it, and feel it. It's my name and my poem. It makes me magic.

I believe in magic - not the phony old stuff you see on TV, with special boxes that hide the lady while the magician cuts her in half - but the magic of words and feelings and love. When I whisper my name into the darkness at night, I feel special and warm and okay. And when I tell someone I've just met what my name is, I feel proud and pretty, even if my hair is all messed up. My name is both a weapon when I need it and a shield from the world around me. It protects me, because it is me.

When I was in third grade and the teacher finally let us write in cursive, my favorite letter was the capital J. It has hills and loops and curves. I used to fill whole pages with my lovely, wonderful initials. I think my mama must have been in a really mellow mood when I was born, to give me a name that sounds so good and looks so good on a piece of paper. She gave me Joy as my middle name because she said that she knew I would be a joy in her life. (Some days, when I'm feeling grumpy and not acting very joyful, I bet she wonders if she did the right thing!) At any rate, I always get joy from writing my name and seeing it on paper. Jasmine Joy Jeffries! Even my friends think it's a slick name.

When I have a daughter, I want to name her something pretty and unusual and special. I like the name Crystal, because it reminds me of shiny things, and I like Jewel because I think diamonds and rubies are pretty. For that matter, Diamond is a good name for a girl. But the name I have picked out for my daughter is Shalimar. It's the name of a perfume my mother likes, but it sounds exotic and mysterious and beautiful. A girl named Shalimar would walk tall and proud and no one could imitate her. A girl with a name like that could be famous.

Some of my friends have wonderful, unusual names. There's a boy at my school whose name is LaDonTon - no kidding! I think it sounds like an African drum. His best friend is a boy named Eagle. I think it's wonderful when people are creative with names. It gives style and individuality to the person. But sometimes it goes too far. There's a boy at school whose last name is Topp and his first name is Table. I feel a little sorry for him. But he likes it, so who am I to criticize? We are what we are what we are.

Friends

I have one best friend. Stephanie is outra-
geous. She makes me laugh. She spent the night
at my house once and we got out the dictio-
nary and looked up all the words we could think
of that had to do with sex. (She knew quite a
few more than I did.) We took turns reading the
definitions out loud. It's amazing what the dic-
tionary will print! We laughed so hard we were
rolling on the floor. Mama came in to see what
we were doing. We held our breath, swallowed
our giggles, looked at her seriously - and told her
we were trying to increase our vocabulary. I
tried to hold the laugh in, but it exploded out of
my mouth and we were rolling hysterically once

again. Mama just smiled, shook her head, and shut the door.

When Stephanie sleeps over, we hardly sleep at all. We order pizza, then we make popcorn or tacos. We talk late into the night about boys and sex and stuff we'd die before we told our mothers. Or sometimes we look at fashion magazines and pretend we're models or pick out outfits we wish we could find at the mall.

When Stephanie and I go to the mall, we always have an adventure. We don't need money to have fun. We try on clothes and shoes and look at the boys who are looking at us. Once we walked into our favorite clothing store - the one that sells stuff in the sizes and styles we like - and the lady asked us if we'd like to model for the day. Talk about being excited! She gave us these really sharp outfits to wear and then told us to stand stiff and unmoving in the window - like mannequins. She said if we could stand there real still for an hour, she'd give us ten dollars each. It was fun at first, but after about five minutes my elbow started to itch, I felt like I had to sneeze, and I really wanted to giggle. I looked over at Stephanie.

She was wiggling only a little, but then a really cute boy started jumping up and down, making monkey faces, and trying to make us laugh. Finally, I sneezed and Stephanie laughed. Then I lost my balance, bumped into her, and we both fell into a heap in the store window. The boy making monkey faces cracked up and then disappeared into the crowd. The lady laughed and told us we'd never make it as professional models. She took our picture, though, and gave us three dollars for trying. Of course, we bought food. Best hamburgers we ever had!

My life isn't very exciting. But last year Stephanie and I had a trip to the mall that ended up being really scary. We decided not to see the movie playing there because she had heard that it was stupid. She bought a pair of earrings for ninety-nine cents, then we wandered down toward the fountain, checking it for coins that people had tossed in there.

Suddenly, a tall man dressed all in black came running full speed toward us! He was sweating and looked scared. He had a brown paper bag in one hand and a gun in the other! I screamed and he looked right at me. Stephanie grabbed my hand and we ran full speed in the other direction, screaming our heads off. People started coming out of stores to see what all the commotion was about.

Then the police came around the corner, with their guns pulled out and ready! Don't they know those things can kill somebody? Screaming even louder, I ran right into a fat policeman who was behind all the rest of them and knocked him down. He grabbed me by my arms, so I screamed and kicked hysterically. I thought I was going to die! Stephanie was yelling and crying, too, and a crowd had gathered around us. The policeman finally got to his feet, let me go, and tried to calm us down. He finally figured out that we had seen the guy who was running. He had just robbed the jewelry store in the mall and had almost made a clean getaway, but we had spotted him. We described what we could remember about him, and the policeman let us go. He never even apologized for grabbing me like I was a criminal.

Five minutes later, we saw the robber in handcuffs at the far end of the mall. We still weren't breathing normally. I called Mama to come and get us right away. She said it's a shame that kids can't even go shopping anymore without being in danger. I've never been so scared in my life. But I don't know who was more dangerous - the robber or the policemen. It was a long time before we went back to the mall.

School

Basically, I like school. But I don't get the best grades in the world. In fact, sometimes my grades are really awful. I'm not dumb - but my mind and my brain don't always work together. I really try to keep my mind on the subject, but while the teacher is talking about battles in the Civil War, I'm thinking about the picture of this soldier in my book. He's pretty cute in an old-fashioned sort of way. I wonder if he liked being a soldier and if his boots hurt when he marched, or if he had socks on. And if he wasn't wearing socks, I start thinking about how his feet must really stink. Then I imagine a whole army full of cute soldiers with stinky feet, and I start to giggle. I look over at my friend Stephanie and she starts laughing, too, and pretty soon the teacher is yelling at me for being disruptive. I couldn't explain what seemed so funny - teachers never understand that kind of stuff. I really was <u>trying</u> to pay attention. I can't help it if my mind jumps on ideas and rides away with them.

Why is it that teachers always tell us they want us to think, but when we do, we get yelled at? In our history book, there's a picture of a knight in armor. He looks awfully uncomfortable. I wondered how hard it would be to walk or ride a horse wearing that heavy armor. And what about the horse? I bet it felt like running the other way when one of those armor-coated guys decided to jump on its back and go riding. And how did knights go to the bathroom? For that matter, what did anybody do before toilet paper was invented? And toilets? And what did the women do about bathroom stuff? Yuck! So when the teacher asks me a question and I can't answer it, I get yelled at for not thinking. I look stupid and feel dumb. How can I explain that I was thinking the whole time?

It doesn't matter what class it is - I just

can't help it. For instance, in science we were reading about gravity. I wrote the definition in my notebook, and then I started thinking. If gravity holds us down, and if the world is round, why don't the people on the bottom fall off? At night, while we're asleep, are we upside down? And is gravity stronger when it's dark? I really want to know, but when I raise my hand and ask the question, the kids laugh and the teacher frowns and I'm in trouble again. School is sometimes a place where questions are never answered and answers end with question marks.

It helps to be able to move around a little. It's hard to sit still for an hour and pay attention to grammar and stuff. That's why so many kids ask to go to the bathroom. It's easier to breathe in the hall and it's fun to walk past other classes and look at kids sitting there who wish they could be in the hall, too.

Once I went to the bathroom and discovered a dead rat floating in the toilet! I ran back to the classroom, screaming. I told the teacher to do something <u>quick!</u> She called the office, the class got all noisy and excited, and we never did get back to doing verbs. I'll never use that bathroom at school again.

I hate having to ask to go to the bathroom at school. Why do I even have to ask? Do I have to ask to breathe? Do I have to ask to see? Some stuff is natural and is nobody's business but mine. It makes me feel embarrassed and I feel like everybody in class is imagining what I look like sitting on the toilet.

One day, when I was in sixth grade, a boy named Tolliver got up and told the teacher, "I gotta pee!" The teacher got an attitude because Tolliver was loud, or because he used bad grammar, or because he was rude, but she told him to sit down and be quiet. Now, when teachers have to go to the bathroom, they just excuse themselves, say they have to get something from the office, and then go. But kids have to ask. Not fair. So Tolliver sat down and wiggled uncomfortably for a while, then he got up and asked again. He was hopping from one foot to the other. It was clear to me, at least, that he <u>really</u> had to go. The teacher knew it, too, but she was in a bad mood and told him no again. So Tolliver stood right there and peed on the floor of the classroom. A big puddle collected under his gym shoes. Then he cried and ran out of the room. The teacher followed him and tried to apologize, but it was too late. Tolliver moved to Cleveland a couple of weeks later. But none of us stepped on that place on the floor where that pee puddle was, not for weeks after the janitors had cleaned it up.

Boys

When I was little, I never even noticed a difference between boys and girls. We played together and nothing made much difference. Of course, some of them got dirtier, and some of them liked trucks and stuff, but mostly we got dirty together and just had fun. When did it change? When did I start feeling self-conscious when a boy was around? When did I start laughing too loud or talking too much when one of them was nearby? And where did this tickly feeling in my stomach come from? Why does it matter? Do they feel stupid when they're around us? I think so.

I've seen some of the boys act pretty stupid when girls are nearby. They punch one another, or punch us, and then run and hang together in a group, like a pack of pimply wolves or something. Most of the boys in my class are still pretty short and skinny - it's the high school boys that I think look good. They ignore girls like me and my friends, but they know we're looking - and they like it.

Yesterday, Stephanie and I were at school, walking down the stairs, giggling and talking about this older boy named Rex. She said his name sounded like a dinosaur, and I said he looked like a dinosaur. But she kept talking about how cute she thought he was and silly stuff like what she would do if she could get her hands on him. We were trying to figure out how to be in the hall when he went to lunch. The plan was to walk close enough to "accidentally" bump into him as we passed him. Just then she turned around and who was on the steps behind us? Rex! He was laughing because he had heard everything we said! Stephanie got so flustered that she lost her balance, fell, and rolled down the last three steps to the floor. Rex walked over, helped her up, and laughed as he walked away. She felt like digging a hole and jumping in.

Sometimes boys are good for laughing at, too. We went on a boat ride once and some boys made it a trip worth remembering. We live near the Ohio River. I guess I take it for granted, maybe like the kids who live near the ocean and ignore it, although I don't see how. The ocean is powerful and beautiful, and the river is just a skinny brown line.

A girl named Ebony had her birthday party on a boat. She had music and lots of food and our class got to have the whole boat to ourselves for three hours. At first, I didn't pay any attention to the water - I'd been on boat rides before. But after I found out that Deon, a cute boy from English class, was spending all his time talking to that skinny-faced Alexandria, I lost interest in the party and started to look at the water. I walked up to the top deck and sat down on one of the deck chairs. The breeze blew peacefully over my face, and the boat chugged along smoothly. The sun was shining brightly and sparkled as it bounced off the water. And even though I could see both shores, I found that the river had a power all its own. It was silent and deep and seemed to be filled with dark mysteries.

Feeling very poetic and satisfied with my deep understanding of nature, I was startled by a splash and a scream. Someone had fallen off the boat! I ran to the rail to see Deon and Marco in the water, looking surprised and scared but laughing. The captain stopped the boat, threw them life preservers, and we watched, fascinated, as the crew rescued the boys. They had been laughing and arguing over Alexandria and were wrestling too close to the edge of the boat. Just as they decided that she wasn't worth the trouble, they lost their balance and toppled over. They were brought back on board, wet, embarrassed, and in really big trouble. Alex kept boasting how two boys were fighting over her. We ignored her. Ebony worried that her party was spoiled. But everybody assured her that it was - for sure - the best birthday party we'd ever been to.

Vacations

The best school days are the days when we don't have to go. On school holidays like Presidents' Day, it feels so delicious to do absolutely nothing. I like to sleep until noon, never get dressed, and eat pie for dinner! I hate when teachers give homework on those days. Weren't they ever kids? Holidays don't come often enough, so summer vacation is what I live for. I start counting the days in April, dreaming of tossing that alarm clock out of my window so I can sleep as late as I want.

But even better are the unplanned holidays - snow days! Snow days, when the TV announcer says, "All public schools are closed today," are rare and wonderful, unless you're lucky enough to live in a rural county. Sometimes you can tell. It starts snowing really hard about midnight and snows heavily all night long - that way the snowplows don't have time to clear the roads by morning. But other times, you wake up to a wonderful surprise. Ten inches of snow and the radio just announced that schools are closed! I feel sorry for kids who live in Florida - there's nothing like the joy of an unexpected snow day.

But Florida has an ocean - and that's my favorite place to go for long, planned vacations with my family. I can sit and just look at the water for hours. The bright blue hugeness rolls and rolls, whether I'm there or not. It speaks to me. It makes me feel safe and scared at the same time. When I get in the water and the sand moves under my feet, I feel like I'm going to be sucked away. But then the waves roll again, and I'm safe. The ocean is even better at night because it's _so_ terrifying. The darkness makes it seem bigger, deeper, and so very powerful! Sometimes the moonlight glows on the waves and the foam seems to shine.

The sound of the waves at night make me shiver. I love it!

Why is ocean water so warm? I think I read in my science book that ocean water and blood were real similar. Is that why I like it? Is it part of me? Ocean water tastes salty, like tears. One year I actually cried when it was time to go back home from Florida. I went down to the ocean one last time to say good-bye to the water and the waves and the sand. I didn't want my brother to see me cry, so I stood there alone, sniffing back tears as they rolled down my face and into my mouth. The salty taste surprised me and then made me laugh. I've got an ocean right inside me! An ocean of tears. That sounds dramatic. I hope we go back next year.

Some years we don't go on a big vacation out of town. We go to Akron to visit relatives sometimes, but Akron is definitely NOT a vacation hot spot. I know kids who have never been on a family vacation, and kids who go to Europe every year. One girl, who's been there several times, told me Paris is about as exciting as Akron. I don't believe her. I'd love to go to Paris or Madagascar - or Nairobi - some really exotic place where no one knows me and I could sip sparkling water from a crystal goblet while sitting on a balcony overlooking the river while soft breezes blow across the plaza below. Or maybe on safari in Africa, where I'd save the rhino from extinction, or discover a new species in the rain forest, or find a leaf that could be made into a chewing gum that cures cancer. But instead, I sit in boring Ohio, where everything has already been discovered and nothing new _ever_ happens.

That's why I like to read. I go to the library during summer vacation and check out stacks of books every week. I've checked out books on angels (they intrigue me), on Nazis (they disgust me), on discoveries (they excite me), and even books on sex (they amaze me). I figure reading is one sure way to find out the answers to all those questions my mother doesn't really want me to ask. Sometimes I check out novels, but I like biographies - books about real people - people so famous they got a book written about them. One day, someone will write a book about me. I just have to figure out what I'm going to do to be famous. Do famous people ever get to take vacations? I guess their whole life must be like a vacation. That's the life for me.

The Senses

I think something must be wrong with my nose. It works too well. I can smell the onions in the soup my mother makes, and I can tell if she put peas in it. I hate peas. They smell green and squishy. I know it sounds dumb, but I think smells and colors go together. It's like the senses all live in the same neighborhood and sometimes they show up at each other's houses.

Now grass, that's a green smell that I love. When my dad cuts the grass in the summer, I like to help him rake the sweet green cuttings. It smells like summer and freshness and fun. But old grass smells disgusting. It smells just like it looks - brownish green. Daddy puts piles of grass behind the garage to be used for mulch on his roses in the winter. It smells sick and dead and makes me want to gag.

Sometimes he cuts the grass just before a rainstorm. The air gets thick and warm and smells yellowish purple. The leaves on the trees turn upward, waiting for the rain, which will make everything smell blue and bright. Outside smells are my favorite. Even snow has a smell. It smells clean and frozen. Does dirt smell brown or do I think that because it is brown? I'm not sure.

Inside smells are usually comforting. My house smells like happiness and safety, maybe like a pale orange. It's a mixture of good food and warm blankets and clean clothes in the washing machine. I've been to some houses that smelled like whiskey or fear. Once I was going to spend the night at a friend's house, but her mother smoked so much that I couldn't breathe and her father screamed and yelled at us while he sat on the sofa, getting drunk. I got scared and went home. I breathed the warm smell of my own house with relief.

Even school smells good sometimes. Not the

tired gray smell at the end of the day when everyone is ready to go home, but the bright new smell of the new school day. The halls are quiet and smell like fresh wax. I feel like this is the chance to have a good day, to grab hold of whatever it is that I'm supposed to find here. The air at school smells like books and chalk dust and hope. What does hope smell like? It smells like bright yellow flowers blooming in the sunshine. Yellow is my favorite color and I guess it's my favorite smell, too.

I don't know what music smells like or what color it is. Maybe the colors and flavors of spice or cinnamon or honey. Since everyone calls me Jazzy, I guess I'm supposed to like jazz, but I don't really understand it. Is it supposed to have a tune? My dad says, "Just feel the rhythm." To make him happy, I told him I did, but I'm not sure what I'm supposed to be feeling.

My parents took me to a jazz concert when I was eight. I was the only kid in a room full of overdressed old people, sitting at little tables covered with tablecloths, sipping drinks, and tapping their feet. I wiggled and complained and went to the bathroom five times in half an hour. Finally, I sat on the floor. I scooted under the table, with the tablecloth as my shield and protector from the music of the older generation. As I sat there, the loud bass notes and the slow saxophone sounds drifted down to my hiding place. The beats of the drum tiptoed to me. All I could see were legs and shoes and shadows from the candles on the tables. Somehow, the music began to make sense.

I think jazz is classical music turned upside down and inside out. I don't often tell my friends that I like Mozart, for instance. They'd laugh at me. When I was little I took ballet and the music seemed glamorous and very grown-up. I felt like I could be a star dancing to that music. When we're in the car and my mother turns the radio to the classical music station, I complain, but I'm really glad she did. I just don't give her the satisfaction of knowing it. I wonder what kind of music those guys Bach and Beethoven would have written if they had been born today. Maybe they'd be rock stars. After all, they wrote that kind of music because that's all there was back then. They didn't have much choice.

I don't know the names of all the rock and rap groups that my friends do, but I pretend that I know what they're talking about when they mention a new song or group. I know the big ones, of course, but I just don't have time to learn them all. So I fake it. I think lots of the kids do, too. Everybody at school claims to be an expert on everything because nobody wants to admit that they don't know something. We're very good at it.

I don't know about other kids, but I see movies in my head all the time. Sometimes they're in black and white, like the old movies that are on TV at three in the morning - the images are grainy and gray. And sometimes I make up full-color productions. Does everyone else do this? There's never a moment that my brain isn't making up stories or songs or conversations in my head. I see a dead squirrel on the side of the road and that makes me think about squirrels and death and cars and smells and blood - all at the same time. I don't understand how my brain can manage to think about so many things and not get mixed up.

Lots of times I think about stuff that probably nobody else does. I worry about people who are sick or suffering. We saw this movie in school about people in other countries and how they have to stand in line all day for a bar of soap or an apple. We Americans have so much stuff in our stores that it rots and we have to throw it away before it can all get sold. We can go to any store in any city and be sure that thousands of necessary food - and even junk food - items will be there for us to choose from. I think we're very spoiled here. We take for granted all that we have. When I see films like the one we saw, I feel guilty and sorry for those people, and a little scared. What if our stores got like that? It could happen, I guess. And what would those people think if they came here?

I'd like to take a girl from one of those movies to the mall with me. I'd like to show her all the choices we have. Would she have fun or would she want to spit on us for being spoiled and having too much? I'm not rich and I can't buy it all - most of the time I don't even have enough money to buy much of anything, but it's still there. And when I get some money, I want to be first in line to buy it all. Is that wrong?

I saw a picture in the newspaper of a little boy who was starving in Africa. His eyes were big and frightened. He was dying. Why do little kids like that have to suffer? And why do I feel so guilty and helpless?

I think I might like to help people like that one day. There are starving people all over the world who are dying for just a piece of bread. I threw away my sandwich yesterday because we were out of ketchup. I don't know what I can do now, but I'm thinking about it. I want everybody in the world to be happy like me. At least I'm happy most of the time. But I know about the sadness in the world. One day I'll help. Maybe.

Sometimes I glance up at the sky, look at the trees against the sunlight, and I'm there - in the trees - flying, breezing, dreaming again.

If I had to choose between being indoors or outside, I'd always choose to be outdoors. I like to feel the wind, or smell the coming rain, or catch snowflakes on my tongue.

I love the sunshine. When other people are complaining about the heat, I go outside on purpose to let the sun warm my face and my hands. The glow makes me feel happy and soothed. Sunshine is friendly and makes me think of golden things like orange juice and lemon pie and candlelight. And when the sun goes down, watching the sky change from bright to night makes me feel peaceful.

It's sunset. I'm sitting on the window seat, watching the day die. The trees, bare of their leaves, empty branches scratching the pale red sky, stand shivering in the fading sunlight. Now dark red, the sky becomes maroon. The branches of the trees look like fuzzy fingers swallowed by shadows. Soon all is swallowed by the breath of night. Darkness rules.

Old People and Death

I have a three-year-old cousin who thinks I'm really old because I'm thirteen. I think my mother is pretty old, but she keeps talking about how young she feels. My teachers are all pretty old, except for my science teacher, who just finished his student teaching and is really cool. He doesn't even wear a tie - he wears jeans and sweaters and running shoes. He carries his books and papers in a gym bag instead of a briefcase. Maybe being old is simply the way you act, not how old you really are.

But some people are just plain old. My grandmother is sixty and my great-grandmother is eighty-three. Both of them are amazing.

Grandma is a forest ranger. She knows the name of every plant and bug and animal ever created. She can climb a tree faster than I can, and can find something interesting while she's up there. I love to go and visit her in the summer. It's always an adventure. Last summer we counted deer for a survey. We saw hundreds of deer and five bears. She wasn't even scared. I was.

I call my great-grandmother Granny. She's unbelievable. She swims often and walks around the track once a week. She eats yogurt and bananas every day. She doesn't drink or smoke or eat candy. I think she'll live to be a hundred and fifty. Granny's face is wrinkled and her hair is gray, and I think she has false teeth, but her smile is very young. When she was born, there weren't any TV sets or fax machines or computers. She's seen so much in her life. She doesn't like to talk about bad things she's witnessed - like the time her husband - my great-grandfather - was killed, or the time the tornado destroyed their house. She knows hundreds of stories that she says her grandmother taught her - tales of goblins and ghosts, or of sailors and soldiers. She makes it all seem so exciting.

I hope I live to be as old as my great-grandmother. I wonder what will happen in the world that hasn't happened yet. I wonder what new inventions I'll use. And I wonder if my great-granddaughter will love me as much as I love Granny.

I hope my grandmother never dies. I went to my first funeral last week. My father's great-aunt Ethel died of a heart attack. I wasn't really close to her, but I had dinner at her house several times when we went to Denver to visit. Her house was large and gloomy. All the furniture was that real dark wood and she had dark green drapes and brown carpets. I remember she always fixed green peas and dark, hard-cooked roast beef. Like I said before, I hate peas. But Aunt Ethel was the kind of lady that you didn't say "no" to. She would stand there and wait until I had eaten every single pea. I finally figured out that if I asked for more lemonade or biscuits, she'd go to the kitchen and I could scrape the peas off my plate into my napkin. My dad smiled and never told Aunt Ethel. But I think she knew.

I don't think Aunt Ethel had much fun in her life. She never got married and she never traveled. Her only joy was her collection of music boxes. She must have had a hundred. They were the only things in her house that were delicate and pretty. The last time we visited, she let me see them, but I was not allowed to touch. She wound a few of them for me. Wonderful tiny sounds from long ago and far away were locked in those glass globes and shiny carved boxes. I looked at her face and she smiled as they played. The sunshine seemed to come into that dark room. It's the only time I ever saw her happy. And then I heard she was dead.

When we walked into the church, the first thing I saw was a huge brown casket in the front with Aunt Ethel, looking very dead, lying in it. I thought I would wet my pants. My parents were quiet and serious. Nobody seemed to notice that I was shaking uncontrollably. We walked slowly down that long aisle of that quiet, spooky church, getting closer to the hard, unsmiling body of Aunt Ethel. I was sure that Death was going to jump up and grab me. I held my breath as we passed the casket, just in case heart attacks were catching. We finally sat down, the music played, the preacher spoke, and the casket was closed and then wheeled away. I cried the whole time, not because she was dead, but because of fear, green peas, and music boxes.

Dreams

There are two kinds of dreams - daydreams and night dreams. Daydreams are thoughts to float on when the day gets long or rough or painful. Night dreams are shadows. Daydreams get me in trouble in school.

Sometimes I daydream on the bus coming home from school. It's always hot and noisy, so I like to sit by the window, ignore all the other kids, and think about the people we pass. There's a bar on one corner. The same little man is sitting in front of it every day. He always wears the same green hat. Summer or winter, he sits on a folding chair, watching the cars and people go by. I bet he's daydreaming like me. Does he sit there all night, too? Where does he live? What does he wish he could do? Or are his wishes all dried up?

I've got lots of wishes left. I want to travel on airplanes to cities all over the world, but I don't want to eat foreign food. Can you get cheeseburgers in Rome? Like I said earlier, I want to be famous. I want people to know who I am, to be excited when they get an autograph from Jasmine Joy Jeffries! I guess I'll have to do something wonderful or amazing first. I'm not sure yet what I'm good at. I can't sing. I'm a pretty good dancer. I'm no superstar in school or even sports. How does an ordinary kid with extraordinary dreams grow up to be famous? I haven't figured that out yet.

I read somewhere once that if you dream you're falling out of an airplane, and you don't wake up, you'll really die. I don't know how <u>that</u> could be proved. I mean, if you kept on falling and didn't wake up, and you really did die, who could you tell? And if you dreamed you died and then woke up, I guess the whole thing is untrue. But everybody I've ever asked about this said they always wake up just in time.

I've never had that dream, but I've had some strange ones. Once I dreamed that I was in a dark room with just a table in it. On the table was a shiny gold box and an ugly brown box. I got to choose which one, and I took the ugly box. I wonder why. If I had been awake, I'm sure I would have taken the shiny box. I bet it had gold and diamonds and stuff in it. The ugly box was full of peas!

Some dreams are funny. Once I dreamed that I was a star, singing in a concert downtown at Fountain Square. Thousands of people were clapping and cheering for me. I felt great until I realized that I didn't have on any clothes! For some reason, none of the people in the audience had noticed, but I didn't know what to do. Should I keep singing or hurry off the stage in case they noticed that I was naked? Then I realized that they might not be cheering because I was such a great singer, but because I was too stupid to know I was naked! I woke up before I could decide.

Another time I dreamed that a tall black monster was coming after me. He was covered in fur and he got closer and closer. I shivered with fear and I couldn't breathe. Just as he was about to touch me, I woke up screaming. When I turned the light on, my big, furry winter coat was hanging over a chair near my bed. If I hadn't been so scared, I would have laughed.

Sometimes I get really scared and I go and get in bed with my mother. I'd never tell my friends that I do that, but no matter how scary a dream might be, and no matter how much I'm shaking, it all goes away when I feel the warmth of Mama breathing close to me. I wrote a poem about how scared I get sometimes. But I never showed it to my mother.

Mama! Mama! hug me quick!
I dreamed you flew away!
you perched on the back
of a large green bird
with feet like clumps of clay

Mama! Mama! hug me tight!
and wake me from my sleep!
you smile as I dance
to a dark stale song
and tears like mud I weep

Mama! Mama! hug me now!
I dream of shadows bright
you watch as I sleep
in your soft warm bed
and you become my light

Writing

I love to write. Sometimes words fall out of my fingertips. My heart starts to beat a little faster when what I really want to say shows up in front of me. I like to think about stuff other people might think is stupid, and then I write about it. I write about rainbows when other people might write about rain.

Sometimes I get out my journal and no words come. It's like my ideas are stuck. I know what I'm thinking, but I just don't know how to write it in words. It really makes me mad when the right words just won't come on a day when the weather is warm and the air smells so good and I feel like I might explode if I don't get the words out of me.

One night I woke up after everyone had gone to sleep. I had remembered a dream and I wanted to write it down. It was dark and silent in the house. The water dripping in the faucet sounded loud and scary like in a horror movie where the monster or the bad guy jumps out from behind a shadow. The air in the hall outside my room looked like thick blue velvet. I could hear a clock ticking downstairs. Even though it was scary, I was excited and I scribbled in my journal with just a flashlight. I felt better after I wrote the dream down and went right back to sleep. The next morning I read it again and I thought it sounded really good. Maybe I should do that more often.

I write stories sometimes, about girls who discover magic raspberries or purple daisies. I like to give them adventures that I'll probably never actually have. Stories take a long time to finish, so I don't always have the patience to keep going. I write poems, too. It would seem like poems, since they're shorter, would be easier to write, but it takes a lot of thinking to make it sound right and not like something off a birthday card. I wrote a poem once about tears. It was so sad it made me cry. I don't know if it would have made anybody else cry because I never showed it to anybody. I'm not ready to do that yet.

Writing for myself and writing for my teacher are two different things. Sometimes the teacher tells us that we have to include six sentences in every paragraph and three adjectives in every sentence. I know why she does that - she wants to make sure kids write enough. I do what she says because it's easier than arguing with her, but sometimes my paragraphs have fifteen sentences and sometimes they only have two. And sometimes adjectives just don't feel like sitting in front of those words like she wants them to do.

Most kids think a paragraph is two inches on a piece of notebook paper, and lots of teachers let us get away with that, but I like my paragraphs to stick around until I'm done with them. Once we had a teacher who made us count every single word we wrote and she would grade us on the number of words. Stephanie wrote, "I am very, very, very, ... and she kept on going until she had written the word <u>very</u>

three hundred times, then she wrote, "happy." She had more words than anybody, so the teacher had to give her an A. But the teacher never made us count words after that.

The best teachers are the ones that show you how to write for school and for yourself, how to make the words on the page sound as good as words in your head, how to make magic with words. Not too many teachers can do that. Maybe I'll be a teacher and show kids how much fun writing can be.

For now, I write to please myself. I write because it feels good and it makes me happy. I write because the words need me to make them real.

Dear Friend,

I love writing in my journal. It's my place to hide from the world, to think, and to dream. It's the only place where I can be totally honest. When I go back and read this, I feel good about myself because I am myself and nobody else. That pleases me.

I hope you wrote some thoughts as well. I enjoyed sharing these words with you. But you don't need me to write your ideas. You can write your own journal and keep your secret fears and special dreams in a place where worries disappear and possibilities bloom. And when you go back and read this, you, too, will feel good about yourself because you are yourself and nobody else. That's good.

'Bye for now.

Love, Jazzy

Extra Journal Pages

Second Chance Proposal

This Large Print Book carries the
Seal of Approval of N.A.V.H.

SECOND CHANCE PROPOSAL

ANNA SCHMIDT

THORNDIKE PRESS
A part of Gale, Cengage Learning

GALE
CENGAGE Learning®

Detroit • New York • San Francisco • New Haven, Conn • Waterville, Maine • London

LP

30.00

GALE
CENGAGE Learning®

LIBRARY OF CONGRESS CATALOGING-IN-PUBLICATION DATA

Schmidt, Anna.
    Second Chance Proposal / by Anna Schmidt. — Large Print edition.
        pages cm. — (Amish Brides of Celery Fields Series) (Thorndike Press
    Large Print Gentle Romance)
    ISBN 978-1-4104-6089-9 (hardcover) — ISBN 1-4104-6089-4 (hardcover) 1.
Amish—Fiction. 2. Courtship—Fiction. 3. Large type books. I. Title.
PS3569.C51527S43 2013
813'.54—dc23   2013016050

Published in 2013 by arrangement with Harlequin Books S.A.

Printed in the United States of America
1 2 3 4 5 6 7 17 16 15 14 13

Show me thy ways, O Lord;
teach me thy paths.
— *Psalms* 25:4

To all who have believed
in the power of love.

CHAPTER ONE

Celery Fields, Florida
January 1938
Lydia Goodloe. Was he seeing things?
  Sweet Liddy.

John Amman closed his eyes, which were crusty with lack of sleep and the dust of days he'd spent making his way west across Florida from one coast to the other. Surely this was nothing more than a mirage born of exhaustion and the need for a solid meal.

But no, there could be no doubt. There she was walking across a fallow field from her father's house to the school. He watched as she entered the school and then a minute later came outside again. She pulled her shawl tighter around her shoulders and began stacking firewood in her arms. They might be in Florida, but it was January and an unseasonably cold one at that. John pulled up the collar of his canvas jacket to block the wind that swept across the open fields.

Lydia went back inside the school and shut the door, and after a few minutes John saw a stream of smoke rising from the chimney. He closed his eyes, savoring the memory of that warm classroom anchored by a pot-bellied stove in one corner and the teacher's desk in the other. He tried to picture Lydia at that desk, but he could only see her as the girl he'd known — the laughing child with the curly dark hair that flew out behind her as she gathered the skirt of her dark cotton dress and raced with him along the path. The teenager — a quiet beauty, the luxurious hair tamed into braided submission under her bonnet and the black prayer covering girls her age wore after joining the church, as he and Liddy had done when they were both sixteen.

He started running across the field, his heart pounding in anticipation of the reunion with this woman he had loved his whole life. This woman he had come back to find after eight long years — to ask why she had not answered his letters, why she had not believed him when he told her that it had all been for her. He had risked everything even to the point of becoming an outcast from their Amish community and indeed his own family so they could have the life they had planned.

But abruptly he stopped. What was he thinking? That he would go to her and she would explain everything and they would be happy again? How could he face her after all this time and admit that he'd failed? Even if she did open her heart to him, what did he have left to offer her? No job. No money. The disdain of his own family . . . of the entire community unless he agreed to publicly admit his wrongdoing and seek their forgiveness.

He crouched down — half from the need to catch his breath and half because the wind was so sharp. The door to the school opened again and, this time when she emerged, Liddy was not wearing her bonnet. She hurried back to the woodpile and took two more logs — one in each hand. But it was not the logs that John noticed. It was what she was wearing on her head in place of the bonnet.

When she had entered the school that first time, her head and much of her face had been covered by the familiar black bonnet that Amish girls and women wore when outside. John had assumed that beneath that bonnet she still wore the black prayer *kapp* of a single woman. But the *kapp* he saw now was not black but white — the mark of a married woman, someone else's wife. The loose ties whipped playfully around her cheeks as she gathered a second load of wood.

His heart sank.

"Fool," he muttered. "Did you really think you would come back here after all this time and find her waiting?"

His stomach growled as he caught the scent of bacon frying, and he glanced toward the house where his family had once lived. After he'd left — and been placed under the *bann* for doing so — his mother had gotten word to him when the farm was sold. She'd written that she and his father and the rest of his siblings were moving back to Pennsylvania. After that he had not heard from his family again, and now someone else owned the small produce farm that would have been his.

John scuffed at the sand with the toe of his work boot — the sole was worn through and the inside was lined with old news- paper. He hefted the satchel that held what remained of his worldly goods to one shoul- der and pulled his faded red cap low over his eyes. He no longer dressed "plain" as he had when he and Lydia had been sweet- hearts. He doubted that she would even recognize him were he to approach her. He had changed that much, at least outwardly. His gaze swept over the rest of the small town past the hardware store, the livery turned machine shop, Yoder's Dry Goods Emporium, the bakery Liddy's family had owned and back to the schoolhouse and that thin trail of smoke that curled across the cloudless sky.

Home.

"Not anymore," John whispered as he turned his back on the town for the second time. There was nothing for him here. He'd been following yet another foolish dream in coming back. Behind him he heard the shouts and laughter of the arriving school-children across the frost-covered field. Then he hitched his satchel over his shoulder and headed east, the way he'd come.

Lydia had a warm fire burning by the time she heard the children gathering in the yard. They were playing tag or hide-and-seek and squealing with delight as someone made it to home base without being caught. She flipped down the seats of the desks and stood for a moment as she did every morn-ing, asking God's guidance for the day. Then she pulled hard on the bell cord, tak-ing pleasure in the familiar sound in the cold air calling the children inside.

As the children scurried into the school, pausing only to hang their coats and hats or bonnets on the pegs, Lydia turned to close the door. Then she saw a man walking across an abandoned produce field that marked the border between the town and the outlying farms. He was wearing a light canvas jacket and a red cap. Her heart went out to him when she realized that he was not dressed warmly enough for the weather. No doubt he was another of those men who wandered into town now and again in search of work or a handout.

She continued to watch the man as the last of her students — a large lumbering boy who would gladly be anywhere but inside this classroom — passed by her. There was something about the way the stranger in the field moved that was unlike the movements of other vagrants she had observed. Most of those men appeared worn down by their troubles and the harsh realities of their circumstances. This man walked with purpose and a rhythm that fairly shouted defiance and determination. Something about his posture stirred a memory that she could not quite grasp.

"Teacher?"

Lydia looked up to find her half sister's

daughter, Bettina, standing at the lectern ready to lead the devotions with which they began every day. Bettina had passed the age when most girls attended school, but she loved being there so much that Lydia had persuaded Pleasant and her husband, Jeremiah, to allow the girl to continue helping her.

She nodded and Bettina opened the Bible, carefully laying aside the purple satin ribbon that had served as a bookmark for as long as Lydia could recall, even back to the days when she and Greta had been students at the school. The days when they had each taken a turn reading the morning devotions. She permitted herself a small smile as she recalled how the girls had eagerly awaited their turn at reading, but not the boys. And especially not John Amman.

John.

Her eyes, which were normally lowered in reverence for the reading, flew open and focused on the closed door at the back of the room. Something about the man she had seen walking across the fields reminded her of John. The broad shoulders unbowed against the wind. The long, determined stride. Suddenly her heart was racing and she felt quite light-headed, to the point that she pressed herself firmly into the safety of the straight-backed chair.

Was it possible that, after all this time, he had come home? But why now? And why had there been no word from him — to anyone — in all this time? Not a single word.

She closed her eyes as a wave of grief and disappointment swept through her. Even after eight long years the sting of John's leaving was as painful as it had ever been. Bettina continued to read the morning's Scripture. The lesson for the day was the story of the prodigal son and the irony of that reading combined with her memories of John Amman made Lydia wince.

John had walked a good six or seven miles away from Celery Fields before he once again changed his mind. How could Lydia have married another man? But then, how could she not when he had given up writing after a year passed with not one of his letters answered? Still, he had to know who that man was. He had to at least be sure that she had married someone worthy of her.

And if she hadn't? What if he learned that she was miserable? Exactly what did he think he could do about that?

John might have lost most of his worldly goods, but the one thing he had not lost was his faith in God. And he had no doubt that God was guiding his steps as he made his way back the way he'd come. There was some plan at work here, a plan that was driving him home to Celery Fields. Home to Liddy. He just had to figure out what it was. He closed his eyes and prayed for guidance. When he opened them he saw Lydia and her students come out into the schoolyard, where they formed a circle and played a round of dodgeball. John smiled. Lydia had always been very good at the game, but he had been better.

It occurred to him that the best way to learn what he needed to know was to go directly to her. Oh, not to her house. He did not want to embarrass or confront either her or her husband. No, he would bide his time and choose the right moment, the perfect place. And after so many years of silence from her he would finally have some answers.

The unusually cold weather continued as Tuesday dawned with a cutting wind from the north and a slanting rain that came very close to being sleet. An umbrella was useless in such a wind so Lydia covered her bonnet and face with her shawl as she picked her way across the rutted path that ran from her house to the schoolhouse. She would need to get the fire going quickly, for the weather was too foul for the children to gather in the schoolyard waiting for the bell to ring.

Then as she neared the school, she caught a whiff of smoke and lifted the edge of her shawl so she could see more clearly. Rising from the chimney was a trail of gray smoke. Lydia smiled as she hurried to the school. Her brother-in-law Luke must have started the fire for her. He was a kind man, the perfect match for Greta, her lively and sometimes capricious younger sister.

"Luke?" she called as she entered the school and the door banged shut behind her. She hung her shawl and bonnet on the first of a double row of wooden pegs by the door. "I came early to light the fire, but I see that you . . ." She froze as she realized that the man kneeling by the door of the woodstove was not her brother-in-law.

She recognized the red cap and light canvas jacket of the man she'd seen crossing the field a day earlier and felt a twinge of alarm. He must have stayed the night in the school. Homes and other buildings in Celery Fields were rarely locked unless they were businesses with wares that had proved worth stealing. Slowly the man turned and pinned her with his gaze as he removed his cap and stood up. He had several days' growth of a beard and his hair curled over his ears. But only one man she'd ever met had those deep-set green eyes.

"Hello, Liddy."

She gasped. "You," she whispered, suddenly unable to find her full voice and at the same time realizing that she should not be speaking to him at all.

John Amman was under the *bann* and as such was to be shunned by all members of the church.

"It's been a long time," he added, his voice hoarse and raspy, and he took a step toward her.

Flustered by the sheer presence of him — taller and broader than she remembered and, in spite of the weariness that lined his face, far more handsome — Lydia resorted to her habit of placing distance between herself and something she could not yet understand. She walked straight past him to the board and began writing the day's assignments on it, her back to him.

"Aren't you going to say anything, Liddy?"

Her fingers tightened on the chalk, snapping it in two. A thousand questions raced through her mind.

Where have you been?

Why didn't you write?

What are you doing here, now?

Do you have a wife? Children?

Are you here to stay?

Do you know that your family moved back north?

What happened to all your plans?

When's the last time you had a decent meal?

And on and on.

She finished writing on the board, laid the chalk precisely in the tray and dusted her hands off by rubbing them together. She kept her back to him, felt the tenseness in her shoulders and listened for his step, praying that he would give up and leave.

But she knew better. John Amman had always been determined to get what he wanted once he set his mind to something. Slowly she turned around. He had not moved from his place next to the stove.

"You're the teacher now," he said with a gesture toward the room filled with desks and the other trappings of the school they had both once attended. "Liddy?" He took another step toward her but stopped when she moved away from him.

"You look terrible," she replied in the voice she used to reprimand a truant student, then she clamped her lips shut. To her surprise he laughed, and the sound of it was a song she had heard again and again over the years whenever she lay awake remembering John Amman.

"I guess I do at that," he said, looking down at his patched and ill-fitted clothing as he ran a hand over his unshaved face.

She placed books on desks, her back to him.

"Are you not glad to see me?"

The question infuriated her because the answer that sprang instantly from deep within her was, *Yes. Oh, yes. How I have worried about you, thought of you, longed to know if you were well. And, most of all, wondered if you ever thought of me.*

"I am pleased to see that you are alive," she replied, unable to prevent the words or stem the tide of years of bitterness in her voice. "As I would be to see any prodigal return," she added, raising her eyes defiantly to his. "And now please go. The children will be here any minute and I . . ."

". . . don't wish to have to explain about me?" He stepped closer and fingered the loose tie of her prayer covering. "When did you marry, Liddy?"

She jerked the tie free and at the same time heard the school door open and shut. She turned to find Bettina standing uncertainly inside the doorway.

"Teacher?"

"Guten morgen," John said, crossing the room to where Bettina waited. "I am John Amman. I expect you know my uncle and aunt, the Hadwells?"

Bettina nodded and looked at Lydia. Lydia considered the best way to get John out of the classroom without raising further questions.

"I am Teacher's niece, Bettina."

"You are Pleasant's daughter?"

Lydia saw Bettina take in John's rumpled clothing, his mud-caked shoes. Her niece was a bright girl, and Lydia knew she was trying to decide if this man was who he said he was or another tramp passing through, trying anything he thought might work to get a handout or a meal. Her eyes darted from Lydia to John and back again as she nodded politely. But at the same time she edged closer to the bell rope, ready to pull it if she deemed them to be in any danger.

"John Amman was kind enough to light the fire, Bettina. Now he will be on his way." Lydia was satisfied that in directing her comment to the girl she had not further violated her responsibility to shun him. She moved to the door and opened it, waiting for John to leave.

He paused for just an instant as he passed

her, his incredible eyes, the green of a lush tropical jungle, locking on hers.

"You may as well know this now, Lydia Goodloe. I've come home to stay."

As Lydia closed the door firmly behind him she noticed that her hand was shaking and her heart was racing and all of a sudden the room seemed far too warm.

John had not meant to say anything about his plans. He didn't know what his future might hold. There were too many unknowns. How would his aunt and uncle, the only family left here, respond to his return? The night before he'd watched them close up shop and head home together and been glad to know they were still there. But could he seek and be granted their forgiveness? Could he find work and a place to live? And most of all, what kind of fool deliberately tormented himself by living in the same small town where the love of his life had settled into a marriage of her own? Still, as he walked the rest of the way into town, oblivious to the rain and wind, he knew that he had spoken the truth. He had come back to stay, for in reality he had nowhere else to go.

When he entered the hardware store it was as if he had stepped back in time. The same bell jangled over the door as he closed it. Instantly he was certain that he could easily fill any order a customer might have because everything was in the same place it had always been. Including his aunt.

He smiled as he watched Gertrude Hadwell chew the stub of the pencil she used to figure the month's finances. She was behind the counter, the ledger open before her, her elbows resting on either side of it as she hummed softly and entered figures into the narrow columns. She looked as if she hadn't aged a day, adding to his sense that nothing had changed.

"Be right there," she called without glancing up. "Roger Hadwell," she shouted, turning her face toward the back of the store as she closed the ledger and walked toward the storeroom. "Customer."

John understood that she was not being rude. His aunt had always felt that their mostly male customers would far rather deal with her husband than with a woman. He removed his hat and smoothed his wet hair as he moved down the narrow aisle past the barrels of screws and nails until he reached the counter.

"*Guten morgen, Tante* Gert," he said softly, not wanting to startle her more than necessary.

She whipped around to face him and immediately her eyes filled with tears. "Johnny," she whispered. Then she hurried around the counter until they were face-to-face and she grabbed his shoulders, squeezing them hard. "Johnny," she repeated.

Behind her John saw his uncle come from the storeroom wiping his hands on a rag as he looked up to welcome his customer. He hesitated when he saw his wife touching a strange man, then rushed forward. "See here, young man," he began, and then his eyes widened. "Gertrude, no," he said firmly, and turned her away from John. "Go in back until he leaves."

John's knees went weak with the realization that his uncle was shunning him. If that were true of these two people whom he had felt closest to all his life then he knew everyone in town would follow their lead. Well, what had he expected? That the entire town would set aside centuries of tradition for him? He sent up a silent prayer begging forgiveness for his prideful ways.

His aunt hesitated, gazing at him as her husband folded his arms across his broad chest and waited for her to follow his instructions.

"Go, Gert," Roger repeated.

"I will not," she replied. "This man needs

our help and I would help him the same as we would any stranger." She brushed by her husband and pulled out a chair. "Come sit by the fire. Why, you're soaked." She pulled a horse blanket from a shelf and handed it to him.

Behind her his uncle took one last look at his wife and then left the room.

"It's good to see you, Gert," John said as he savored her motherly nurturing.

"Where have you been?" she fumed, then quickly added, "No, I do not wish to know the details of your foolishness. It is enough that God has brought you back to us in one piece." She studied him critically. "You're too thin, John Amman. When did you last have a decent meal?"

John shrugged as she tucked the blanket around his shoulders then handed him a bakery box that had been sitting on the counter. It was filled with large glazed doughnuts. He bit into one and licked his lips. "I see Pleasant Obermeier still makes the best doughnut anywhere," he said as he devoured the rest of the pastry and licked the sticky sugar coating from his fingers.

"She's Pleasant Troyer now," his aunt informed him as she busied herself setting a teakettle on the wood-burning stove. "Obermeier died a few years back and shortly

26

after that Bishop Troyer's nephew, Jeremiah, came to town. He opened up that ice-cream shop next to the bakery and it wasn't long before Pleasant and him married and adopted all four of Obermeier's children. Now they have a couple of their own."

"But she still has the bakery?"

"She does. After her *dat* died she managed on her own for a while and then once she married Jeremiah . . ."

Pleasant was not the Goodloe sister John wanted to know about, but he thought it best to hide his curiosity about Lydia until he knew just how much things had changed in Celery Fields. "They live up there in the old Obermeier house at the end of Main Street then?"

Gert perched on the edge of a chair across from him to watch him eat. "No, Jeremiah bought a small farm just outside of town for them. Greta Goodloe married the blacksmith a year after Pleasant married. It was her husband, Luke Starns, who bought the Obermeier place." She poured him a mug of strong black tea. "Drink this. You're shivering."

"And Liddy?" he asked as the hot liquid warmed his insides.

"Still teaching," Gert replied. "Pleasant's oldest girl, Bettina, helps her out, not that there's any need. So few children these days. Lots of folks have moved away and until Greta's brood and a few other little ones reach school age, well, it's getting harder to justify keeping that schoolhouse open."

"She ever marry?" John mumbled around a mouth filled with a second doughnut. He kept his head lowered and steeled himself to hear the name of some former friend, some boy he'd grown up with who had known very well that Liddy Goodloe was taken.

"Liddy?" Gert said, as if the name was unfamiliar. "No. She lives up the lane there in her father's house all alone now that Greta's married. I doubt she has any plans in that direction."

John thought he must be hallucinating. Had he imagined the white prayer covering? No. He'd touched one of the ties and Liddy had pulled it away from him. That had happened. Of course, he could hardly ask his aunt about that unless he was ready to admit he'd already seen Liddy and spoken with her.

"You'll need to see Bishop Troyer and the sooner the better," Gert instructed. "We have services this coming Sunday so there's time enough to have everything in place so that you can make your apology and seek forgiveness and get the *bann* lifted. Then you'll be needing a job and a place to stay." Gert ticked each item off on her fingers as if she were filling a customer's order. "And some decent clothes."

She reached for her shawl and bonnet. "I'm going across to Yoder's to get a few things and when I come back we'll get you settled in." She headed for the rear of the store. "Roger Hadwell, go fetch Bishop Troyer," she instructed. "And then go see if Luke Starns is willing to let John stay in his old rooms above the livery until he gets back on his feet."

John watched as Roger came to the front of the store and retrieved a black rain slicker and his hat from a peg behind the counter. Without so much as a glance at John his uncle left by the front door.

By suppertime John had a place to stay as well as two sets of new clothes. He'd shaved and washed and enjoyed his first solid meal in days, wolfing down three bowls of the beef stew his aunt kept simmering in the back room of the hardware store along with half a loaf of Pleasant's crusty wheat bread. In exchange for being able to live above the blacksmith's shop, Roger had agreed that John would take charge of the stables behind the shop and care for any animals

29

housed there overnight. All of this had been arranged between his uncle and the black-smith. Roger had yet to utter a single word to John.

But his aunt seemed to have made her choice. It appeared that having him home was worth breaking the traditions of shunning.

"Like old times," she said as she and Roger closed the shop. She turned to John and added, "I left you some of that stew for your supper and there's coffee and enough bread for breakfast tomorrow." She cupped his cheek gently. "You look exhausted, John. Get some rest."

Not wanting to contribute to her disobedience of the shunning, John nodded. It was just as well. He probably could not have gotten his thanks out around the lump of relief and gratitude that clogged his throat. The idea of spending the night sleeping under one of his aunt's handmade quilts seemed unbelievable after all the nights he'd had to find shelter wherever he could.

"Come along, Gert," Roger instructed, refusing to make eye contact with John.

"Oh, stop your fussing," Gert chastised as they walked down the street. "By morning everybody is going to know the prodigal has returned and on Sunday he can put things to right once and for all."

The prodigal. That's what Lydia had called him.

CHAPTER TWO

The day had been unsettling to say the least. After her encounter with John, Lydia had barely been able to concentrate on the lessons she tried to teach the children. After they had eaten their lunches she surrendered to her complete inability to concentrate and let Bettina teach the little ones. In the meantime she gave the older students assignments they could do on their own. Then she sat at her desk studying her Bible in hopes that God would send her answers to the questions that crowded her mind.

At the end of the day she hurried home, thankful that the rain had let up and that John Amman had not waited for her outside as she had feared he might. Perhaps he had come to his senses and walked back the way he came. He clearly thought she was married and, given the shunning, surely no one in town would have told him the real story. She could only pray that this was the case.

It was unimaginable to even consider living in the same town with John after all this time, after everything that had happened between them.

"Impossible," she muttered as she climbed the porch steps to her house. She was eager to have a quiet supper and settle in for the evening to correct work she had collected from the students. That would surely calm her nerves. She would retire early and pray that John Amman would not haunt her dreams.

But as she reached for the doorknob, the door swung open and there stood her sister Greta, her baby daughter riding her hip while her two boisterous sons — only a year apart — raced from the kitchen to greet Lydia. "Tante Liddy," they squealed in unison as they threw themselves against her.

She set the large basket that she used to carry books and papers to and from school on the table inside the front hallway and bent to give the boys a hug. "This is a surprise," she said, glancing up at Greta.

"I have news," Greta said in a conspiratorial whisper. "Boys, go finish your milk," she instructed as she led the way into the front room. "You should sit," she instructed as she shifted the baby in her arms.

This could be anything, Lydia warned

33

herself. Greta was given to melodrama, and even the simplest news could seem monumental to her. Lydia sat in her rocking chair and reached for her niece. Greta handed her the child, clearly relieved to sit down herself. She was nearly eight months along in her latest pregnancy, and she sank heavily into the nearest chair.

"John Amman has returned," Greta announced. "Gert Hadwell told Hilda Yoder that he just walked into the hardware store this morning as if he'd last been there yesterday." She waited, her eyebrows raised expectantly. "Well?"

Lydia would not sugarcoat the facts, especially with Greta.

"I know. He was at the school when I arrived this morning. He had started the stove to warm the building."

"Well, what happened? What did you say? What did *he* say? Where's he been all this time and why didn't he ever write to you and why come back now? Is he staying?" All of the questions Lydia had refused to voice came tumbling from her sister's lips. Greta covered her mouth with her fist. "But, of course, you couldn't say anything. He's still under the *bann.*"

"Of course. How could I have any information about whether or not he plans to stay?" *But he had said as much as he walked away from the school.*

"Oh, he's staying. He's taken the rooms above Luke's shop. Gert sent Roger to arrange everything with Luke earlier today."

So close? The distance between Lydia's house and Luke's building was less than fifty yards. "Well, there's your answer," Lydia murmured, and wondered at the way her heart lurched at the news that he had found a place to live already. That they were to be neighbors.

"If you ask me, there's more to this than it seems," Greta pressed.

"What do you mean?"

"What if he's come back for *you*?"

Lydia stood and bounced the child as she walked to the window that looked directly down to where the blacksmith shop sat and where even now John might be standing at the kitchen window of the upstairs apartment looking at her house, watching for any sign of her. "Don't be silly," she said briskly. "It's been years. If John has come back to Celery Fields, it's because he needs a place to work and live."

"Then why not go north to his family's farm?"

Because he was never a farmer.

With a sigh she turned to face her sister.

35

"You'll have to ask him that question, Greta."

"Well, I just might," Greta replied. "Of course, I'll wait until he's seen the bishop and makes his plea for forgiveness on Sunday. But if he has any idea that he can just come back here after all this time, after no word to you for years, and . . ."

"Let the past go, Greta," Lydia warned. "Be happy for the Hadwells. I'm sure Gertrude is beside herself with joy. John was always her favorite nephew."

"I am happy for them," Greta said petulantly. "It's just that . . ." She frowned.

"It was kind of Luke to offer him the apartment," Lydia said, hoping the shift in the conversation would take Greta's mind off worrying about her.

Her sister sighed. "We took most of the furnishings out of there when we moved to the house, so he's going to need some things if he intends to stay. Luke also says we should invite him to supper on Sunday evening. I don't know what that man is thinking sometimes."

"Luke doesn't know John from the past," Lydia reminded her. "And do I need to remind you that Luke himself was under a similar *bann* when he moved here from Canada?"

Greta blushed. "I guess you've got a point. Luke's more understanding of this whole matter."

"And a kind man always doing what he can for others," Lydia reminded her sister.

"Hmm. Still, Sunday is Samuel's birthday," Greta said with a nod toward the kitchen, where the boys could be heard whispering and giggling. Suddenly her eyes widened. "Even if John comes you'll still be there, won't you? Samuel would be so disappointed if . . ."

"Of course I'm coming," Lydia assured her.

"I mean I could just tell Luke not to . . ."

"Greta, if John Amman has indeed come home to stay then we will need to adjust to that — all of us."

"If you're sure . . ."

"I'm sure. Now shouldn't you be getting home? Luke will be wanting his supper."

Greta smiled as she heaved herself out of the chair and waited a minute to catch her breath. Then she took her daughter from Lydia, called for the boys and herded them onto the porch. "I left you something for your supper," she said as she and the children headed back toward town.

Greta had been the homemaker for Lydia and their father from the time she'd been old enough to reach the stove and counters in the kitchen. Even with her own house and brood to care for she still felt the need to make sure that Lydia was eating.

"I do know how to cook," Lydia reminded her.

"Not well," Greta shot back, and both sisters laughed.

Lydia stood on the porch watching Greta waddle down the path toward her own house at the end of town. As she turned to go back inside, a movement on the landing above the livery caught her eye.

John Amman was standing in the open doorway of the apartment Greta's husband had once occupied. He was watching her and, as Lydia stared back, he raised his hand, palm out flat in the signal they had shared as teenagers.

He remembered.

By week's end everyone in Celery Fields and the surrounding area made up of small produce farms owned by Amish families knew the story of John Amman. And as far as Lydia could see, John did not need a forgiving father on the scene to kill the fatted calf in celebration of his return. He had his aunt. Gertrude Hadwell took John in as if he were her beloved son.

Only a day after his return he was working in the hardware store as if he'd never left. Oh, to be sure, at Roger Hadwell's insistence, John's chores were confined to the loading area in back. That way no customers would be placed in the awkward position of having to openly shun him. But Gert made it clear that by Monday he would take his place behind the counter.

In the meantime his aunt had organized a frolic, the name given to occasions when Amish women gathered for some large work project such as cleaning someone's home or completing a quilt top. To Lydia it seemed exactly the right word for such events. No matter how difficult the work, the women always enjoyed themselves — sharing news and rumors and laughter. This time, the cause for gathering on Saturday morning was to properly clean and furnish the rooms above the livery for John. Of course, everyone in town knew how Gert Hadwell had grieved the fact that she had never had children of her own. It was understandable that people would put their happiness for her above their concern about John's past. Besides, John would not be on-site for the cleaning.

So on Saturday morning Liddy sat on a stool in the barn behind her house squeezing warm milk from the cow as she tried to decide her next course of action. Much as she dreaded it, Lydia could hardly refuse to join the other women. If she failed to attend the frolic the day's chatter would no doubt focus on her at some point. She could not bear the thought of the others gossiping and recalling how she and John had once been sweethearts. The newcomers would have to be filled in on the romance that had ended when John left town. Lydia had no doubt that she would be forced to endure curious glances and abject pity when she attended services on Sunday.

No, better to do whatever seemed prudent to get through the first rush of excitement over John's homecoming. Not much happened in Celery Fields and John's return was, indeed, cause for excitement. It had certainly taken everyone's mind off her own stunning break from tradition a few weeks earlier, when Lydia had decided to forego the black prayer *kapp* of a single woman and the habit of sitting on one of the two front benches with her nieces and the other unmarried girls. Rather, she had taken a seat in the rear of the section reserved for the married women and widows. To punctuate her action she had replaced the black *kapp* that she had worn since joining the church with one of white.

As she had hoped, during the service the other women had not wanted to create a stir and so had simply focused their attention on the words of the hymn and sermon. One or two had gently nudged those girls in the first two rows, who had turned to stare. Of course, once the service ended and the women gathered in the kitchen to prepare the after-services meal, there had been whispers and knowing nods until Lydia had realized she would have to say something.

"It seems plain that there is little likelihood that I shall ever marry," she announced, drawing the immediate and rapt attention of the others. "As I grow older — having nearly reached my thirtieth year now — and having served the community and the congregation for several years since my baptism, is it too much to ask that I be allowed to sit with the women of my age?"

She had taken her time then meeting the eyes of each woman in turn. Some had looked away. Others had registered sympathy, even pity, for her plight. Hilda Yoder, wife of the owner of the dry-goods store, had chewed her lower lip for what seemed an eternity and then given Lydia's decision her blessing.

"Makes perfect sense," she said with the

crisp efficiency with which she pronounced most of her edicts. "Now, shall we attend to the business at hand and get this food set out?"

And that had been the end of any public discussion on the matter. So at least John's return had taken people's attention away from that. Of course, if she didn't go to the frolic . . .

Lydia would go to the frolic — and to supper at Greta's after services on Sunday. By that time John would have contritely sought the forgiveness of the congregation and been officially welcomed home. If she could just get through the next few days, surely by the end of the coming week everything and everyone would settle back into the normal routine of life in Celery Fields. Oh, no doubt, she and John would cross paths in town or at some gathering, but in time . . .

"Hello, Liddy."

Lydia had been so lost in thought that she'd been unaware of anyone coming into the barn — much less John Amman. He was dressed "plain" in clothes that were obviously new and store-bought. The pants were half an inch too short and the shirt stretched a little too tightly over his shoulders. He was clean shaven and his face was shaded by the stiff wide brim of his straw hat. His blond hair had been recently washed and trimmed in the style of other Amish men, although it was more wavy and unruly than most.

She turned her attention to the cow, determined not to allow John or any thought of him to further disrupt her plans for the day.

"Why do you wear the prayer covering of a married woman, Liddy?" He leaned against the door frame, one ankle crossed over the other. "My aunt tells me you have never married — and in her view you have little thought of ever doing so."

Lydia bit her lip to keep from speaking. He was to be shunned at least until the congregation could hear from the bishop and take a vote to reinstate him. She squeezed the last of the milk from the cow's udder and stood up.

John reached for the bucket of warm milk and his boldness unnerved her. Someone could be watching — people were always passing by on their way to and from town and it was Saturday, the busiest day for such traffic. If she were seen standing right next to John Amman tongues would surely wag, no matter whether she shunned him or not.

She wrestled the bucket from him and quickened her pace as she headed out into

43

the sunlight. Surely, he would not follow her where everyone could see him.

But he did. He had not changed at all. John Amman had always been one for testing boundaries. "We will talk about this, Liddy," he said. "I think I deserve an explanation."

She almost broke her silence at that. *He* deserved an explanation? This man who had promised to write, had promised to come back to her? This man from whom she had heard nothing for eight long years? This man whose memory had so dogged her through the years that he had made it impossible for her even to consider accepting the attention of any other man in his stead?

She kept her eyes on the sandy lane before her and concentrated on covering the ground between the barn and the house as quickly as possible without spilling the milk. But the path was narrow and he was walking far too closely. Their arms were in real danger of brushing if she wasn't careful. She had to do something before they came into Hilda Yoder's view. Surely at this hour the wife of the dry-goods store owner would be at her usual post by the shop window watching the goings-on in town.

John said nothing more as he continued

to keep pace with her. In truth he seemed to be unaware of the awkward situation. Not knowing what else to do, she broke into a run, not caring whether the milk sloshed over the sides of her pail. To her relief he made no attempt to follow her. He just stood where she'd left him on the path watching her go. "See you tomorrow at services, then," he called after her. "And after I've been forgiven and reinstated you'll be free to speak with me. I expect to have your explanation, Liddy."

Her explanation? She ran up the steps to her back door and hurried inside.

Safe in her kitchen with the door tightly closed, she scanned the lane that led to town and the parts of Celery Fields' main street that she could see from her window. She cringed at the idea that anyone might have heard him call out to her. Her breathing was coming in gasps as if she'd run a good distance instead of a mere few feet, and she found it necessary to sit down for a moment.

It was not exertion that caused her breath to suddenly be in short supply. It was John — being close to him like that, remembering all the times they had walked together, and facing the reality that he was back in Celery Fields and gave every appearance of

45

intending to stay.

She moaned as she buried her face in her hands.

After a moment she sat up straight and forced her breathing to calm. She would do what she always did when faced with a challenge. She would set boundaries for herself, and for John Amman, as well. They were no longer children. He would simply have to accept that she had certain duties as a member of the community — duties that did not include answering to him.

With her confidence restored, she stood, smoothed the skirt of her dress and put the milk in a glass pitcher before storing it in the icebox. Then she took a deep breath as if preparing to dive into the sea and set forth once again, this time to do her part to clean and refurbish the place next door where John Amman had taken up residence as her neighbor.

John knew he should not have called out after Lydia ran from him. Even as a girl she had hated anything that drew attention to her. For that matter the entire encounter could have caused her grave discomfort if anyone had seen or heard. "Not exactly the best way to worm your way back into her good graces," he muttered as he headed for the hardware store.

On the other hand, why should he be the one trying to win her favor? Wasn't she the one who had said she would wait and then shunned him as had everyone else? He'd written to assure her that he had every intention of returning once he'd made enough money to set up a business of his own. She had always understood his aversion to farming. She had even been the one to encourage him to start some sort of shop and they would live above it and she would help out on Saturdays and after school. But when he'd explained to her that it would take money to start a business and his father would never accept the idea that John would not one day take over the family farm, she'd insisted that God would provide.

He knew what she meant. In her mind if owning his own business were God's plan for his life then the opportunity would simply present itself. "You just have to be patient — and vigilant for God's signs," she had instructed.

But patience had never been one of John's attributes. When he reached the age of eighteen with no sign from God, he decided to seek out other possibilities. After all, hadn't Bishop Troyer taught them that God helps those who help themselves?

"And where did that get you?" he grumbled as he put on the denim apron his aunt had left for him and began sweeping the loading dock behind the hardware store. He brushed the accumulated debris into a dustpan and dumped it in the bin next to the loading dock. Then he set the broom and dustpan inside the door and rubbed his hands together as he moved to a place where he could better listen in on his uncle and Luke Starns as they sat outside Luke's shop. With no one allowed to converse with him, this was his only recourse for gathering information.

"Warmer today," Roger said. "After the last spell of frosty mornings I thought we might be in for a stretch of cold weather."

"Good for the crops that it's passed," replied the blacksmith, who was sipping a cup of coffee. He was a quiet man, as John had observed earlier that morning when the blacksmith handed Gertrude a box of kitchen items that Greta had gathered from her own supply to place in the rooms above his business. The idea of this silent giant of a man married to the vibrant and petite Greta made John smile.

A few minutes passed while the men discussed weather and crops and business. Then Bishop Troyer crossed the street from the dry-goods store and joined them.

"Bishop Troyer," Roger said as he stood and offered the head of their congregation his chair. "Did you speak yet with John Amman?"

"*Yah.* We have spoken already twice. I am convinced that he has learned the error of his ways and come home to make amends," the bishop replied. "Everything seems to be in order for tomorrow's service."

"Then I can have him working the counter come Monday." This was not a question but something John realized his uncle had been dreading.

"Should bring you a bunch of business," Luke said with a chuckle. "Folks will want to get a look at him after all this time. They'll be curious about where he's been and all."

"They can look all they want at services. On Monday I need him to be working, although I'm not sure how we're going to have enough business to support the three of us."

"I seem to recall that this entire matter had its beginning in John wanting to start a business of his own," Bishop Troyer said.

Roger let out a mirthless laugh. "With what? He has nothing. Gert had to buy him the clothes he's wearing now and he owes a debt of gratitude to Luke here that he has a place to stay."

"Still, he must have a skill if the plan was to open his own shop."

"He's a tolerable woodworker," Roger allowed. "Clocks and furniture mostly. He built that cabinet where Gert keeps her quilting fabrics. And the clock we have in the store — that's his work."

John saw the bishop exchange a look with Luke. "I reckon Josef Bontrager took up that business in John's absence," Luke observed.

Roger stared out at the street. "You've got a point there. Not much call for handmade furniture these days."

Was it John's imagination or had his uncle raised his voice as if to make sure John heard this last bit of information? It hardly mattered. He was in no position to take up his trade. Over the past several months he had sold off his tools one by one or bartered them for a meal or a night's lodging.

"Well, until something comes along he's got work with you. The Lord has surely blessed him in having you and Gertrude still here," the bishop said.

"Speaking of work I'd best get back to it," Luke said as he drained the last of his coffee.

As the bishop took his leave and Roger walked slowly back to the hardware store, John stepped from the shadows of the storeroom into the sunlight that bathed the loading dock. There was work to be done — a pile of newly delivered lumber that his uncle had instructed him to sort and stack by size and type in the pole shed outside the store. But when he stepped into the yard he heard feminine laughter coming from the rooms above the livery.

He took a moment to enjoy the sight of the women moving in and out of the apartment, up and down the outside stairs carrying various items they seemed to think he might need. Then Lydia came out onto the tiny landing at the top of the stairs to shake out a rag rug.

She was laughing at something one of the other women had said, her head thrown back the way he remembered from when they'd been teenagers. And in that laughter he heard more clearly than any words could have expressed exactly why he had decided to return to Celery Fields. He had come back to find answers to the questions that had plagued him. He had come back to the only place where he knew there was a path to forgiveness and from there a safe haven to rest in while he found his way. He had come back because even eight long years had not erased the memory of this girl turned woman whose laughter had always had the power to stir his heart.

CHAPTER THREE

When Lydia glanced up and saw John watching her from the loading dock, the laughter she'd been sharing with the other women died on her lips. How could she possibly have gotten so caught up in the pleasure of the work and companionship with the others that she had been able to forget that he was back in her life, whether she wanted it or not? That the place the women were scouring and setting to order was where John would live — was already living? How had she forgotten who would be eating off those mismatched dishes that she had washed and dried and stacked so precisely on the open shelf above the stove?

She had helped scrub the walls and floors and even made up the narrow bed that occupied one corner while engaged in the normal chatter. At events like this, women enjoyed catching up on news from families that had moved back north when the hard times hit, or the decision of the newest member of their cleaning party and her husband to move to Florida and start fresh after a tornado had destroyed the family's farm in Iowa. And so the morning had passed without a single thought about John Amman. His presence in town was far too recent and their encounters had been rare enough that it was easy to lose herself in the work and the conversation. It was truly amazing how easily she had been able to simply dismiss the man from her mind.

But now seeing him standing in the back doorway of the hardware store, filling the space with his tall, lanky frame, she could not seem to stop the images of him living in that small apartment from coming. He would rinse the dishes she had washed for him at the sink as he looked out the small square window with its view of her house. He would hang his clothes on the pegs that she had wiped free of dust above the bed. He would sleep in that bed under a quilt that Greta had brought to add an extra layer to the one already there. It was a quilt that Lydia and Greta's grandmother had made. A quilt that had once covered the bed Lydia and Greta shared when they were children.

She felt the heat rise to her cheeks as these images assailed her and John stepped closer to the edge of the dock, his bold gaze fixed directly on her. The other women went about their work, glancing shyly in his direction as their laughter and discussion dissolved into expectant silence. Lydia stood frozen on the steps, her fingers gripping the small rag rug until her knuckles went white. She felt as if her cheeks must be glowing like two polished red apples.

Greta stepped onto the porch landing next to her. "He's watching you," she whispered.

Hilda Yoder cleared her throat. "We have more work to do," she instructed with a glance at John and then a lift of her eyebrows to Lydia. "Greta, take this mop bucket and get us some clean rinse water."

"I'll do it," Lydia said firmly. Greta had no business hauling buckets of water up and down that steep staircase.

"I hardly think that . . ." Hilda began but then pressed her lips into a thin line and said no more.

Lydia handed the rag rug to Greta and took the bucket. She descended the stairs without looking at John, but she knew he was following her every move. Dumping the soapy water, she set the bucket aside and prepared to prime the pump until the faucet spit out fresh water. Above her she knew Hilda Yoder was watching with disapproval.

She saw John leap down from the loading dock and walk slowly toward her. She could not help feeling a little like the sandpiper she'd once seen caught in a fisherman's abandoned net at the beach.

She reached for the pump handle but John was there first, his fingers closing around the handle and brushing hers. "Let me," he said softly. Lydia snatched her hand away as if she'd gotten too close to a hot stove. Then, not knowing what else she might do, she looked away while he primed the pump until the faucet squirted clear water into the pail.

Without a word he carried the full, heavy pail up the steps and set it on the landing careful to keep his eyes lowered so as not to give offense to any of the women Hilda had herded quickly inside. His delivery complete, he hurried back down the steps, past Lydia, who had waited in the yard, and back to the loading dock where he turned his back to them and began sorting through a lumber pile of mixed-size pieces.

"That man has been too much out in the world," Hilda Yoder huffed as Lydia mounted the steps and all the women went back to their work.

"It may take him some time to settle back into the old ways," Pleasant said with a glance at Gert, who was clearly embarrassed by her nephew's action. "After all, he has been eight years in their world. Still, the important thing is that he has seen the error of his youthful decision and come home to us."

There was a general murmur of agreement among the women. But Lydia had her doubts that John would ever truly return to their ways. The only reason he'd come back now was because he'd clearly had nowhere else to turn. In Celery Fields he could be assured of forgiveness and the care of the community. From what she knew of outsiders, they were not quite so generous to those who were down on their luck. No, she knew John Amman perhaps better than any of them or, at least, she had once a long time ago. It simply was not possible for a man to change so completely, was it? To have finally learned his lesson and abandoned the wanderlust of his youth? To be satisfied at last with the quiet, simple life of his Amish roots?

"Hilda, you don't think there's any possibility for someone to vote against him tomorrow, do you?" Greta asked, her eyes wide with worry.

"John Amman has sought his forgiveness from Bishop Troyer," Pleasant reminded

Greta. "We will wait to hear his recommendation tomorrow."

"Nevertheless, the congregation has to be unified in its acceptance," Hilda reminded them. Lydia saw Gert Hadwell press her fist to her mouth. She hoped, for Gert's sake, that Hilda had not got it into her head to vote against John. Not that she would put it past the older woman. Hilda saw herself as carrying the standard for what was right in their small community. In many ways her opinion carried almost as much weight as the bishop's.

But to Lydia's relief Hilda positioned herself next to Gert in a gesture that could only be read as one of support as she glanced around the room. "I think we have done as best we can here."

Gert smoothed the quilt on the bed and nodded. "It does look nice," she said with a smile. "Perhaps," she added wistfully, "with such nice quarters John will find his peace here."

"Well, I'll say one thing," Pleasant announced. "It smells a good deal better than it did when we came in."

All the women laughed as they gathered their supplies and trooped down the outside steps to the yard below.

All except Lydia.

She lingered to wipe the oilcloth that covered the small wooden table and glance around the room one last time. She told herself she was only making sure they had left none of their cleaning supplies behind. But she knew better.

In spite of the aroma of the strong lye soap they'd used, offset by the sweetness of the furniture wax, John's essence filled the space. And as she closed the door behind her she recalled the scent of John — the sheer warmth of his nearness when he'd bent to take the bucket from her. A memory stirred, of him standing so close to her one time when they had gone to the beach together. That day he had smelled of the sun and the sea. And that was the day they had shared their first kiss. They had been fourteen years old.

A lifetime ago, she thought, shaking off the memory as she followed the others down the steps and into the lane where they said their goodbyes. Greta glanced back at her. "Coming to the house, sister?" she called.

"I'm a little tired," Lydia replied. "You go on." She was aware that John had paused in the sorting of the wood the minute she spoke. He did not turn around, but everything about his posture told her he was listening.

Greta hesitated then nodded. "All right. See you tomorrow then."

Ah, yes, tomorrow. First, the services where John will no doubt be fully embraced back into the community. After all, forgiveness is the very foundation of our Amish faith. And later Samuel's birthday party, Lydia thought. And John would be there for all of it. She drew in a deep breath and forced a smile. It had already been a long and difficult day but the events scheduled for *Sunndaag* promised to test her even further. "*Yah,* tomorrow," she replied.

On Sunday morning John was awake well before dawn. He lay on the narrow bed beneath two faded hand-stitched quilts and thought about the bed he'd slept in as a boy in a room shared by his three brothers. Where were they now? Married with families of their own? And his sisters? He tried to imagine them all grown-up.

And his parents. *Dat. Maemm.* Did they think of him? Speak of him?

He rolled onto his side and watched the rays of sun creep through the window that looked out onto Lydia's property, and his thoughts turned to the day before him. He was confident that the congregation would vote to accept the bishop's recommendation of forgiveness. But what about Lydia?

So far she had given not the slightest sign that once the *bann* was lifted she would be willing to resume the friendship they'd once shared. If he was going to live here they would be neighbors at the very least. And, given the way the community's population had shrunk over the years, they could hardly avoid spending time in each other's company from time to time. There would be gatherings where they would both be present, like the birthday party for Greta and Luke's oldest child. Maybe once the *bann* was lifted Lydia Goodloe would meet his eyes instead of averting her gaze. Or would she? He was certain that part of the way she'd been acting had to do with her thinking she would never see him again. And now that he was here she had no idea what to do.

Well, by this time tomorrow — in fact by later this very evening, when they all gathered at Luke and Greta's for supper, he would have made clear that she could no longer use the excuse of his shunning for refusing to talk to him. The congregation would vote to accept Bishop Troyer's recommendation for forgiveness and full reinstatement, for that was the way of his people. They would vote in his favor for his aunt's sake even if they still had doubts about him. He had missed the traditions of his faith; never in all the years he was gone had he once been tempted to follow the faith of outsiders. Without question there were any number of good and pious people out there, but their ways were far too complicated for John to fully grasp. He liked the simple ways of his own people.

He had made a mistake in not coming home after he'd saved up the money that he needed. Instead, he'd allowed his business partner and friend to invest for him. He'd had no idea what a stock market was, but he had trusted his partner and been drawn in by pure greed at the prospect of doubling his savings in a short time with no work at all. Now he realized that he should have known better. The day he'd turned that money over to his friend was the day he'd realized that he had lost his way — his purpose in leaving Celery Fields in the first place.

But now he was back. He had returned for many reasons — to reconnect with his faith and his community was certainly something that had driven him as he made his way west across the state. He had missed his family, although with them moved north again there was little he could do about that for now. But he had also missed his neighbors and friends. And as hurt and upset as he had been with Liddy, he could not get her out of his mind. Every day as he made his way back to Celery Fields he had thought about her. Through pouring rain and cold, blustery nights when he had to sleep outside, he warmed himself by remembering the times they had spent together, the dreams they had shared, the plans they had made.

Now that he was back he was more confused than ever by her behavior toward him. There was the business of the white prayer *kapp* for one thing, and then she had barely said ten words to him. Of course, that could be explained by his being under the *bann,* but still as a girl Liddy had had little use for such rules if they got in the way of what she thought made more sense.

John kicked the covers off and sat up on the side of the bed. Liddy had always been stubborn. She had her opinion on almost any subject and not much tolerance for those who did not see things as she did. The two of them had always been alike in that way and it had caused them no end of arguments when their individual views on a subject differed. But seeing her these past few days since his return — being able to observe her for the most part without actually being able to talk to her — John's impression was that she had changed. She was more like her half sister, Pleasant, than she'd been as a girl. Then she had been as lighthearted as her younger sister, Greta. But from what he'd observed she had developed the pursed lips and tense posture of their former teacher — a woman Liddy had declared she would never ever want to emulate. But then there had been moments — like when he pumped the water for her — when she had glanced at him and he'd seen the girl he'd fallen in love with, the girl for whom he'd risked everything.

Well, that girl-turned-woman had some explaining to do. And once he'd gotten through the service and then the supper at Luke and Greta's, he fully intended to find out why Lydia Goodloe had never acknowledged his attempts to write to her.

John stood and surrendered to the wide smile that stretched across his face. He raked his fingers through his thick hair and it flopped back over his ears, reminding him that he was once again Amish. In a matter of less than a week he had cast aside the trappings of the outside world and now presented himself as every other man in Celery Fields did. He knew one thing for certain: Liddy Goodloe had always been one who wanted to know exactly what to expect at all times. She liked being in charge. That was one of the things that made her a good teacher. Well, just maybe it was time the teacher became the student. And if anyone could teach her the lessons of surviving and even thriving on the unpredictability of life, it was John Amman.

He dressed and then prepared a hearty breakfast of eggs, fried potatoes and thick slices of Pleasant's rye bread slathered with butter and jam. He set his plate of food on the table and bowed his head, thanking God for leading him back to this place and these people.

Anxious now for the day to begin, for this life he'd come back to retrieve to begin, John gobbled down his breakfast. He set the dishes in water to soak and was out the door and on his way to meet Bishop Troyer and the second preacher before the sun was fully above the horizon.

Usually Luke, Greta and the children called for Lydia early on Sunday morning. Services were held every other week in one of the homes that made up the community. On this day the service would take place in the Yoder house behind the dry-goods store in town and, as was her habit whenever the venue was so close, Lydia planned to walk. There was one problem, though.

To walk from her place to the Yoder house she would have to pass by Luke's shop — and the residence of John Amman. Her plan was to delay leaving her house until she had seen him go. That way there would be no possibility of running into him. And so, dressed for over an hour already, the morning chores done, her breakfast eaten and her dishes washed, dried and back on the shelf, she waited. And waited.

The clock chimed eight and still there had been no sign of life in the rooms above the livery. She would be late. Greta would be worried, perhaps send Luke to fetch her. Everyone would be talking about her, about whether or not she had decided against coming because of John, about . . .

"Oh, just go," she ordered herself.

She tied the ribbons of her black bonnet and wrapped her shawl around her shoulders. The morning air was still chilly although a soft westerly wind held the promise that by the time services ended she would have no need of the shawl's extra warmth. She picked up the basket holding the jars of pickled beets and peaches that would be her contribution to the community meal that always followed the three-hour service. Then she stood at the door and closed her eyes, praying for God's strength to get her through this day.

By the time she reached the Yoder house her sister had indeed worked herself into a state. "I thought perhaps you weren't coming," she whispered as she relieved Lydia of her basket and handed it to one of the Yoder daughters. "I know how difficult this —"

"I am here," Lydia interrupted as she saw that most of the congregation had already taken their places in the rows of black wooden benches that traveled from house to house depending on where services were scheduled. "We should sit."

Pleasant slid closer to the women next to her, making room for Lydia and Greta. She gave Lydia a sympathetic look, as did two other women who turned to look at her. *Oh, will this ever end?* Lydia thought even as she manufactured a reassuring smile of greeting for each of the women.

She and Greta had barely taken their places when the first hymn began. Lydia felt the comfort of verses that had been passed down from generation to generation for centuries as she chanted the words in unison with her neighbors. There was something so powerful in the sound of many voices chorusing the same words without benefit of a pipe organ or other musical support. By the time the hymn ended twenty minutes later Lydia felt fully prepared to face whatever the day might bring.

Of course, it helped that John was nowhere in sight. No doubt, he was sequestered in one of the bedrooms where the elders and bishop had met with him before the service. Either that or he had lost his nerve and run away again in the dark of night.

That thought gave Lydia a start. What if he had done exactly that? She struggled to focus her attention on the message as Levi Harnischer, the deacon of their congregation, preached. But as he rambled from one Biblical story to another she found her thoughts, as well as her gaze, wandering.

More than once she glanced toward the hallway that she knew led to the bedrooms. Was he there waiting to be called before the congregation to make his plea for forgiveness and reinstatement once the regular service ended?

Greta nudged her as the second hymn began and gave her a strange look. *Are you all right?* she mouthed.

Lydia frowned and nodded but Greta continued to stare at her.

"You are quite pale, Liddy," she whispered.

"I am fine," Lydia assured her, forcing a gentle tone through gritted teeth.

Bishop Troyer's sermon followed the singing, and there could be no doubt of his message. He quoted the story of the prodigal son and then focused much of his attention on the young people seated in the front two rows of benches on either side of a center aisle. For over an hour he spoke of lambs wandering away from the flock, tempted by the promise of greener pastures. He spoke of the dangers that awaited such runaways and the importance of returning to the stability of the fold.

All around her Lydia saw her neighbors sitting up very straight as they listened with rapt attention to the bishop's words. They knew what was coming. At the meeting following the service they expected John would enter the room and face them. Did not one of them entertain the notion that he might once again have lost his nerve and run away?

The final hymn began and as each verse was sung Lydia felt her heart beat faster. She focused her gaze on Gertrude Hadwell, who clearly could barely contain her joy at having John back in her life. If he left again, Gert would be devastated.

Please let him be here, Lydia prayed silently even as she understood that life would be far easier for her if John had surrendered yet again to the temptations of the adventures he'd found in the outside world.

John followed the sounds and silences of the service from his position in one of the small bedrooms near the two large front rooms of the Yoder home. The hymns, chanted slowly in unison verse by verse, had a beauty all their own. It was so different from the music he'd heard on the rare occasions when he'd attended an *Englisch* service. In the outside world hymns were always accompanied by some musical instrument — most often a pipe organ that huffed and thudded as the organist pushed or pulled the stops and pressed down on the row of pedals beneath her feet.

He had missed the quiet rhythm of hymns from the *Ausband* — hymns passed down through the generations, hymns that could run on for dozens of verses, hymns he had memorized as a boy. He heard the drone of the preacher's voice as the first of the two sermons was delivered. Since the door to the bedroom was closed, he did not hear the actual words until he was called to seek his forgiveness.

He folded his hands and leaned his elbows on his knees. He ought to be praying for God's guidance. He ought to be using this time to figure out how he was going to state his case without sounding either arrogant or insincere. He ought to be trying to understand exactly what he hoped to achieve by coming back here — what his life was going to look like after today. He ought to be doing all of that but, instead, his mind was filled with thoughts of Liddy.

She would be there sitting with the other women and girls, all of them dressed in the solid dark-colored dresses and aprons topped by the starched prayer *kapps* of their faith. They would wear their hair the same, as well, for in the Amish world sameness was a sign of commitment to the community at large; individuality in dress or style was seen as rebellious. Male and female would sit shoulder to shoulder on their respective sides of the room, their eyes either on the minister or lowered in prayer. None of them would be distinguishable from their neighbor. For that was their way. The community was everything and the individual was nothing.

That was, of course, why he had to apologize and seek forgiveness. He had put his personal dreams and plans above what was considered in the best interest of the community. In the outside world such actions would be considered laudable. He would be praised for his ambition and determination to make something of himself. But not in Celery Fields or any other Amish community.

And not in the eyes of Liddy Goodloe.

He knew why the rest of the community had failed to understand his purpose in leaving eight years earlier, but he had thought that Liddy of all people knew why he'd done the only thing he'd felt he could do if the two of them were to have a future. She had counseled patience then but how long was he expected to wait? And she, too, had wanted to marry and start their life together. He was certain of that — or at least he had been.

He stood and paced the confines of the room, the leather soles of his new work boots meeting the polished planks of the wooden floor with a distinct click like the ticking of a clock. He straightened his suspenders and tucked his shirt more firmly into the waistband of his wool trousers. He heard more singing and then the hum of Bishop Troyer's deep voice as the elderly man delivered the second and final sermon for the day.

Soon the deacon would come for him.

Soon he would face them.

Soon one way or another it would be decided.

And if someone voted against him? What then?

He would have little choice but to leave Celery Fields for good. Mentally he considered each of his neighbors and friends, picturing them waiting to seal his fate. By this time tomorrow he would either be settled back into the fold of the community or once again miles away from everything he had once cherished.

The final hymn began. John stood next to the closed door listening for the deacon's footsteps. He closed his eyes and prayed for God to show him the way. Liddy would say that if it was God's will he would be forgiven and just like that, in the eyes of the community, the last eight years would be gone. People would greet him as if he had been in town the whole time. Liddy would no longer look at him with the eyes of a cornered animal . . . or would she?

CHAPTER FOUR

The vote was unanimous in John's favor.

The *bann* had been lifted and in the yard, where the members of the congregation had gathered to share the light fare of the after-services meal, the atmosphere was that of a celebration. As Lydia brought out platters of food the women had prepared in Greta's kitchen she saw John surrounded by a circle of men, his full-throated laughter at something one of the men had just said filling the air around her. It was as if the past eight years had never happened. She froze suddenly, her eyes riveted on John, her ears attuned to his voice, so familiar, so dear.

"Oh, it is so good to have this matter decided!" Greta exclaimed as she came alongside Lydia and followed her gaze to where John was standing. "Now things can return to normal around here." She wiped away beads of sweat from her forehead with the back of one hand. "Is it me or is it unusually hot today?"

"It's you and that extra weight you're carrying," Pleasant replied as she nodded toward the protrusion of Greta's pregnancy and relieved Lydia of the platter she'd nearly forgotten she was holding. "Liddy, find your sister a place in the shade before she passes out."

"Please do not make a fuss," Greta protested, but Lydia saw the way her younger sister pressed one hand against her side and the grimace that followed.

"Come and sit, anyway," Lydia instructed. "You still have Samuel's birthday supper to manage. It will do you good to rest some." She saw Luke glance up and excuse himself from the group of men, then move quickly to his wife's side.

"Are you all right?"

"I am fine," Greta assured him.

"I'll get you some water," Luke said, but before he could do so John was there with a glass filled with cold lemonade.

"I seem to remember you liked your lemonade extra tart, Greta." He grinned at her and Greta giggled as she accepted the glass.

"It is so good to have you back, John," she said. "Everyone is truly pleased."

Lydia did not miss the way her sister cut

her eyes in her direction as she said this.

"It is certain that we have been losing more people than we have gained here in Celery Fields," Pleasant added. "What are your plans, John Amman?"

Lydia hid her smile at her half sister's well-known habit of speaking her thoughts bluntly, not taking time to temper them with discretion.

John chuckled. "Ah, Pleasant, I've missed your forthright way of coming to the heart of any matter."

"That does not answer my question."

"For now I will work at the hardware store with my uncle. In time . . ."

Lydia almost gasped when she glanced at John as he paused. In his eyes she saw the faraway look she remembered so well from their youth, as if he were already miles away from this place and time.

He had not changed at all, she thought. He was still the dreamer.

"In time?" Pleasant prompted.

John shrugged. "Only God can say." He focused his gaze on Lydia.

"I forgot the bread," she murmured, and hurried back inside the house. From the kitchen she watched out the window. She saw Gert tug on John's arm and lead him across the yard to be introduced to people who had moved to Celery Fields since his departure.

She saw him smile as he spoke to those families that had moved to Celery Fields since he'd been gone. She saw him nod sympathetically as Gert introduced him to a young couple who had lost everything in a recent fire. She watched as he admired children and bent to their height to speak with them, charming them with some chatter that made their eyes go wide or their faces break out in smiles.

Oh, how she had loved him once long ago. Loved him for all of these things. But he had left her, and seeing the way he had looked away when Pleasant questioned him, Lydia had no doubt that in time he would leave again.

By the time he walked back to his rooms following the services, John had heard the story of how Lydia had one Sunday simply decided that she would no longer sit with the unmarried girls. He chuckled as he imagined her walking into the service, looking neither left nor right as she took her place in the back row with the married and widowed women. And no one protested.

Of course, that was Liddy. She might not be as free-spirited as he had often been but even as a girl she had demonstrated a streak of independence that had worried her father and older half sister. It had been that very inclination toward questioning things that had attracted John to her. From the first day he'd worked up the nerve to walk home from school with her he had felt she was someone who could perhaps understand his own restless spirit. And as they had spent more and more time together, his certainty had grown that they were meant to be together — destined to share a life filled with happiness beyond anything they could imagine. While at home he had to face his father's constant disapproval, when he was with Liddy none of that mattered. *She* listened. *She* encouraged him to pursue his love of carpentry. *She* believed in him. *She* loved him — or so he had thought.

But in the end she had chosen the community over him, as any good Amish girl would have. She had conducted herself as any Amish girl would when dealing with someone under the *bann.* She had let his letters go unanswered, shunning him as tradition required. That single action had told him more forcefully than any words she might have written that, in her eyes, he had chosen the wrong path and she could not — would not — stand by him.

He stared down at the house he'd visited so often as a boy. He, Liddy and Greta had played tag or hide-and-seek, and he had helped Liddy get through her chores so the two of them could go to the beach. He had sat with Liddy on the porch after a Sunday-evening hymn singing and a ride to her house in the brand-new courting buggy every Amish boy received when joining the congregation. And although no one had spoken openly about it, the expectation had been that he and Liddy would soon marry and start a family of their own.

As he stood at the window lost in memories of the past they had shared — a time when everything had seemed possible — John couldn't help but wonder if the old wooden swing on the porch of Liddy's house still squeaked. He smiled as he recalled a day when he had offered to oil the connection between the hook and the chain that held the swing in place. Liddy's father had thanked him for the offer but said with a wink, "Now, if I let you fix that squeak, how will I know what you and that daughter of mine are up to?"

How Liddy had laughed when he told her that. "We'll just have to find a quieter place, then," she'd said with a twinkle that matched her father's.

And they had. At every opportunity he would meet her at the bay that separated the town of Sarasota from the barrier islands standing between the community and the Gulf of Mexico. At the bay they would walk out on the mudflats where Liddy would collect shells while he fished. In the late afternoon they would walk their bikes along the unpaved roads that led east to Celery Fields. Sometimes they walked the entire distance across the causeway from downtown Sarasota to the islands beyond and the wide sandy beaches of the Gulf of Mexico. They walked instead of riding in his buggy or taking their bicycles because it gave them more time. More time to plan their future together.

"So much for that," John muttered as he plucked his hat from the peg near the door and headed for Greta's house. He was not sure why he had agreed to attend the supper and birthday celebration, but a promise was a promise. At least Greta's boys had been excited to know he would be there.

"He'll be here," Greta murmured as she worked next to Lydia, peeling vegetables for the stew she was making for their supper.

It did no good for Lydia to pretend she didn't care but she tried, anyway. "It hardly matters to me, after all. He's your guest," she said, licking her thumb after she nicked it with the paring knife.

"You're nervous," Greta said with a sharp nod. "It's to be expected. After all, if the congregation had rejected him he would probably be long gone by now. I mean, what would he have left to stay around for? But they didn't reject him and now you have to decide what to do."

"About what?"

"About the fact that you are still in love with him. And about the fact that he has come back here for one reason — you."

Sometimes Greta's certainty could be so annoying. To disguise her irritation, Lydia laughed. "Greta, John Amman and I have not seen each other in years. He was not much more than a boy when he left here and I was . . ."

"You were both of age to be married," Greta reminded her. "You had both been baptized into the faith and you were on your way to starting a life together." She placed her hand on Lydia's. "What happened? You never talked about it to me or anyone else."

Greta had still been a child oblivious to the heartaches of courtship when John boarded the train that took him away from Celery Fields to a job in St. Augustine on the east coast of Florida — a job he'd only read about in the Sarasota newspaper. A job he did not yet have but one he was certain was the key to their future that did not rely on his becoming a farmer.

"He left." Lydia pulled away from her sister's touch and scooped the chopped vegetables into the boiling water.

"And now he has returned," Greta continued. She sat down in one of the wooden kitchen chairs and pulled a bowl of frosting toward her. "He certainly did not come back to work in the hardware store," she commented as she swirled the creamy confection onto each layer of her son's birthday cake.

"He had nowhere else to go." Lydia clamped her lips together. Why was she even attempting to reason with her romantic sister?

Greta gave a hoot of a laugh. "Admit it, Liddy. He came back because of you. So what are you going to do about it?"

"Nothing," Lydia replied as she picked up a stack of plates and utensils and went to set the long table in the front room. From the yard she could hear the children's laughter as they played and, after a moment, through the open window that overlooked the porch, she heard male voices drifting into where she worked. Her heart skipped a beat as she realized that one of those voices belonged to John. He was talking to her brother-in-law Luke. *This is how it might have been every Sunday evening,* she thought as she centered each plate precisely in front of each chair. *This is the life John and I might have shared if he had not left.*

She felt the sting of tears even as she felt the sting of the memory that not once had he written or tried to contact her after that day. Everyone knew that John Amman was the only boy she'd ever come close to marrying. Almost from that first day when John had caught up to her on her way home from school they had been inseparable. Once they reached their teens their families, as well as the rest of the town, simply assumed that they would wed. But late one night John had left Celery Fields to seek his fortune in the outside world. She fought unsuccessfully against the memory of that night when her entire life had changed forever. It had been raining. She had followed him to the train station hoping to talk sense into him. He had listened impatiently and then he had begged Lydia to come with him, painting her a picture of the adventures they would share, the money he would make, the material things he would buy for her.

"I don't want such a life," she had argued. "I just want you."

"Then promise me you will wait," he'd pleaded. She had known in that instant that nothing she could say would change his mind.

"I will wait for you to come to your senses, John Amman," she had told him, tears streaming down her cheeks.

But he never had. No one had seen or heard from him — certainly not Lydia. His family had worn their shame like a hair shirt until the day they sold their farm and moved back to Pennsylvania. Lydia's father had forbidden any mention of John in his presence. Her mother was dead. Greta was too young to understand what had happened, and Pleasant — in those days — had not been someone that either Greta or Lydia could go to for solace.

So Lydia had turned all of her attention to her teaching, pouring herself into the lives of her students and their families and quickly establishing her place in the community. Through the years there had been hints that this man or that was interested in her and would be a good provider. But when it had come to even considering a match with any other man, Lydia had refused. She had loved only one man in her life and she would not settle for less — even if that man surely had to be the most obstinate and opinionated man that God had ever set His hand to creating.

She set the rest of the plates around the table and then surrounded them with flatware and glasses, ignoring the low murmur of John's voice and his occasional laughter as he visited with Luke. As she set the last glass in place, the crunch of bicycle tires and buggy wheels on crushed shells told her that other guests were arriving. She gave one final glance at the table to assure herself that nothing was missing and then called out to her sister, "Greta, company." She smoothed her apron and went to greet Pleasant and her family, Levi and Hannah and their children, the bishop and his wife and John's aunt and uncle.

In the clamor surrounding the arrival of the other guests Lydia was certain she would be able to avoid John's presence. Once they sat down for supper she had already planned to let him find a place first and then to take a chair as far from him as possible. The very fact that she was making such elaborate plans told her that John Amman was too much on her mind.

He is here, in Celery Fields and at this party, as he will no doubt be often where you are, she scolded herself silently. *Best get used to it.*

And having made up her mind to face whatever she must to get through the evening Lydia squared her shoulders and went out onto the porch. She greeted the women and invited them to carry their contributions into the kitchen. Then she turned to the men. "Supper is almost ready," she said, and forced herself to meet John's gaze before looking at the gathering of men as a group. "We can sit down as soon as the children have washed their hands."

Clapping her hands, she stepped off the porch and into the yard and called for the children to stop their games. When they immediately abandoned the tree swing and seesaw that Luke had built and came running, she heard Roger Hadwell chuckle.

"The children mind their teacher better than they do their parents," he said. But then Lydia noticed a clouded expression pass over his features. "Just wish there were more of the little ones around," he added softly as he made his way past her and into the house.

"What did he mean by that?" John asked. He and Lydia were the only adults left on the porch.

"Enrollment is down at the school and it

may have to be closed," Lydia explained. She was so relieved that his first attempt at conversing with her had nothing to do with their personal history that she was able to speak easily. She saw John's eyes widen in surprise and concern.

"But that's your . . . that's the way you . . ."

"Times are hard, John. You know that perhaps better than anyone in Celery Fields. If the school building and land can be put to better purpose for the good of the community then that's the way of it." She herded the children into a single line and pointed to a basin and towel set up on the porch. "Wash your hands," she instructed.

"But what about you — what's best for you?" John persisted. He reached around her to hold open the door so the children could file into the house.

She looked at him for a long moment. "You are still too much with the outside world, John," she said. "You have forgotten the lesson of joy."

"Joy?"

"Jesus first, you last and others in between." She actually ticked off each item on her fingers the same way she might if teaching one of her students the lesson. Embarrassed by her primness, she followed the last child into the house, leaving John standing on the porch.

She had not intended to engage in any true exchange of conversation with him, anything that might let him know more of her life after all this time. Her plan had been to remain polite but distant. Still, the realization that he had forgotten the old ways — the idea that community came first — was just one more bit of evidence that John Amman would struggle against the bonds that the people of Celery Fields lived by.

Why should she concern herself with his happiness? He had left her before and he would leave her again.

After Lydia moved the children into the house, John stayed on the porch staring out over the single street that ran from Luke and Greta's house to the far end of town where the bakery and ice-cream shop sat. He found it hard to absorb how much the community had changed in eight years and yet so much was familiar and comforting about being back here. In the distance he heard a train whistle and he remembered how as a boy he had dreamed about where that train might one day take him, the adventures he might have. The adventures he and Liddy might have together. But the destinations of that train held no attraction for him now. He knew all too well what was out there.

"John?"

Greta stood on the other side of the screen door watching him with an uncertain smile. She was so very different from Lydia in both physical appearance and demeanor. Greta's smile came readily while Lydia's had to be coaxed. Greta's vivacious personality drew people to her while Lydia's reserve kept them at arm's length.

"We are ready for supper," Greta said.

John pulled open the screen door. *"Gut,"* he said with a grin intended to erase the lines of concern from Greta's forehead. "It's been three hours since I last ate."

Greta glanced back at him and then she giggled. "Ah, John Amman, it is good to have you back. We have missed you."

They were still talking and laughing when they entered the large front room where a table stretched into the hallway to accommodate all the adults and children. John paused for a moment to enjoy the scene. This was one of the things he had missed most about the life he'd left behind — this gathering of friends and family on any excuse to share in food and conversation and the special occasions of life. He recalled one time when he had attended a Thanksgiving dinner at the home of his business partner in the outside world. There the adults had sat at a dining-room table set with such obviously expensive crystal and china that John had spent the entire meal worrying that he might break something. The children had been shooed away to the kitchen and a separate table set for them with the more practical everyday crockery.

He liked the Amish way of having all generations in one room much better, he decided as he pulled out a vacant chair. He glanced around until he located Lydia taking a seat on the same side of the table but with the safety of his aunt and three small children separating them. Luke took his place at the head of the table and all conversation stopped as every head bowed in silent prayer.

John thanked God for the food and for the willingness of the townspeople to forgive him and take him back into the fold of the community — and for second chances. After a long moment he heard Luke clear his throat, signaling that the meal could begin. Instantly the room came alive with the clink of dishes being passed. Conversation buzzed as the adults talked crops and weather while the children whispered excitedly. No doubt they were all anticipating a piece of Samuel's birthday cake — a treat Greta told them would not be forthcoming until every child had devoured all of his or her peas.

From farther down the table he picked out the low murmur of Lydia's voice and found himself leaning forward, straining to catch whatever she was saying to Pleasant's husband, Jeremiah. She was smiling as she cut small slices of the sausage and then placed the meat on Samuel's plate.

It struck John that she performed this task so naturally that she might have been the boy's mother. And for the rest of the meal, while he fielded the questions of those around him about his plans for the future, John found his thoughts going back to a time when he had first thought what a good mother Liddy would be. The time when he had imagined her as the mother of the children they would have together. And he could not help but wonder if she regretted never marrying.

She glanced up then, her gaze meeting his and she did not look away as she continued to speak to young Samuel, reassuring the boy that she had seen his birthday cake and it was his favorite — banana with chocolate frosting. John wondered if she was remembering that this was his favorite, as well. He wondered if she was remembering a day when the two of them had shared a single piece of cake, their fingers sticky with the frosting as they fed each other bites while sitting in the loft of her father's barn.

How they had laughed together that day, and on so many other days. But now her expression was as serious as it had been each time he had seen her since his return. In her eyes he saw questions and could not help but wonder if her questions were the same as his.

CHAPTER FIVE

Lydia had managed to convince herself that once she settled into the daily routine of morning and evening chores separated by her duties as teacher, John Amman would be less of a problem for her. Surely, once everyone in Celery Fields returned to the regular business of living and working, John would cease to be the topic of discussion and speculation. He would be busy with his work at the hardware store all day every day except Sundays. The chores he had taken on for Luke in exchange for living above the livery would occupy him in the early mornings and after the store had closed for the day.

But when she returned home on Monday she found a basket filled with oranges next to her door. There were orange trees in Greta's yard and her first thought was that the gift had come from her sister. But she and Greta had sat on the back porch after they'd finished cleaning up after the party on Sunday and Lydia had noticed that the fruit on her sister's tree was not quite ripe enough to pick yet.

"The tree outside Luke's shop is loaded with fruit," Greta had said. "Every day he brings me a basket filled with the largest, sweetest oranges I've ever tasted."

Lydia hesitated before reaching for the basket. She glanced down toward the livery where she could see the tree, its orange bounty reflected in the bright sunlight of late afternoon. The tree stood just outside the stables at the back of Luke's shop and she was well aware it was a tree that John passed every time he descended or climbed the stairs to his living quarters.

A square of white paper tucked in with the fruit caught her eye.

"Remember the day we picked oranges?"

She folded the paper slowly as the memory he'd awakened overcame her. They could not have been much more than ten or eleven. It had been Christmastime and the children and their teacher had planned a special program to celebrate the season. Their teacher had sent the older children — Lydia and John among them — to pick oranges from a grove of trees at the Harnischer farm to be handed out as a treat at the end of the evening.

"We will need a gross at least," their teacher had instructed. "How many is that, John Amman?"

"One hundred and forty-four," he'd replied without hesitation. Even then John was good with numbers.

"And there are how many dozen?"

"Twelve."

Their teacher had smiled and then counted the older children. "There are six of you so how many must each of you bring back?"

"Two dozen," the students had chorused.

"Two dozen of the most perfect specimens you can gather," their teacher had added. "Now off you go."

The other children had finished the task within half an hour of arriving at the orange grove. And so had John. But Lydia had lingered over every orange until he'd lost patience. This one was not as large as that one was. Another had a slight blemish. And wasn't it more desirable to have the fruit's stem and perhaps a leaf or two still showing? But the leaves would dry and wither and that was no good.

"We're going back!" he had shouted.

"I'll be right there," she had replied as she made her way deeper into the grove, oblivious to the waning daylight. The Harnischers had gone away for the holidays to visit relatives and as the shadows lengthened Lydia had been unaware that all the other students, including John, had returned to the school. By the time she realized she was alone and she had wandered to the farthest end of the large grove of trees, it was dark.

She shuddered as she recalled how terrified she'd been as she fumbled blindly along the rows of trees trying to find her way back to the farmhouse and the road so she could return to town. Every night sound that she thought of as almost a lullaby when she lay safe in her bed seemed ominous in the dark. Fallen fruit made the way more challenging as she tripped over the oranges on the ground. By the time she reached the Harnischers' house she was choking back tears.

She knew it was not that late, but in the country the darkness was like a blanket thrown over any possibility of light. There was no moon that night. She knew that her family thought she was at the school rehearsing the pageant with the other children. No one would come looking for her for hours. She had sat on the steps of the porch, her arms wrapped around herself as she cried and tried to think what to do.

Then she had heard a sound, faint and in

the distance — someone was calling her name.

"Here!" she had shouted, running toward the sound. "I am here."

She had slipped on the root of a banyan tree and gone sprawling onto her stomach, the breath knocked out of her as she tried without success to call again.

"Liddy Goodloe!"

It was the voice of John Amman. Although the two of them had had their differences over the years, she had never been so happy to hear him calling out to her.

"Here," she managed, and only minutes later he was there beside her, placing a kerosene lantern carefully on the ground as he bent to help her.

"What hurts?" he asked.

"I scraped my palms when I fell," she admitted, holding her hands out to him, "but really, I am all right." She started to stand up but he blocked her way.

"Stay still," he ordered, and he removed his wide-brimmed hat, as if it might block the light while he examined her palms.

"Really, I am . . ."

He let out a heavy sigh. "Why do you always have to be so stubborn, Liddy Goodloe?"

"I am certainly not as stubborn as you

are, John Amman. Now, please move so I can stand up. It's a long way back to town and Dat will be worried."

But instead of doing what she asked, he continued holding her hands as he ran his thumbs lightly over her palms. "You frightened me, Liddy," he said softly. "You said you would be along shortly so I went back with the others. But when it got dark and you still had not come . . ."

Liddy pulled her fingers free and, with one hand, brushed back his flaxen hair from his forehead. "I did not mean to frighten you, John," she said. She thought she might faint from the rush of pure joy she felt at the realization that he cared, truly cared for her the way she did for him. "We should go back," she said softly.

Without a word John replaced his hat and retrieved the lantern and her basket of oranges. He handed her the lantern, and as they walked back toward town she slipped her hand in his and did not let go.

Remember the day we picked oranges?

"I remember," she whispered as she carried the basket of fruit inside and set it on the table. Then she went to place John's note in the box where she had kept all of her special treasures when she and John were courting.

■ ■ ■ ■

By the end of his second week in Celery Fields John had settled back into life in the town as if the years he'd spent in the *Englischer* world had been no more than a bad dream. He took up his duties in his uncle's hardware store with a familiarity born of the years he had worked there as a teenager. He waited on customers, filled and delivered orders, and even managed the store on his own one day when his uncle took ill and Gert stayed home to care for him.

He was aware that gossip around town had it that he would one day take over the business permanently, but the Hadwells were still in their prime and it would be years before anything like that might happen. In the meantime, stretching the income of the business to cover the needs of three adults took some doing. To make matters easier on his aunt and uncle, John continued the arrangement of bartering his services at the stables with Luke so that he had no rent to pay and his uncle could keep his wages low. He had revived his habit of going to the bay after finishing work. Twice already he'd brought back buckets of clams and a string of fresh-caught fish that his aunt prepared for the noon meal the three of them always shared at the store. He also planted a kitchen garden behind the store so he could tend it when business was slow, which was often. He planned to give the harvest to his aunt in return for the steady supply of covered dishes she kept bringing him for his supper.

The main problem John faced was trying to decide whether he and Liddy might have a future, after all. She did not appear to be trying to avoid him. They were both so busy with their work that most days he barely caught a glimpse of her and, when he did, she was usually surrounded by others — her sister, her students or some of the women in town. On the one hand he was glad he had some time to consider his options. If he and Liddy were to find their way back to each other he wanted to make sure that this time he would be fully ready for them to start the life they had postponed for all these years.

The one thing his father had taught him was the responsibility of a man to provide properly for his wife and children. Of course, his father had insisted that farming was the only way to do that. In his eyes — weather notwithstanding — the land was God's gift and the only living a man needed to secure a future for his family. He had never understood John's attraction to building things and found his curiosity about how some machine or tool worked as bordering on dangerous.

"Never mind how it works," he would grumble. "Just thank the Lord that it does."

In spite of his father's disapproval, John had continued to focus his interest on ways he might make a living other than by farming. And Liddy had encouraged that. How many hours had they spent thinking about all the ways he might put his talent for carpentry to use to establish a business once they were married?

They had finally settled on the idea of John setting himself up as a clockmaker and furniture builder. Liddy had assured him that in time his father would come around, even when his father accused him of willfully disobeying his elders and from that day refused to speak further of John's future. Instead, he focused all of his attention and praise on John's younger brothers — boys as dedicated to farming as their father was.

"We'll be fine," Liddy had said repeatedly. But he could not help but recall how her small hands had tightened into fists as if she alone would make sure that everything turned out for the best.

But providing for the family was a man's job and he had been determined to prove himself — to his father and to Liddy. He'd been so sure that she would understand why it was so important for him to succeed.

"But you haven't succeeded, have you?" he muttered to himself as he loaded lumber for a neighbor's new barn onto his uncle's delivery wagon. "It's going to take years before you have enough to support a family — even if Liddy were willing . . . even if you and she . . ."

They were both almost thirty years old. Not that age mattered, but if they wanted children . . . and they did. . . . Or at least they had once upon a time. Surely she still did want children of her own. In their courting days they had talked often of the offspring they would have, how things would be different for them, how John would encourage them to find the talents God had given them and build a future with those. They had so often talked about how their children would be native Floridians, not transplants like their parents and grandparents. They would have different opportunities.

But what if Lydia had changed her mind? What if having spent years teaching other people's children she had decided that was enough? Night after night John had fought his inclination to go to Liddy's house and ask her point-blank what she was thinking, feeling. And as he considered how he'd failed to achieve anything he began to understand why Lydia might have decided to make a clean break of it with him by refusing to answer his letters. He had asked for and received the forgiveness of his friends and neighbors, but he wondered if God had truly forgiven him for his foolish and prideful ways. What if never having enough to support Liddy and make a home with her was to be God's punishment?

"You're getting ahead of yourself," he muttered as he scooped up the last of the powdered cleaning compound that his uncle used to sweep out the store at the end of every day. "What makes you think she's even interested in a future?"

The bell above the front door jangled. "Be right there," John called, chastising himself for forgetting the turn the latch on the door. On the other hand a customer was a customer. He wiped his hands on a clean rag as he walked to the front of the store.

Of all the people he imagined might be standing just inside the door, her hand still on the doorknob as if she might change her mind and leave, the last person he would have guessed was Liddy Goodloe.

"Oh," she said when she saw him coming toward her, "I thought . . . I had wanted to . . . Is Gertrude not here?"

John slowed his step, keeping some distance between them as he might have were he approaching a skittish mare. "Just me, I'm afraid," he replied with a smile. "Can I help?" She was clutching a basket.

"I brought her . . . these are scraps she needs for . . . We're making a quilt for Greta's baby," she finally managed. She fumbled with the doorknob. "I'll just. . . ."

John stepped forward and relieved her of the basket. "My aunt will be back tomorrow. I can give these to her then if you like."

"She wanted to work on the quilt this evening. I got delayed at the school and . . ."

"It's not that far. Why don't I walk them over to Gert's house?"

"I can manage," she replied, seeming to conquer her obvious bout of nerves. She held out her hand for the basket. "Thank you for offering." Her tone again was prim and proper.

"Liddy, don't be stubborn. It's nearly dark and you know there have been some incidents in the town — vagrants wandering through and such."

"The last incident like that was months ago, before . . ." She pressed her hand to her lips as if to stem the tide of her words.

"Before I wandered into town?" He handed her the basket. "Humor me, Liddy. Let me walk with you to my uncle's house. If you like I'll wait in the shadows. They won't even know I'm there."

"Gert will want me to come inside."

He bit back a smile, knowing she was wavering. "I can wait," he said softly. *For as long as it takes to win you back.*

She chewed her bottom lip as she looked around the store, dimly lit now as the shadows of evening gathered. "All right," she agreed, and then her eyes pinned him with their glitter of determination. "But you will stay back and no one is to know . . ."

"I'll just put these away," John said, picking up the push broom and bucket of cleaning compound. "Won't be a minute," he added, backing away and afraid that the minute she saw her opportunity she would change her mind and leave.

In the back room he took a minute to remove his hat and smooth his hair, then brush sawdust off his trousers. At the same time he sent up a silent prayer of thanks that God had provided this unexpected opportunity for him to walk with Liddy. It would bring back all the wonderful memories of the times they had kept company together, the times they had laughed together. The times they had stopped under the shadow of a live oak tree and shared a kiss.

"Are you coming or not?" Liddy demanded using her teacher's voice.

"*Yah. Ich bin . . .*" He gave his trousers one more swipe with his palms and headed for the front of the store.

Once they were outside he noticed that Liddy kept glancing around as if she feared being spotted by one of their neighbors. At the end of the street kerosene lanterns lighted her sister's house, but otherwise the thoroughfare was dark. All of the shops were closed for the night, their owners at home finishing their suppers, readying their children for bed or reading their evening Scripture.

"Do you think it might be too late?" Liddy wondered aloud.

"I don't think so. Gert was late leaving the shop this evening and Roger was out making a delivery. I expect they might just be sitting down to their meal."

Lydia stopped walking and seemed about to turn away from the lane leading to the Hadwell house. "I wouldn't want to interrupt their supper," she said.

"But if my aunt needs the scraps for the quilt . . ." he reminded her. To his relief this seemed to give her the impetus she needed to press on. "When is the baby coming?" he asked, and immediately realized that such a statement could be taken as the invasion of a private family matter among the Amish. "Sorry," he muttered.

"You are going to have to watch your ways, John, if you truly wish to make your place in this community," Liddy admonished him, and the fact that she was frowning in disapproval was evident in her tone.

"Perhaps, but when we were younger Greta was like a sister to me." He chuckled at the memory. "A pesky little sister but nevertheless . . ."

To his surprise and delight, Liddy laughed. "You came up with so many schemes for escaping her notice," she said.

"And not one of them worked. I doubt those children of hers can get away with much," he added.

Liddy sighed. "It is hard to believe that she's a mother herself, almost four times over now."

"She is certainly providing future students for you to teach," he said. When Liddy grew quiet as they walked away from town and down the lane that led to his uncle's house he knew that once again he had said the wrong thing. Still, having broached the subject, he decided to persevere. "Tell me more about this business of shutting down the school."

"I told you, John. The elders are thinking that for the time being the building and land might be put to better use. They will do what is best."

"But if a community is to thrive, surely it needs to have a school," he argued.

"Whatever the children need to learn can be taught at home," she replied, but her voice sounded as if she were simply repeating some argument given for closing the school. "And these hard times are bound to pass. Once more people come here to live, we can start another school."

"And what about —"

"Ah, here we are," she interrupted as they approached the gate that led to the small cottage his uncle and aunt occupied. "Wait here. I won't be long."

He crouched down in the gathering darkness, resting his elbows on his knees while she walked up the path and knocked on the front door. Her voice and his aunt's were muffled, but the tone of their words told him that Gert had invited her inside and she had refused. He heard her laugh as she retreated down the porch steps and called out her good-night. How he had missed the lilt of that laughter!

He was about to rise to meet her when he heard her hiss, "Stay down." Then she turned back toward the house and waved. *"Guten nacht,"* she called out.

John watched as Liddy continued on her way back toward town. If his aunt were watching she would see only Liddy walking with her usual determined stride.

"Well, come along," she said in a normal tone when she'd already gotten several yards past him.

He caught up to her and she started to walk faster. He kept pace and even moved a little ahead of her as he turned to face her. She giggled as she raced past him. Then they both started to run as they had when they were children and had just gotten away with avoiding Greta or John's stern father and were running off to the shore to wade in the shallow water and collect shells. And it was the most natural thing in the world for John to grasp her hand in his as they ran back toward town.

Lydia was not only giggling like one of her students, she was also gasping for breath by the time she and John reached her front porch. It felt like old times — the two of them out together on some adventure, the wind in their faces and hair, her one hand clutching his while the other held fast to her bonnet. Their fingers were so entwined that it was as if he never intended to let go and Lydia found that she liked that feeling — she liked it very much.

Too much, she thought as caution and common sense overcame her giddiness. She slid her hand from his and pressed it to her chest as she forced her breathing to slow. "Thank you for going with me, John. You were right — I would have been nervous in the dark alone," she admitted. "And I did not thank you for the oranges you left for me. They were very . . . sweet."

It was the wrong word but the only one that came to mind. She found that she could not look at him, and yet even if she closed her eyes she could see him clearly: the wide smile that lit his entire face as if his features had been bathed in sunlight; the eyes that twinkled and teased and dared her to take the kinds of risks that he had more often than she cared to recall talked her into taking as teenagers; the mouth that so often had kissed hers in those long ago years.

A moment before she had been babbling like a brook, the words tumbling out almost faster than she could think them. But with the sudden image of his lips meeting hers she felt as if she had been struck dumb.

"*Guten nacht,* John," she whispered as she prepared to flee such thoughts of him in favor of the secure isolation of her house. But he caught hold of her hand before she could move more than a step away from him.

And then he waited. John had never been more eloquent than when he said nothing. Everything he might have said was contained in the compelling silence that was heavy with expectation and unasked questions.

"John," she whispered, and her voice was a plea that she could not have defined. Was she asking him to stop or to come closer? Did she want him to leave or to stay? She had no idea what her feelings were. "You confuse me," she added petulantly.

He chuckled and stroked her cheek with the tips of his fingers. She closed her eyes, savoring that touch.

"*Gut,*" he replied as he kissed her lightly on her forehead.

And then he was gone.

■ ■ ■ ■

Slow and steady, John reminded himself as he walked from Lydia's house to his rooms above the stables. And although he had to fight against the urge to look back at her, he kept walking, knowing she was still standing where he'd left her. He could not keep the smile off his face. He had his answer. Whatever she had felt about his leaving all those years earlier he was sure now she was glad he was back. A man could build something on that.

Later, as he lay in bed waiting for sleep to come, he thought about the many good days he'd had since returning to Celery Fields. That first day when he'd gone to the school and Lydia had walked into the schoolroom. Later, when he'd surprised his aunt. The meeting with Bishop Troyer when he'd known by the man's kindness and complete absence of censure that he would be forgiven. Then, that Sunday when he had stood before the congregation — some faces familiar while others were new to him — and without question they had welcomed him back into the fold of their community. *All except Lydia.*

She had maintained her caution and

reserve, while remaining polite.

Until tonight.

He folded his hands behind his head and gazed out the small window at a strip of clouds sailing across the moon. The way things were going he had every reason to hope that he might win her back. They might have a real future just like the one they had planned years earlier.

Slowly John's smile and the high spirits behind it dissolved into the worried frown that had been his constant companion when he and Lydia had first talked of marriage. Nothing had changed. Or maybe now things were worse than they'd been when he left. He still had no means to start a business of his own — he was a carpenter with no tools. And he could hardly expect to earn enough from clerking at the hardware store to make the kind of life he wanted for Liddy.

He sat up, his bare feet resting on the polished floor, his fingers buried in his hair as he realized that unlike before when he'd so foolishly left, these days he literally had nothing to offer Liddy. Everything he had earned in the world was gone, taken by creditors along with the business he'd built with George Stevens, the son of a wealthy *Englischer* family. The Stevenses had absorbed their son's part of the losses. They had even offered John some money "to tide him over" but he had refused.

"You'll do all right," his partner had assured him. "You've got a gift for building things, fine things that one day people will be wanting again," he added. "These hard times won't last forever, John, and one day . . ."

John couldn't afford to dwell on *one day.* He needed to find work he could do today and tomorrow and next year. He thought about some of the furniture pieces he had designed and built — pieces that were then mass produced in their factory and sold to stores all up and down the East Coast. Tables and chests and bureaus and desks. And the clocks. How he had loved figuring out the intricate workings of fine clocks — each cog and wheel and wire set just so.

But those days are gone, as are my tools, he reminded himself as he flopped back on the bed and stared at the ceiling. He had a trade, a skill with which he might make a decent living, but without the tools or the money it would take to purchase lumber and the other materials he would need, how was he going to build a business? And without a way of earning a living, there could be no future for him with Liddy.

He closed his eyes against the sting of

tears. What a mess he'd made of everything. He and Liddy were no longer teenagers flush with the certainty of youth that all things were possible. "Oh, Liddy, what are we going to do?"

He got up and paced the confines of the tiny apartment, finally coming to rest at the kitchen window that looked down on Liddy's house, which was dark now. She would be sleeping. But then he saw a light in the window of an upstairs room and the silhouette of Liddy herself seated in a chair, her head bent as if in prayer. And even though he had no idea whether she was also struggling with thoughts of the evening they had shared — of his touch, his light kiss on her forehead — he needed to believe that such a thing was likely. Because believing that she held him in her thoughts and prayers, he would find a way.

God would show him a way.

CHAPTER SIX

Lydia saw John only from a distance over the next several days. Sometimes when she was on her way to school she would see him grooming one of the horses from Luke's livery. He would pause for a moment in his work and lift his hand, palm out, to her. At first she simply nodded in his direction and kept walking. But after a week of such silent greetings she found herself responding in kind. She took some pleasure in the blossoming of his smile when he saw her return the special signal they had devised in their youth.

Each of them worked long hours and they both had chores. Ever since the evening that John had walked with her to the Hadwells' and then seen her home again, Lydia had begun staying after school to tutor a child, correct the children's work or prepare the lessons for the following day. After a few days she realized that she was unconsciously timing her departure from the school for when John might be finishing his work at the hardware store. Such schoolgirl foolishness was more Greta's way than Lydia's and yet she simply could not seem to help herself. John Amman was constantly in her thoughts.

Not that her careful timing did any good. Even if she stayed at school until nearly suppertime, John was always still at the hardware store. She knew Roger and Gert closed at five, as did every other merchant in Celery Fields. But many an evening John stayed there until well after dark. What could he be doing?

Unable to suppress her curiosity, she left school one day at her regular time, went home and spent some time squeezing lemons from Greta's garden to make lemonade. She told herself that her purpose was to use the lemons before they spoiled, and then she ended up with far more of the product than she could hope to use herself. It was only prudent that she share.

Through her open kitchen window she heard the rhythmic sound of a handsaw passing back and forth across a piece of lumber. The sound was faint but definitely coming from the rear of the hardware. It was well past five. The sun was low on the horizon, but the heat and humidity that earlier had led Lydia to release the children to sit under the shade of a banyan tree to work on their lessons had not abated.

Before she could change her mind or overanalyze her motives, Lydia filled a crockery pitcher with the fresh lemonade, chipped in some ice from the block that Jeremiah had delivered to her earlier that week and carried the pitcher and two glasses outside to the porch. Her plan was to sit on the swing and wait until she saw John walking from the store to the steps leading up to his rooms. She would offer him the lemonade, as she would to any neighbor she saw coming home from a long, hot working day, she told herself firmly.

With her plan decided she took her place on the swing. From this vantage point she had a clear view of the stables with the stairway that led up to John's rooms as well as the hardware store. She poured half a glass of lemonade for herself. Then she realized that it would be odd for her to simply be sitting idly sipping lemonade at this time of day. She should be doing something — reading or needlework.

She went back inside and retrieved her sewing basket. Taking her place again on the porch swing, she pulled out the pieces for a nine-patch quilt square and began stitching them together. Yes, this was better. She could keep an eye on things and yet not appear to be laying in wait.

But as the shadows lengthened and it became harder to see the small pieces of the patchwork, much less measure her stitches properly, Lydia grew restless. The sounds of the wind rustling the large palm fronds, dry from the days without rain, were usually a comfort to her after a long day at school. Tonight the sound grated on her nerves. Through the open window she could hear the clock in the front room clicking off the seconds as the brass hands made their way toward six-thirty. The chatter of the birds as they settled into the shrubs surrounding her house for the night seemed louder than usual. A horse in the stables whinnied. The ice in the pitcher settled into melting.

And still John stayed at the hardware. She saw the unmistakable glow of a lantern spilling its light onto the loading dock through the open back door of the shop. The sawing had been replaced by hammering, a light tapping that matched the restless rhythm of her foot.

"This is ridiculous," Lydia muttered as she put aside her sewing and stood. Without bothering to retrieve her bonnet, she picked up the extra glass and the pitcher of watery lemonade and struck out across the yard toward the rear of the hardware store. With each step she told herself that she simply needed to satisfy her curiosity about what John was doing at the shop so late. It was nothing more than that. She would take him the cool beverage on the pretense of having noticed that he was still working. She would see whatever he was doing and, satisfied at last, she would walk home and get some rest.

But when she reached the hardware's loading dock, she stopped short, her mouth open in surprise and admiration. Inside John had set his hammer aside and was sanding the arms of the most beautiful rocking chair Lydia had ever seen. It was small and slender and the lines were as graceful as the woman who would surely sit there cradling her child.

"Is that for Greta?" she asked as she climbed the three steps to the loading dock.

John glanced up and grinned. "Shh," he whispered, putting his finger to his lips. "Luke wants it to be a surprise." He stood and set the sanding block on a stool near the chair. "Is that for me?" he asked, nodding toward the pitcher and glass she held as he wiped his forehead with the back of his arm.

He was so incredibly handsome, his features lit by the soft glow of the lantern. Lydia felt her heart race, and her hand shook a little as she filled a glass and handed it to him. "It's watery," she said.

He drank it down without pausing for breath and held the glass out for her to refill. "It's perfect," he replied.

He was not wearing his hat. His hair was damp with sweat and clung to the edges of his face. He had rolled back his sleeves, exposing tanned and muscular forearms, and he was covered in a fine coat of sawdust.

"This is very kind of you, making a chair for Greta," she began, needing to say something to break the silence that surrounded them, a silence filled with unspoken possibilities.

"Not kind at all. Luke hired me to do it. Seems he preferred not to do business with Josef Bontrager even though from what I've been told Josef has the furniture-making trade pretty well sewn up in these parts."

"Greta will be very surprised. She already has a rocking chair, the one our mother used when we were born."

John frowned. "Do you think she won't want to replace that one? Luke tells me that after three children already, the chair is in need of some repair. Maybe he should have . . ."

Instinctively she placed her hand on his arm. "She will be very, very pleased," she assured him.

John drank the second glass of lemonade more slowly than the first. "Come to think of it, I seem to recall that Greta and Josef Bontrager were pretty close. What happened?"

"They were just children in those days. Greta and Luke are a good match and Josef seems to have made an equally good match with the Yoders' eldest daughter, Esther. It has all turned out well, as God intended," Lydia assured him.

John grinned. "It certainly has for me. Luke is paying me a nice sum to make this chair for Greta, and if others see the work, perhaps they will . . ." He stopped abruptly.

She hated the shadow of defeat that passed over his features. He set down the empty glass and took up his sanding block again.

"It's just something I was able to do for Luke," he told her. "Roger said I could use the space here and his tools in the evenings to work on it. With the money Luke is paying me I can start replacing some of the tools that I used to have."

Lydia waited for him to say more but he just worked the sanding block across the curve of the rockers.

"Will you tell me what happened, John?" Lydia set the pitcher next to his glass and folded her arms in her apron as she leaned against the doorjamb. She knew that she should simply let the past go, but she had so many questions.

He shrugged and kept on working, not looking at her. "Surely you know the story. It's the same for everyone out there. Things were going well — and then they weren't."

"You made a good living then?"

"For a while. Most of the time."

She could see that the memory caused him pain so she stopped asking about it. Instead, she watched him work. "Have you eaten?" she asked after several minutes.

"Yah." He did not look at her and she wondered if he was still lost in the thoughts of happier times, before he'd been forced to come back to Celery Fields. And from there logic took her to the more obvious point.

He had come home to Celery Fields. That did not mean he had come back because of her. John had a ready smile and friendly wave for everyone he saw. Why was she imagining that she was special to him? Or was it John's true motive to win her back because out in the world he had fallen so far that he had decided she represented a safe haven? He had come back to his past and she was nothing more to him than a part of that past. She was making a fool of herself for all the town to see.

Without a word she collected the pitcher and glass and walked back out to the loading dock.

"Wait," he called.

"It's late," she replied, and kept walking.

John caught up to her before she cleared the last step of the loading dock. He closed his fingers around her upper arms and turned her so that she was facing him. "It's hard, Liddy," he said. "Going back over those times — the fool I made of myself, the losses I suffered."

"But you are back now and safe again."

"And you think that's what I want? When did I want what was safe, Liddy? When did *you* want that?"

Finally she looked up at him and in the light spilling out from the shop he saw that she studied him not with the longing and love he'd hoped for, but with pity. He released her arm and stepped back.

"We were so young then, John." He hated the way her lips pursed in the disapproving manner of their former teacher.

"You were not a child that Sunday when you decided to take your place with the married women at services," he reminded her. "That was an act of defiance by the girl I once knew, the girl I . . ."

Her expression softened as she pressed her fingers over his lips. "Do not say things you will regret," she whispered. "Please. You are too soon trying to set things the way you remember them, the way you want them to be. But you are not the boy who left here, John. And I am not that girl. We cannot go back in this world — only forward."

She pulled away from him and continued walking back to her house — *her* house, *her* school, *her* life.

"We could be if you're willing to work things out with me," he said, and was gratified to see her step falter. "We could find a way to . . ."

She turned around but her features remained in shadow. "I am glad that you've come home, John. Is that not enough for now?"

"It's a beginning," he admitted. "But . . ."

"And that's the point, John Amman. We are beginning again and you must allow time for things to develop according to

God's will." She took half a step toward him and stopped. "You must think of me as someone you are just getting to know, John."

"Is that how you see me? As some stranger?"

"Not a stranger exactly. Just not . . ." Her voice trailed off.

"Just not the same person you once loved?"

For a long moment she said nothing. Then very softly she said, "There are glimpses of him, John Amman. That I will grant you, but it has been eight years and whether you are willing to admit it or not, each of us has changed — grown, hopefully — taught and shaped by the lives we have lived while apart."

He knew she was right but he didn't want her to be. "So what are we, Liddy?" He knew he sounded annoyed.

"We have made a good start as neighbors."

He snorted. "Neighbors? I barely see you these days."

"Friends, then — friends who have not seen each other for many years and are looking forward to getting reacquainted."

He could see that it was the best answer he was likely to get on this occasion. "Truly? You're looking forward to getting to know me again?"

She laughed and the lightness of it floated on the air between them. "I am, John Amman. I seem to remember that you were always a most interesting man. Now, *guten nacht.*"

He let her go, watching until she let herself into the dark house, waiting for the light in the window of the front room that never came.

Lydia was actually shaking as she stepped inside the dark house and closed the door behind her with a soft click. It wasn't a chill or fear that overcame her. It was her understanding that after all these years — after assuring herself that she had made a life for herself — she still had deep feelings for John. But surely such feelings were born of reflection on things past. John's very presence in Celery Fields was bound to stir up scenes they had shared when they were younger. His laughter would naturally bring back those times when they had laughed together. His touch would evoke the sensation of times in the past when he had held her hand, stroked her cheek, kissed her.

She closed her eyes against the flood of sensations that swept through her as she leaned against the closed door. Having John Amman back in town was going to be much harder than she could have imagined.

"Well, there's nothing for it but to take things one day at a time," she admonished herself. She pushed away from the door and in the dark went through the familiar regimen of preparing for the next day's teaching and for bed. But, after assembling the items she would need for the following school day, she bypassed the rocking chair in the front room where she was accustomed to ending her day by reading passages from her Bible and silently praying for her students, her family and her neighbors.

Her chair, the one her father had sat in when he was alive, was nothing at all like the chair that John had been making for Greta. But it was enough that it was a rocking chair and that alone brought to mind the image of the beautifully shaped wood, the smooth gracefulness of the back and arms, the sheer simple beauty of John's handiwork. From there it took little to make the leap to recalling her fingers touching his lips. She found herself standing next to her father's rocking chair, her fingers moving slowly over her own lips.

"You are being ridiculous, Lydia Goodloe," she said as if she were lecturing one of her students. "Go to bed."

She followed her own advice but sleep did

not come. Instead, she lay awake next to the open window. Every night sound seemed exaggerated and she kept thinking she was hearing the swoosh of a handsaw slicing into wood or the light tapping of a hammer. Surely John was not still at work on the chair. Like her he had to work long hours the following day, and yet she recalled that even as a boy he had been single-minded when it came to completing an important project. And John would see the perfection of that chair as vital to his goal of impressing Luke and anyone else who might see his handiwork.

Lydia frowned. He was clearly aware that Josef Bontrager had been the carpenter that the people of Celery Fields had turned to for years. John must understand that loyalty, if nothing else, would keep them from abandoning Josef in favor of buying from him. And, besides, there were two other issues that made questionable his chances of succeeding in establishing himself as a furniture maker. For one thing, the families still living in Celery Fields had been there for years and their homes were already furnished. And second, even if someone did need to replace a cabinet or chair, most likely the purchase would be postponed until the economy was stable again.

She should warn him of the folly of his plan.

Why me? Surely his uncle . . .

But I know him so well.

She sat up and pulled the heavy braid of her hair over one shoulder, fingering the ends that curled round her forefinger as she tried to calm herself. Again she thought John Amman was too much on her mind. From the moment she'd seen him kneeling next to the stove at the schoolhouse he had been a constant presence, and she was only fooling herself if she believed that living practically next door to the man was going to be easy.

Didn't she have troubles enough of her own to worry about? If the school closed and she had no income she would have to consider selling this house, and then what? Move in with Greta? Pleasant? She shuddered at the image of the rest of her life spent as the spinster aunt whose only purpose in life was to make herself useful so as not to be a burden to her sisters and their husbands. Yes, she had more than enough to worry about without adding John Amman to the list. Neighbors? Fine. Friends? Of course. But anything more? Far too risky.

■ ■ ■ ■

After Liddy left, John returned to the shop and continued working on the chair. Only now, as he sanded and stained the smooth wood, he imagined he was making a chair for Liddy. He imagined them married and her rocking their child and singing softly to the baby. As he recalled she had a lovely voice, as sweet and clear as the air on a spring morning. He pictured the way she would look up at him from under her long lashes, her eyes brimming with love for him and their baby.

Liddy would be a wonderful mother.

But what kind of a father would he be? How would his natural inclination toward restlessness and adventure affect their children?

He paused in his work and closed his eyes.

How long would it be before he could no longer stand the sameness of the life he'd come home to in Celery Fields? At least when he was building something, he had the freedom of his creative imagination. There were always problems to be solved so that the piece turned out different.

He set down his paintbrush and wiped his hands on a rag. That was the crux of it. John had always been different, had always needed to stray from the path set for him first by his parents and then by his community. But, while he readily admitted that he had rebelled against those norms, he had never in all of his life felt that he was straying from the way God was leading him. Even when he left Celery Fields, he had felt he was doing what God intended him to do.

At first, he reminded himself sternly. For he had left with the best of intentions to go out and earn the money he would need to return, establish a business and marry Liddy. But when she had not replied to his letters — when there had been no word at all — he had turned his mind to the ways of the outsiders. Making his fortune became the one driving force that got him up every morning, and in time it had replaced everything else — his family, his religion . . . even Liddy.

Liddy. Liddy. Liddy.

She was everything he wanted in this life and yet he had nothing to offer her.

CHAPTER SEVEN

After that night, Lydia managed to keep her distance from John until the community gathered once again for their biweekly worship. But avoiding him at Sunday services and especially at the social gathering afterward proved more difficult. As she carried food out to the gathering in Josef Bontrager's large yard, John never seemed to be more than a few feet away from her. And even though he was engaged in conversation with the other men, his soft voice settled around her like blossoms from an orange tree blown free by a tropical breeze. When she sought refuge inside the large farmhouse, assuring Josef's wife, Esther, that she simply needed a break from the heat, she certainly did not expect to wander into the front room and find John there.

He was running the flat of his palm over the closed cover of Josef's tilt-top desk. The piece dominated one corner of the otherwise mostly barren front room. The expression on John's face was hard to read, but Lydia decided that it showed something between admiration and disappointment. Either way, she felt that it would not do for her to interrupt his reverie or for others to see them alone together. She turned to go.

"Josef Bontrager is a fine carpenter," John said without turning.

"*Yah.*" She was rooted to the spot, one foot half-turned to leave.

"I can see why he's earned the loyalty of his customers," he continued, moving on to the fireplace, studying the way Josef had so expertly matched the wood grain of each side piece and crossbeam the way a woman might precisely match the square of a quilt to form a border between the rows.

As the sun streamed in through the open windows, Lydia was glad for the breeze that filled the room with the fragrance of the bougainvillea blossoms matting the trellis outside the open window. She stepped into the room, the leather heels of her shoes echoing on the bare wooden floor that an hour earlier had been filled with the benches used for worship, benches now moved outside.

John turned to her with a wry smile. "My uncle has repeatedly reminded me that there is not much call for handmade furniture these days — hard times."

The words held an aura of bitterness and regret that seemed to cover him like a cloak. Lydia instinctively stepped closer as she searched for any gesture that might offer some comfort. "The chair you are making for Greta is fine," she said.

He smiled. "Are you complimenting me twice in one week, Lydia Goodloe?"

"I am simply stating a truth," she replied, hating the edge of contention that colored her words. Why did she always have to sound so prudish when she spoke with him?

"I could make you a chair — or a desk or anything you might like," he said, moving away from the fireplace and closer to her.

"My father furnished our home when he was alive. Besides, I have no money for such . . ." He kept coming until he was standing so near that if she moved an inch his breath would surely fan her suddenly hot cheeks.

"It would be a gift," he said, his eyes roaming over her features, her hair and finally settling on her eyes. "I have missed seeing you these last days, Liddy."

As have I missed you. "I was at the school and the evenings I spent with Greta helping her with the little ones. She has not been feeling well." *That's right. Stay with mundane, impersonal topics. Neighborly, friendly topics.*

John frowned. "The baby?"

It was not appropriate that she should discuss such matters with him — no woman would. But she was worried and, because she had promised Greta that she would say nothing to anyone lest talk get back to Luke, she had kept her concerns to herself. But this was John and she had always been able to confide in him.

"I'm worried," she admitted.

He lifted his hand as if to touch her then lowered it back to his side. "Can I help?"

She realized that he already was. The relief that flooded her with the ability to finally say aloud the thoughts she had carried with her for days now was like a great weight had been taken from her.

"You know Greta," she said, the words flowing like a rushing stream now. "She is determined to put on a brave face, but when it is just the two of us I see that she is so very uncomfortable. With the first three babies she had no problems at all, but this time is different."

"I can see now that Luke is also concerned. He's been quieter than usual these last days. I thought perhaps his distraction was due to the fact that business is slow, as it is for everyone. I expect he understands more than Greta realizes."

"Yes, they are so loving and caring with each other. Luke wants her to agree to see one of his customers, an *Englischer* doctor from Sarasota, but she refuses. She insists that she will be fine with the catcher."

John smiled. "I haven't heard that term for a very long time, Liddy."

"Do they not have catchers in the outside?"

His smile broadened. "Only in the game of baseball," he said with a chuckle. "Never applied to the woman who attends the mother in a birthing."

"Greta will be in good hands."

"Hilda Yoder is still the catcher for Celery Fields?"

Lydia nodded.

"She has certainly been present for the delivery of her share of the children of Celery Fields," John said. "And if Greta trusts her . . ."

"Oh, she does. Everyone does. It's just that . . ." Unexpectedly her eyes filled with tears. "Oh, John if I were to lose Greta . . ."

He caught the single escaping tear with his thumb. "She's not going to die," he said softly.

"You can't know that," she argued, but

she did not pull away from his touch.

"No," he said softly. "Just like you can't be sure that she might, so why worry about something we cannot control?"

He had a point. Lydia gave him a tentative smile. "You were always one to find the brighter side of the matter," she said.

He chuckled, his thumb still lightly touching her cheek. "And you were always the worrier."

Behind them a woman cleared her throat and they turned to find Hilda Yoder frowning at them. "Here you are, Lydia," she said, as if making a pronouncement for all those in the yard to hear. "I thought you must have already gone back to town to see how Greta is doing. I cannot recall a time when she and Luke missed services. We are all quite worried."

Lydia put several steps between herself and John by heading for the door where Hilda stood waiting. "There's no need for concern, Hilda. Greta is just a bit under the weather."

"Still, it would ease all our minds to know that you were with her — at this time," she added with a look that conveyed her reluctance to mention Greta's pregnancy.

"Yes, you are right. I was just about to . . ."

"Let me drive you there," John said.

"I really do not think that you and Lydia should be seen . . ." Hilda began.

But John gave her the smile that Lydia remembered charming every female in Celery Fields, regardless of her age, from the time John was a young boy. "Ah, now Hilda Yoder, let me do my part in setting your mind at rest. As it happens my uncle and aunt and I were late coming this morning so there was no time to stable their horse. Why spend time hitching up Liddy's buggy when God has already seen to our having one ready to go?"

Lydia saw what he was doing. By turning things around so that he seemed to be trying to put Hilda at ease he would no doubt win her approval.

"Well, I suppose . . . perhaps I should ride along, then."

"That might be all right," John said hesitantly as he frowned and scratched his clean-shaven chin.

"But?" Hilda asked impatiently.

"Well, that might give folks the wrong idea about Liddy here. With you appearing to be acting as chaperone, it might look like we had taken up courting again and, well, it's just that . . ."

Lydia thought her cheeks must be ready

to burst into actual flames. "Really, John, I can —"

"No, John is absolutely right," Hilda interrupted. "The two of you go along, and should there be speculation I'll be here to assure everyone that it is exactly what it appears to be — John giving you a ride so you can get to Greta's as quickly as possible. You should take along some of the food we haven't yet put out," she added, leading the way to the kitchen, where she loaded a basket with partially filled containers of their meal. She handed the basket to Lydia. "For Luke and the children, even if Greta doesn't feel like eating."

"Greta will appreciate your thoughtfulness," Lydia said.

"Well, go on," Hilda instructed. "I'll tell Roger and Gert that they need to drive your buggy back to town, Lydia." She shooed the two of them out the back door in the direction of the barn, where a row of identical black buggies sat lined up at precise angles to one another.

John helped Lydia onto the seat and then waved to Hilda as he climbed up and took the reins. "That was close," he murmured with a grin.

Lydia could not help herself. She burst into laughter and nearly choked trying to cover her mirth as he guided the buggy past the house and out to the road with Hilda Yoder still watching them from the back porch. The tears that spilled down her cheeks were of pure joy, and she could not remember a time when she had felt so light-hearted.

Then she saw John give her a sideways glance, his own face wreathed in a smile, his eyes twinkling with mischief, and she remembered that there had been times — many of them — when she had felt this way. Back when she and John had been courting, there had been so many times like this.

"I see Hilda Yoder hasn't changed much," John said as he let the reins go slack, knowing the horse would find the way back to town without his help. "When we were children she was always kind of the town overseer, and that seems to still be her role."

"She means well."

He glanced at Lydia, aware that in the close confines of the buggy their shoulders would touch whenever the vehicle swayed. He sent up a silent prayer of thanks for rutted roads.

"I expect there is someone like Hilda in most small communities," Liddy added, "someone who takes it upon herself to make sure things run smoothly — or at least the way she believes is right and proper."

"You've got a point. My partner's mother was that woman when . . ."

He stopped talking. Rarely, since he'd returned to Celery Fields, had he allowed himself to speak of those years he'd spent living in the outside world. He knew that his neighbors did not wish to hear about such things — certainly Liddy would not want to know the details of his life then. Even if she had raised the question herself that night when he was working on Greta's chair.

They rode in silence for several minutes, the mood now stifled by his slip of the tongue.

"What was it like?" Liddy murmured so softly that at first he wasn't certain she had really spoken. "Out there, what was it like, John?"

He took a moment to consider his answer. How much should he say? How much did she really want to know?

"Did you like that life?" Liddy asked before he could find words to answer her initial question.

"It was . . . it was so very different from life here," he began, glad that the horse seemed content to plod slowly along, giving

142

them more time. "At first it was all so strange. Their ways are not our ways. It took time for me to find my place."

"And did you find your place in their world?" There was no accusation or judgment in her words, just curiosity.

"Once I met George Stevens, things got easier." He smiled at the memory of that first meeting with the man who would become his friend and business partner. "I had taken a job with his father's company. The building industry was booming and new orders were coming every day. One day George's father brought George to me and told me that my job was to take him in hand, teach him how to do the work I was doing."

"And you became friends?"

John chuckled. "Not at first. George certainly wasn't used to working with his hands. I think he began to hate me a little in those early days, but I knew that his father was preparing him to take over the business and he believed that to be successful you had to know everything about it."

"So you became a teacher."

"I suppose you could say that. In time, as we worked, we started to talk. He'd had a harder life than I first thought. His father was a true taskmaster, and especially with

George. Then his father was in an accident and suddenly George was in charge." He shook his head. "It's still hard for me to understand, but the very next day he called me to his father's office — his office then — and promoted me to foreman for the entire company. A year later, after his father died, he made me a partner in the business."

"But surely as a partner you would need money to invest . . ."

"I had built up quite a savings by then," he said, and swallowed the words that would have reminded her that his whole purpose in going away had been to make the money necessary to return and start his own business and marry her. "George could never understand what he called my 'living on the cheap.' " He smiled. "He spent money almost before he had it in hand. Anyway, he offered me stock in the company at a price that would take all my savings — two years' worth — but would make me a major shareholder."

"And you gave him your money?"

Now he heard the faintest hint of disapproval creep into her voice. He tightened his grip on the reins. *"Yah,"* he said, and snapped the reins to urge the horse into a faster pace.

"So what happened?"

John's lips thinned into a hard line as he recalled those difficult times. "The stock market crashed and it seemed like overnight everything just changed. People had no money for clocks or furniture — or to pay for furniture that they had already ordered. The company was heavily invested in bad stocks and had to close up shop."

"And the money you had invested?"

"Gone. Everything was gone — my savings, my job, my ability to find work . . ." *You and the life we had planned together.*

"But surely your friend was in the same position and the two of you . . ."

"First of all, he'd lost his business and a lot of money in the bargain, but he still had his family and the means to make it through. Times would be hard, but he assured me that the day would come when things would be better again and then the two of us would start fresh."

"So he was able to help see you through these —"

"That is not their way, Liddy. He offered me a loan, but how was I ever going to repay him?"

"What did you do?"

This was the part of his story that John was most reluctant to talk about. He shut his eyes against the images of begging for handouts and working in the citrus groves picking fruit for hours and hours in exchange for a place to sleep and a hot meal. "I came back here," he said after a moment. *I came home to you.*

In silence they approached the cluster of shops and homes that made up the center of Celery Fields. Just before John turned the buggy onto the street that led to Greta and Luke's house, Liddy reached over and covered his hand with hers.

"You made the right decision," she said, and her hand remained on his, her warmth seeping into his fingers and spreading up his arm to settle in his chest as he pulled the buggy to a stop.

Lydia was glad for the wide brim of her bonnet that hid her face from John. His story of the years he had spent away from her had not only touched her, it had infuriated her. So much time wasted and lost when they might have shared those years. And what of this so-called friend and business partner? Did he not care that while he apparently remained in his home with his family, John was left to make do as best he could? What kind of people were these *Englischers*? By the time she stepped down from the buggy she was fuming about how

146

the people who had called themselves John's friends had abandoned him. So lost in her own thoughts was she that she marched straight up to the front door and entered her sister's house without knocking.

"Tante Lydia!" Samuel shouted as he came racing toward her from the back of the house.

Almost immediately Luke stepped into the hallway, shushing the boy as he tried to balance the two younger children, one in each arm. Lydia immediately reached to relieve him of one of the children, but he shook his head. "I've got them. Could you go and see about Greta?" His eyes shifted toward the stairs and Lydia saw that he looked more haggard and worried than usual. "She's been ill all through the afternoon."

Lydia turned to mount the stairs and saw John waiting uncertainly in the doorway, the basket of food in his hand. "We brought this for you and the children, Luke. Perhaps John could help feed the children while you make Greta some tea?"

To her relief John did not shy away from the duty she had assigned him. Instead, he looped the handle of the basket over one arm and scooped Samuel into the other. "I'm starving," he announced. "How about you?"

"Me, too," Samuel agreed, and the other two children echoed his words.

As he passed the stairway on his way to follow Luke to the kitchen, John glanced up at her. In his eyes she saw his concern for her and for Greta and also his assurance that he had things in hand with Luke and the children. She could focus on her sister.

Lydia removed her bonnet on her way up the stairs, and when she reached the landing she followed the sound of low moaning to the large bedroom at the end of the hall. As soon as she saw her sister, she dropped her bonnet onto a dresser and ran to the bedside where Greta was thrashing about. Her eyes were closed, her lips were parched and her forehead gleamed with perspiration.

Lydia soaked a cloth in a nearby basin of tepid water and wiped her sister's face, smoothing back the strands of golden hair that clung to Greta's cheeks. "Shh," she crooned. "I'm here now."

Greta's eyes flew open and she tried to sit up. "Services are over? What time is it? Luke and the children haven't eaten and . . ."

Gently Lydia pushed her back onto the pillows. "They are eating now. I brought a basket of food from services and John is downstairs helping Luke with the children."

"John? Here? With you?" She managed a smile. "Progress at last," she murmured as she relaxed against the pillows and closed her eyes. After several more minutes of restlessness, her breathing settled into the steady rhythm of sleep.

Lydia studied her sister's wan face. After a moment she rested her hand on the mound of Greta's stomach and then instantly removed it when she felt the movement of the child inside. What would it feel like to carry a living being? What would a child of hers look like were she to ever know the joy of motherhood?

John, she thought as she imagined a towheaded boy running from the house where she lived down to the hardware where John worked. *His child — and mine.*

She heard steps in the hallway and got up expecting to see Luke bringing the tea. "She's resting," she said softly at the same moment that John entered the room carrying a tray with a teapot and two cups. "You shouldn't be here," she said, but at the same time she felt such gladness that he was.

"Luke has his hands full downstairs. I'll just set this here and go." He kept his eyes averted from the bed and Greta's sleeping form. "Is she . . . ?"

"Resting a little easier," Lydia assured

him. She did not look at him as she relieved him of the tray and set it on the top of a bureau next to the door. "When she wakes, I'll try to get her to sip a little tea."

"You should have a cup, as well," John said, and she could feel him watching her.

"I'll be fine. Thank you for . . . everything," she said, and knew that it came out as if she were dismissing him even as everything inside her cried out for him to stay.

"I'll go, then." He turned back toward the stairs and she followed him. "You'll be all right?"

"It is Greta we must pray for," she reminded him.

"I know, but she has a whole town looking out for her. Who do you have, Liddy? Who takes care of you?"

There was a time when I hoped you and I would take care of each other, she thought as she met his intense stare that demanded an answer. "I am fine," she said instead.

She walked with him to the top of the stairs. From below, Lydia heard the laughter of the children. Behind her she heard Greta begin to moan again. "I have to go to her," she said, but it came out a whisper as if she weren't yet ready to let John go.

"I know," he answered as he took hold of her hand and brought her fingertips to his lips. "Drink the tea," he added. He kissed her fingers then walked slowly back down the stairs and out the front door.

Could they find their way back to each other? Was it possible to re-create the past — the time when they had been everything the other needed or wanted?

"Liddy," Greta moaned.

"Coming," she replied.

CHAPTER EIGHT

John knew that he could not work on Sunday without enduring the disapproval of Hilda Yoder, not to mention his uncle. Sundays were reserved for the activities of faith and family. Even though the Amish met only every other week for formal services, the alternate Sundays were given to more leisure activities. On Sunday evenings the single young people in the community would gather for a hymn singing and, more important, a rare opportunity to explore the possibility of a courtship that could eventually lead to marriage. In their youth he and Liddy had attended such gatherings and afterward he had driven her home in his courting buggy as the two of them talked of the day when they would marry and start a home of their own.

Many times they had sat long into the night on the front porch of her father's house planning their future, oblivious to hours passing or the oppressive summer heat, the mosquitoes and pesky gnats known as no-see-ums that were native to Florida. On Sundays when there were no services they often went to the beach. John would borrow a small rowboat and row them along the shore, weaving close to the tangled roots of the mangrove trees that formed a barrier between the water and land. Liddy would bring a picnic lunch and they would spend the whole day together.

Having been assured that there was no more he could do for Luke and the children, John drove his uncle's buggy to the Hadwell house on the edge of town and arrived just as Gert and Roger did with Liddy's buggy.

"Is everything all right, John?" Gert asked.

"Liddy's with her. Luke thinks it might be something she caught from one of the children — a stomach bug." He unhitched and stabled their horse, then returned to climb onto the seat of Liddy's buggy. "I'll take care of this for her," he said.

"You'll come back?" Gert called from her position at the back door of their small cottage.

The idea of sitting for an entire evening with his aunt and uncle in the small, dark house while Gert read Scripture and Roger dozed was not at all appealing. "I thought I might keep Luke company — maybe carve the children a soap animal to keep them quiet while Greta rests."

"Tell Luke I'll bring them some supper," Gert said.

By the time John had unhitched and stabled Liddy's horse and walked back down the street toward Luke and Greta's he saw another buggy parked outside the house. Luke was sitting on the porch with one child while the other two played in the yard. Sitting across from him was Jeremiah Troyer, Liddy's half brother-in-law and Bishop Troyer's great-nephew.

Jeremiah's story was not all that different from John's. He'd left home, settled in a new community, started one business — the ice-cream shop — and eventually bought another — the ice-packing company.

Not so different in some ways. Worlds of difference in others, John thought as he walked down the street. For one thing, Jeremiah Troyer had had the good sense to seek out a new Amish community instead of trying to make his way in the *Englischer* world. For another, by the time he was ready to court Pleasant, he was making a good living and had a secure future to offer her.

And what do you have to offer Liddy? The

question was never far from his thoughts.

He should stay away from her. But he willingly admitted that the reason he was heading back to Luke's house had little to do with wanting to help out. It was because Liddy was there and he was drawn like a moth to a lantern to wherever she might be.

"John Amman!" Samuel shouted when he saw John approaching. John smiled as he recalled how George's son had once called him by his given name and been reprimanded by George's wife. "This is *Mr. Amman,* young man," she had instructed. But in the Amish world such titles were never used, although often a person would be called by his or her full name.

"Did you forget something?" Samuel asked, his eyes wide with curiosity as he walked alongside John up the steps of the porch.

"In a way I did," he said as he nodded to Luke and Jeremiah and took a seat on the top porch step. He pulled out his pocketknife and the bar of soap he'd picked up after stabling Liddy's horse. "Do you like horses, Samuel Starns?" he asked as he started to carve the soap made pliable by the warmth of the day.

"Yah."

Samuel's younger brother scrambled

down from his father's lap and took his position beside her brother. "I do, too," he announced.

"Das ist gut," John replied as he concentrated on shaping the rectangular bar into the form of a pony. "Ask your *dat* if he might have an extra bar of soap around and we'll make a team of horses."

Behind him Luke chuckled as the boy, Eli, looked imploringly at him. "In the house," he said. "By the kitchen sink."

Eli was gone and back in an instant, presenting the partially used bar of lye soap to John as if it were a bar of gold. "Ah, looks like these ponies will be a matched set," John said, showing him that the two bars were identical in color.

Eli giggled. "They'll be *bruders* like me and Samuel." Then he frowned as he glanced back to where his little sister was crawling around the porch. "My *maet* is getting a brother or sister for Sarah there," he whispered. "We're not supposed to talk about it. It's a surprise."

John nodded. "I won't tell anyone," he whispered, and Eli giggled again.

He finished Samuel's horse and turned his attention to carving one for Eli. "Greta feeling any better?" he asked as the two children sat apart, admiring Samuel's soap horse and plotting out the game they would play as soon as John finished the second one.

"Lydia and Pleasant are with her. Pleasant said they were able to get her to take a little of the clear broth that she brought." Luke sounded tired and more than a little worried. "She's never had trouble before," he added, and his voice trailed off as if he hadn't meant to say this part aloud.

Jeremiah cleared his throat. "John, Luke tells me that you're making a rocking chair for him to give Greta. That's your trade, then? Making furniture?"

Normally John was reluctant to discuss his work, always aware that the discussion might eventually stray to those years he'd spent in the outside world. But he understood what Jeremiah was doing. He wanted to turn Luke's attention away from his sick wife. "It is a gift that God has given me," he replied.

"I'm in need of some extra tables for the ice-cream shop," Jeremiah continued. "If you have the time you could stop by the shop tomorrow and see if that might be something that would interest you."

Ever since John had lost everything he'd ever acquired, he had been especially sensitive to strangers who might think they were doing him a favor by offering some charity. He glanced up at Jeremiah, trying to gauge the man's purpose.

"I have a bid from Josef Bontrager for the work," Jeremiah continued. "Seems high."

"Josef has not known much competition in this," Luke said, and John realized that Luke was encouraging him to agree to at least consider the project.

"Tomorrow, then," John said as he blew the last shavings off the second horse and handed it to Eli. The youngster squealed with delight and ran off with his brother to play under the shade of the live oak tree that dominated the front yard.

John leaned back against the column that supported the porch roof. He could hear the women moving around upstairs and speaking softly to each other, their voices drifting out through the open windows.

"Have the elders come to a decision about the school?" Jeremiah asked Luke.

John's ears perked up.

"It's still under discussion."

"But Liddy . . ." John blurted. The other two men exchanged a look. "Teaching is her whole life," he added.

"She'll still be able to teach — privately in her home," Luke said.

"But in Celery Fields not many have

money for private lessons. How will she make her way?"

"The final decision is not yet made," Jeremiah assured him. "Perhaps there will be a way that the elders have not yet seen. God will show us in time the decision we must make for the good of the community."

And Liddy?

Lydia was sure that she must be imagining things. She thought she heard John's voice rising up to the open windows from the porch. He sounded upset. She edged closer to the window and listened.

She sighed. They were talking about closing the school. It was a topic that was often discussed when men gathered these days. Waiting for the decision to be finalized had been a little like waiting for the next nibble on her line in the days when she and her father used to go fishing in the bay. But she had no doubt that the school would close. She was a practical woman with simple needs. She had put aside a portion of her stipend from the past year in preparation for the time after the school closed. And she had other skills. If all else failed she could clean houses for families in Sarasota, although she did not like the idea of working for outsiders. She took comfort in knowing that whatever happened with the school, this was Celery Fields. Her family and friends would make sure she had everything she needed.

What truly bothered her about John's comment was the focus on her and not what was best for the community. Perhaps his coming back here had been a mistake. Still, she had begun to allow herself to hope that in time . . .

"Liddy?"

Pleasant was studying her curiously and Lydia realized that a question had been posed to her, one she had not heard. "Sorry," she said, moving away from the window.

"I was just saying that the worst seems to have passed. Greta's fever is down and she's likely to sleep through the night now. Jeremiah and I need to get back for the milking and other chores. But I can send Bettina to take charge of the little ones and stay the night so Luke can get some sleep. What do you think?"

"It is a good plan, Pleasant. I'll stay until Bettina gets here. I can fix supper for Luke and the children."

"And eat something yourself?"

Lydia smiled sheepishly. It was well-known that she often got so caught up in her teaching or her chores at home or some other project that she forgot all about meals. "I will eat."

"Bettina will bring back one of the peach pies I made for services today. No one touched it," Pleasant grumbled. As the town's bakery owner she was frequently irritated when others did not line up to devour her wares, especially when they were freely offered as they were at any community gathering.

"Your peach pie is my favorite — you know that," Lydia replied, and was relieved to see her half sister smile.

From outside they heard a buggy approach and then stop outside the gate. Pleasant glanced out the window. "It's Roger and Gert Hadwell," she announced. "From the looks of it they've brought enough supper for half the town."

"I'll go help them bring things to the kitchen," Lydia said, glad of the excuse to go downstairs and see for herself that John was there, that he had returned. *Because of me?* Her heart beat a little faster as she digested that thought. But then she forced her steps to a slower pace as she descended the stairs. Sitting with Greta while she slept, Liddy had allowed herself to get lost in the memories of the Sunday afternoons she had shared with John when they were younger. She had gotten so caught up in those pleasant daydreams that she'd actually begun to convince herself that maybe they might find their way back to what they once felt for each other.

But she had seen that faraway look cross John's handsome features more often than it should if indeed he had come back to stay. He might be deceiving himself but she knew him too well. His determination to make a success of himself was the one thing that had not changed. And she could think of nothing that she might do to persuade him that such things did not matter to her and *should* not matter to him.

You are a foolish woman, Lydia Goodloe.

The chorus of voices from the gathering on the porch brought Lydia back to the present. She smoothed her apron over her dress, tucked a wisp of her hair back under her prayer covering and then went to open the screen door for Gert.

"Let me take that for you," she said as she relieved John's aunt of a heavy basket and led the way to the kitchen. "You'll stay for supper?"

"That's the plan," Roger Hadwell said with a chuckle as he set down a second basket filled to the brim. "I don't think my

162

wife left us a single thing to eat at home."

"Oh, stop that," Gert said, but she was smiling.

It had been a day for Lydia to be surrounded with couples whose marriages were strong and even inspiring. Watching Luke worry and fuss over Greta, then seeing how Jeremiah took his lead from Pleasant and got Luke and the children settled on the porch so that she and Pleasant could minister to Greta, had made Lydia more aware than usual of the beauty of a shared life. Now the Hadwells were taking over Greta's kitchen, their gentle teasing and laughter a testimony to the comfort and security they had found in each other's company.

There was a time when she and John had thought to have a marriage like any one of these. There was a time when they had assumed that they would grow old together. But at this moment she had to face reality. And the reality was that she was a single woman and would likely always be so.

She turned to get a platter from Greta's cabinet and found John watching her. Surely in time she would not feel her heart lurch with unexpected joy every time their eyes met. Surely in time they would be able to settle into the kind of easy friendship she shared with her brothers-in-law. She stood on tiptoe to reach the platter from the top shelf.

"I can get it," John said as he stood behind her and easily retrieved the platter. He stepped back so that she could turn and take it from him. "What else?" he asked.

"Nothing," she said, her voice barely audible. "It's fine. I'm. . . ."

"You men go back outside while Liddy and I take care of things here," Gert instructed, shooing the men from the kitchen. "We'll never get this meal on the table with you in the way," she added as she swatted at Roger's hand when he tried to take a slice of the cheese she'd just unwrapped.

In the commotion that followed, John leaned in closer. "May I come by tonight?"

Lydia's nod of agreement was automatic. She should have refused. She should have used the excuse that Greta might need her. But Greta would be fine under Bettina's care. He was asking to see her in a way that could hold only one meaning.

John Amman is asking to court me again.

The shy smile that thought carried to her lips froze when he added, "We need to talk about this business with the school."

"That will be decided by others," she replied curtly, and walked back to the kitchen.

While the others ate supper together in Greta's large kitchen, Lydia insisted on sitting with Greta.

"She's sleeping," Gert said. "And you have to eat something. You came directly from services and Pleasant told me that you haven't eaten a thing since I arrived."

"I'll take a tray up with some broth for Greta and something for myself, as well. I don't want to leave her alone until we're certain her fever has run its course."

Gert wasn't one to give up easily, but she agreed to Lydia's terms on the promise that she would let the older woman prepare the tray of food and send it up with Bettina as soon as the girl arrived.

Over Gert's shoulder Lydia saw John watching her from his position on the front porch. He was scowling at her. John had never been pleased when she dared to dispute something he had said. But the closing of the school was not for him to decide, or her, either. The elders would do what was best for all, and John's need to discuss the matter only served as more evidence that he might have moved back to Celery Fields but he had not entirely left the ways of the outside world behind.

John left as soon as supper was over. He accepted Luke's heartfelt thanks for his part in bringing Lydia to care for Greta and encouraged him to follow up on giving Jeremiah a bid for the tables he needed for the ice-cream shop. His aunt tried hard to get him to stay for a second piece of pie but he declined, having realized that Liddy had no intention of coming downstairs as long as he was still there.

He walked back down the main street, deserted now and nearly dark with shadows. The woman was as stubborn as ever. Did she not understand that what he wanted to do was help her devise some alternate plan that she could bring to the elders to perhaps keep the school open and her job secure?

She hadn't even given him the opportunity to discuss the possibilities, rejecting any such conversation out of hand from sheer obstinacy. It was becoming an old story with them, this refusal to even consider his ideas for making things better. It was as if, having not trusted him when he left to make enough money to get his business going, she had decided never to trust his thinking again.

He frowned. What kind of a marriage could they build on that? He would agree that his leaving Celery Fields had not turned out at all the way he'd intended. In fact, he had made matters far worse. If he had stayed and worked for his uncle through the good years they might be married by now with a house filled with children of their own. On the other hand he had stayed away far longer than he had intended mostly because she had rejected him. He had written her time and again, trying with each letter to make her understand his intention to return as soon as he had earned his financial stake. But her refusal to even acknowledge his letters had been his answer.

So why are you here? Why do you care so much whether she maintains her job or not? Why should it matter to you when it doesn't seem to matter to her?

Because, having failed her once, he was intent on making certain that she was happy and content in her life, even if he were not to be a part of it beyond living in the same community. If John was sure of anything it was that Liddy loved teaching and that taking that away from her would be devastating, whether she wanted to admit it or not. And whether she wanted his help or not he was determined to find some way that the school could hold on for at least a couple of years. By that time Luke and Greta's children would be ready to attend, as would other youngsters from the outlying farms that he had seen at Sunday services.

Instead of going directly to his rooms above the stables he walked over to the schoolhouse and stood outside the closed double doors considering the possibilities. The building was in good shape — no peeling paint, no loose shingles on the steep-pitched roof. The windows were not cracked or broken and the yard surrounding it was well tended and neat. It was close enough to the businesses in town that John could understand why the elders might be thinking it would bring in some much-needed income if turned into a shop of some sort.

He stepped onto the well-worn footpath that connected the school to Liddy's house. No doubt she had walked this path thousands of times over the years. In those first days after he'd left, he imagined her walking slowly from her father's house to the school, her head bent low, her heart missing him as he had missed her. But then as the weeks and months and years passed, being Liddy, she would have raised her eyes from the ground to the school itself and walked with new purpose. She would have set her mind on becoming the very best teacher she possibly could.

And these days? He thought about the woman he'd watched making her daily trips to and from the school and realized that there had been little difference in her posture or stride even as she must have already been facing the likelihood that this would be her last year of teaching. She would simply accept that whatever happened was God's will and that there would be some new purpose for her life.

So why bother trying to change things?

Because I love her — always have and always will.

"Whether she wants me to or not," he muttered aloud as he crossed the yard. He stomped his way up the outside stairs and into the rooms that Liddy and the other women had made into a home for him. But the home he truly wanted was the house across the way, shared with Liddy and their children. In spite of everything that had happened, he still wanted to marry her. Nothing about that had changed. All he had to do was persuade her that being with him was surely God's will.

CHAPTER NINE

If the week in late January that John returned to Celery Fields had been unseasonably cold, six weeks later saw the humidity and unsettled skies of storms that usually did not arrive until the hurricane season began in early summer. There was no need for a fire at the school on these days. Instead, Lydia made sure the windows were open to allow whatever breeze there might be to flow freely through the single room.

As Greta's time to deliver grew nearer, Lydia spent most of her days either at school or caring for Luke, Greta and their children. To Greta's dismay Hilda Yoder — in her role as the town's midwife — had injured her back in a fall and was laid up in bed on doctor's orders until it had a chance to heal. On Hilda's orders Greta was also confined to complete bed rest for the duration of her pregnancy. So Lydia closed up her own house and moved in with her sister and Luke. The irony of her circumstances did not escape her. She believed that God was offering them the opportunity to become accustomed to an arrangement that would almost certainly be their future — the school shut down and Lydia living with Greta and Luke.

It also did not escape her notice that there was a blessing in all of this. By living with Luke and Greta she could avoid seeing John. Her feelings for John were incredibly confusing and rushed at her like a wave on the beach whenever she was in his presence. Her only defense seemed to be avoiding him whenever possible. No longer would he be able to watch from the vantage point of his uncle's hardware or his own living quarters above Luke's business as she came from and went to school or did chores around her house. Luke now handled milking Lydia's cow and gathering the eggs her chickens laid.

She also had not attended any of the community gatherings in town since moving to Greta's, offering the excuse that someone needed to be with her sister at all times. This included missing services for the first time in her life. And although John had stopped by on several occasions, she had always made sure to be sequestered upstairs with Greta, an area of the house off-limits to him.

"Is it your intention to avoid him forever?" Greta asked one afternoon as Lydia sat by her bedside mending some of the children's clothing. Greta had been feeling much better the past few days, enough so that she and Lydia had both urged Luke to go to Sarasota on business for the day. He was not expected back until late that evening. Pleasant had insisted on taking the children and Lydia had turned her duties at school over to Bettina in order to stay with Greta.

"I am not avoiding anyone."

Greta snorted and shifted her large bulk so that she lay on her side. "Yes, you are. What I want to know is why? In the weeks that have passed since his return has John Amman not proven his sincerity in wanting to be part of the community again? When will you let go of the past, Liddy?"

Lydia put down her sewing as she faced her sister with a sigh. She knew Greta would not give up on this conversation so they might as well have it. "I am not clinging to the past, Greta," she explained patiently. "John Amman left Celery Fields — and me — eight years ago. We are both very different people now. Why, it is almost as if he is a stranger to me, he's so unlike the boy he was."

"The boy you loved, have always loved, will always love," Greta insisted. "And he seems quite the same to me." Her eyes went all dreamy, the way they sometimes did when she thought or spoke of her husband. "That smile of his has not changed one bit and, if anything, age has made him more handsome. And the way he looks at you."

Outside the open window, thunder roiled in the distance like a giant's unsettled stomach. They would have the welcome relief of rain before the day was out. Lydia could smell it in the heavy air that hung over the room. It reminded her of the day that John had left. It had rained then, a harsh, cold, pelting rain that had slapped at her face as she watched him go. She pressed back a wisp of her hair that had clung to her cheek as she took up her sewing again. "That boy is no more," she reminded her sister.

"No he is now a man, a very eligible man. You'd best wake up, sister, before some other single woman sets her eye on him."

Lydia felt the color rise to her cheeks. John was indeed handsome, in the way that drew attention especially from women, despite the Amish leaning toward sameness. He stood out. He was taller and broader than many of the men in Celery Fields. "And that is exactly the point. Since he is so fine looking, why would he be interested in a spinster like me?" She felt she was making an excellent argument.

"Because he does not see the years, Liddy. He sees you. Everyone can see it except you. I don't understand why you think you must ignore the reality before you." She twisted around to reach for the cardboard fan they sometimes used during summer services and let out a cry of distress.

Lydia kicked over her sewing basket as she stood up. "What is it?" she asked as she eased Greta back onto the pillows. She noticed that her sister was biting hard on her lower lip to keep further cries at bay. "Where does it hurt, Greta?"

"Everywhere," Greta managed through gritted teeth.

"I'll go make you some peppermint tea. That always eases the cramping."

Greta nodded as she closed her eyes against the pain.

Downstairs, Lydia hurried to prepare the tea. From the day she had moved into the house, she had made sure a kettle was always filled and kept simmering on the wood stove in the kitchen. And as Greta's time grew closer she had made other preparations, as well — a stack of clean rags placed on the bureau in the bedroom, along with newspaper and two pads they would use to line the bed during the delivery. Greta had finally finished stitching the dark blue gown and blankets that she had made to wrap the newborn in after the delivery.

They had planned that when the time came, Luke would go fetch Hilda, who would attend Greta through the delivery with Lydia's help. Luke would be there, too, while the children would go to stay with Pleasant again. Everything was prepared. And Greta had been through the entire process three times already. There was no need to worry, Lydia assured herself as she prepared the tea and carried a steaming mug back up the stairs as large drops of rain splattered against the windows. Except, if the baby came today, Luke was not there and Hilda was still confined to bed.

By the time Lydia reached the room Greta was collapsed against the pile of pillows, her eyes closed, her breathing coming in shallow gasps. Rain was dripping onto the wood-planked floor through the open window. Lydia set the mug of tea on the bedside table and closed the window then sat on the side of the bed.

"Greta? I have some tea," she said softly.

Greta's eyes fluttered opened. "Did you send for Hilda?"

"Hilda cannot come, remember? She took a fall and injured her back."

Greta closed her eyes again and nodded as a single tear leaked down her cheek. "Something is not right, Liddy," she said, and her voice shook with fear. "This isn't like any of the others. I know that something is terribly wrong."

"Lie still," Lydia instructed as Greta began to writhe in pain. "I'm going for help." She set the tea aside and ran back down the stairs and out onto the porch. The sky was pitch-black and the rain now fell in sheets that made seeing more than a couple of feet impossible.

Normally someone was always out on the street in Celery Fields at this time of day, but with the storm everyone had sought shelter. She needed to send someone to fetch the *Englisch* doctor that the citizens of Celery Fields hesitated to call except in emergencies. Well, this was definitely an emergency, and the only telephone in town was the one at Hadwell's Hardware.

From upstairs she heard Greta cry out and she did not wait another second before dashing into the street and running as fast

176

as she could to the hardware. She was soaked through by the time she pushed open the door and clutched at a counter displaying a variety of pocketknives to catch her breath.

"It's Greta," she gasped when Gert glanced up and then hurried forward. "I think the baby is coming but there is a problem — a serious problem. I think we should call for the doctor."

Gert ran to the wall phone and lifted the receiver. She yelled into the phone. "Hello! Hello?" Her shouts into the phone brought John and Roger from the storeroom.

"It's dead," Gert announced. "The wires must be down with this wind."

"What's going on?" Roger demanded.

Once again Lydia explained the urgency to reach the doctor, and all the while her mind raced with thoughts of what she would do if they couldn't get him there in time. "I need to get back. Greta is alone and . . ."

"I'll go for the doctor," Roger said, grabbing his rain slicker. "John, you go with Lydia."

"Shouldn't I . . ." Gert began but she was already shaking like a leaf, her nerves evident to all.

"Someone has to manage the store," Roger reminded her gently. And although

Lydia knew the store could simply be closed for the time being, she also understood that Roger was protecting Gert. Gertrude Hadwell tended toward hysteria when faced with any crisis.

"John?" Roger nodded toward Lydia.

John took down a second black rain slicker and held it over his head and shoulders indicating that Lydia should join him under the shelter of the coat. "Let's go," he ordered as he held out one arm, ready to envelope her against him under the coat.

"I . . ."

"For once in your life stop worrying about what is proper, Liddy. Greta needs you."

Her sister's name galvanized Lydia into action. She huddled close to John as he opened the shop's door, and together they headed out into the storm. All around them thunder rumbled and lightning cracked the blackness of the sky in jagged flashes. John held her close, half carrying her forward as they ran back to the house.

The front door stood open. As they stepped into the front hallway and John dropped the coat and shut the door against the noise of the storm, Lydia realized that the house had an eerie, empty sound. She glanced up the stairway, her ears peeled for any cry from Greta.

Nothing.

"Oh, please, do not let her have . . ." Lydia did not finish her prayer as she raced up the stairs with John right behind her.

When they reached the bedroom, Greta was on her hands and knees in the middle of the bed. Because her face was buried in a pillow they could barely hear her moans. The linens on the bed were soaked through with perspiration as well as what Lydia realized was the rush of water that was a preamble to the baby's coming.

"There's water simmering on the stove. Fill this basin," she instructed John, thrusting a washbasin at him as she rushed to her sister's side. "Greta, we're right here."

"Luke?"

"Not yet. Remember, he had to go out on a job and there's a storm? I'm sure he'll be back as soon as he can." As she talked, she took a clean rag from the stack by the bed and wiped Greta's forehead.

"The mattress," Greta said. "It's ruined."

"It's wet," Lydia corrected, "and it will dry."

To her surprise Greta managed a laugh. "Oh, Liddy, there is ever so much more than water coming," she said. "Get the newspapers and pads."

Relieved to have her sister take charge

Lydia did as she was told, managing to spread the pad, layers of papers and another pad while she helped Greta balance back and forth on her hands and knees. "Do you want to lie down?"

"No. This is better," Greta said, and then gasped as another contraction took hold.

What was taking John so long?

As if in answer, she heard footsteps on the stairs and he came to the door with the basin of steaming water. "There wasn't enough in the kettle," he said, and Lydia remembered that she had taken water for the peppermint tea earlier.

"I refilled the kettle." He sounded as nervous as she felt.

She took the water from him. "How long before Roger comes with the doctor?" she whispered.

John glanced at the window where the wind was so strong that palm fronds lashed at the sides of the house like fingers scratching on a chalkboard. The sky was so dark that it seemed more like midnight than mid-afternoon. He shook his head. "Just tell me what to do, Liddy, and we'll get through this together."

I don't know what to do, she wanted to tell him, but behind her Greta let out a half moan and half cry and rolled onto her side.

"Just stay close in case I need you, and watch for the doctor," she said as she returned to Greta's bedside. "Right here, Greta," she chanted as she dipped a rag in the water and pressed it to her sister's swollen belly as she had seen Hilda do when delivering Greta's other children. "Just tell me what to do," she whispered, and was not at all sure if she was directing this plea to Greta or to God.

"That's good," Greta managed as the contraction passed and she shifted into a half sitting position. "The heat helps." She sounded almost normal, but her face was flushed a blotched red and her breathing sounded as if she had run a great distance. "Better," she added, and found the strength to smile at Lydia and clutch her hand.

Within seconds she was squeezing Lydia's fingers as her face contorted into a grimace. "Coming," she managed to gasp as she pushed herself higher onto the pillows.

Lydia had never found the term "catcher" more accurate than she did as she watched the head of the baby appear. Surrounded by the sounds of the storm, Greta's labored breathing and John pacing back and forth just outside the bedroom door, she instinctively cradled the emerging head of the child in one hand as she gently guided this wonder into the world. She looked up once to find Greta grimacing through the strain of one final push and suddenly the rest of the baby landed in Lydia's hands.

She was shaking and laughing at the same time and there were tears of pure joy rolling down her cheeks. "It's a girl, Greta. A beautiful daughter," she said. She turned the child, still connected to her mother by the umbilical cord, so Greta could see her. But then her heart raced with panic as she realized the baby was making no sound and was not breathing.

"You need to give her a slap," Greta instructed, her voice faint.

Lydia was horrified at the very idea of striking such a precious being.

"Get her breathing," Greta urged, half leaning forward as if to do it herself.

Lydia patted the baby girl sharply on her tiny back still slick with the afterbirth. After what seemed like an eternity the baby gasped and then let out a wail. Lydia smiled and turned to her sister. "She's lovely, Greta."

Greta smiled as she cradled her newborn. "Another girl," she whispered.

Lydia laughed. "*Yah.* You have a pair of boys and now a pair of girls."

She felt more confident now that the baby

was out and breathing. The rest would not be that different from the time she had helped her father deliver a calf. There would be the afterbirth that Luke would take and bury in the field behind the house. Once she had cut the cord, she would take the baby away to wash her and coat her in baby oil before dressing her in the gown that Greta had prepared and wrapping her in the blankets.

"John!" she shouted, and heard him come running. When he got to the door his eyes were wide with fear. "Is it . . . ?" But as soon as he saw the baby, he started to smile. "You did it," he said, softly edging into the room and peering over Lydia, who stood between him and Greta as she tried to protect her sister's modesty.

"I was only the catcher," she said, handing him the basin that now held the afterbirth. "Take this downstairs so Luke can bury it when he gets home. Then I need you to bring me fresh water and warm these blankets on the stove — try not to let them catch fire. Oh, and Greta will need a cup of that mint tea."

She shooed him from the room as he struggled to balance the basin and the blankets she had draped over his arm. Just then a crack of thunder shook the house and was followed immediately by a flash of lightning that seemed to arc right through the window in Greta's bedroom. Lydia turned back to her sister and newest niece and cried out in panic as she saw Greta's eyes roll back and a gush of bright red blood soak the padding.

John was halfway down the stairs when he heard Liddy's shriek of sheer terror. Carefully he set down the basin on a step and, still clutching the blankets, he raced back up the stairs. When he entered the room, Lydia thrust the tiny slippery, squirming bundle into his hands and then turned back to her sister, grabbing rags from a pile on the bedside and placing them between Greta's legs.

"The doctor has to come now, John. I don't know what to do." He realized that she was crying and shaking and he wanted to pull her into his arms and reassure her. But he was holding the baby and he could see the blood that soaked through the rags even as Liddy added more. Spying the cradle in the corner of the room, John laid the baby girl down and covered her as best he could with the blankets still clutched in his arms.

"I'm going for help," he said.

"Don't leave me," Lydia begged.

It was exactly what she had said to him that day eight years earlier when he had boarded the train. She had been sobbing then and she was sobbing now. Then he had left, certain that he knew best. Now he hesitated, knowing that what they needed was for him to find help and yet feeling reluctant to leave her alone.

He crossed the small room and placed his hands on her shoulders. "I'm going for help, Liddy. I'll be back."

She caught her breath and nodded. Then she looked up at him, her eyes pleading with him to make this all right. "Yes, go," she whispered as she cupped his cheek with one bloodstained hand. "Go now."

He kissed her forehead damp with perspiration. "I won't be long," he promised. On his way out the front door, John grabbed the still-wet rain slicker and covered his head as he dashed into the street and barely missed being run over by a motorcar coming toward the house. The car squealed to a stop and a gray-haired man carrying a doctor's bag got out. "Is this the house? Starns?" he shouted above the driving wind and rain.

"*Yah. Kommen Sie,*" John urged, reverting to the German his grandparents and parents

185

had spoken. He led the way back inside the house and up the stairs. "This way."

"You're the father?"

"A friend," he replied as he stood aside for the doctor to enter Greta and Luke's room.

"Mrs. Starns," the doctor said in a loud, firm voice. "I'm Dr. Benson."

John heard Greta give a low moan of acknowledgment and then he heard Lydia answer the questions the doctor asked as he opened his bag and began examining Greta. Not knowing what else to do, John took the bowl with the afterbirth down to the kitchen and left it so Luke could bury it. He returned and waited outside the door as the sounds coming from the bedroom took on a rhythm of their own. Liddy's voice, calm now, then the doctor's. Occasionally, the gurgle or cry of the baby.

The clock in the front room chimed five o'clock. Outside, the wind had calmed and the rain let up. His uncle had brought Pleasant, who immediately joined the doctor and her half sisters in the bedroom. "Bettina is staying with the other children," Roger explained. "I thought it best. Is Luke back?"

"Not yet," John said. He glanced toward the closed bedroom door. "What if . . ."

His uncle clasped his shoulder. "God will

show us the way, John. Come downstairs."

John followed his uncle down to the kitchen and accepted the cup of tea Pleasant handed him. The house seemed suddenly filled with people and he could not help but wonder where they had all come from and why they hadn't arrived sooner. He could not shake off the feeling that only the intervention of God's own hand had made everything turn out right for Greta and Luke and their new baby. He understood just how close this young family had come to the day ending in tragedy. And he could not help but put himself in Luke's place — Luke who knew nothing as he drove his wagon back from Sarasota where he had gone on business that day. What if Luke had come home to find that Greta had died in childbirth?

He wandered out to the back porch, sipping his tea as he stared at the fields that lay beyond the town. Fields he and his father had once plowed and planted together. Fields he had abandoned in his zeal to do things his way. The time he had squandered on his foolish pride were years he and Liddy might have shared the joys of marriage and started a family of their own. What did it matter if he farmed or ran a business like his uncle did? What mattered was Liddy.

He glanced up at the sky, beginning to clear now that the storm had passed. A double rainbow arched its way across the horizon, enveloping the house and town in prisms of color. John felt his chest tighten with tears of gratitude, for surely this was a sign that he'd been given a second chance. And this time he was determined to get things right.

When Luke arrived and heard the news, he raced up the stairs and into the bedroom without even bothering to shed his rain slicker. Greta was sitting up holding their daughter, an exhausted smile on her lips. Lydia made the excuse of showing the doctor out and closed the door behind her with a soft click before leading the way back downstairs.

"Thank you for coming," she said.

"You did everything right for your sister," he told her. "These things happen. I'm just glad I was able to help. Tell your sister and her husband that they have a fine, healthy baby girl there and, given the demanding nature of her cries, I expect they will have their hands full raising her." He chuckled as he stepped off the porch and climbed into his car.

Lydia wrapped her arms in her apron and hugged herself as she closed her eyes and thanked God for the way this day had turned out. She was bone weary and there was still a great deal to be done, but she felt happy.

"Liddy?" John stepped out onto the porch and stood next to her. "We need to talk," he said, and she saw that the deep lines of a frown creased his brow.

"Oh, John, not right now. Can you not be happy for my sister and Luke, for the blessing of this new life?"

"It is because of their joy that we need to talk," he persisted. "What happened today and the way things might have gone had God not blessed them with your quick thinking has brought me to my senses. I have wasted so much time, Liddy, so many years I might have shared with you and the children we might have had."

Lydia felt her cheeks go pink as she glanced toward the open front door, hoping no one was close enough to overhear this very personal conversation. "John Amman, this is neither the time nor —"

"This is exactly the time, Liddy," he argued as he stepped closer, his fists clenched at his sides as he stared down at her. "This is past the time."

"You are speaking in riddles, John Amman, and I am very tired and have no patience for —"

"Will you marry me or not, Lydia Goodloe?"

Her first instinct was to laugh. Surely he was making a joke, a cruel one at that. But she did not laugh. Instead, she met his gaze. "I answered this question once before — eight years ago," she reminded him. "It was you who . . ."

"You said yes then. Are you saying the same now?"

Without warning, the years fell away and the man she was looking up at was the man she had loved then. The man against whom all others had been measured and come up short. "I . . ." She swallowed hard and shook her head to clear it. Had there ever been a stranger day than this one had turned out to be?

She closed her eyes and thought of the hours just past, the baby she had lovingly washed and wiped with baby oil while the doctor worked with Greta to stop the bleeding. She thought about the cotton birthing gown and the soft blankets she had wrapped the baby in before presenting Greta with her new daughter. It had been like handing her sister a very precious gift. And yes, she

190

thought of the envy she had felt that this gift was not hers, might never be hers.

But perhaps God was giving her another chance, giving John and her another chance to make a fresh start and have the life together they had planned.

"Liddy?" His voice was husky with pleading. "Open your eyes. I am right here. Can we not begin again?"

Oh, how she wanted to say yes to his plea. How she wanted to set aside the doubts that had hardened inside her in the years he had been gone and sent no word. But if he left again surely her heart would be shattered forever. Caution had become her proverb and she would not abandon it now. "I will stay here for the next month caring for Greta and her family," she said slowly. "I cannot stop you should you decide to call on Luke and Greta in the evenings after your work is finished." She watched as a grin twitched at the corners of his mouth and knew that he understood she was giving him permission to court her.

"And you will sit with me sometimes on those evenings, Liddy?"

His smile was contagious, and to hide the joy she felt building inside her she ducked her head. "It would be rude not to," she admitted.

"And at the end of that month, will I have my answer?"

It was a reasonable request especially given their ages. And she did love him, had always loved only him. But would a month be long enough for her to find trust again? "You will have your answer," she said softly.

CHAPTER TEN

On more than one occasion John had heard his partner, George, use the expression "walking on air" to describe his feelings whenever he had a business success. Finally John thought he understood what George had meant. On his way home from Luke's house, with Liddy's promise echoing in his mind, he did feel a certain bounce in his step. Oh, she had doubts and they would not be easily put to rest, but he had a month to prove to her that he was home to stay and intent on making a life with her.

He stopped by the hardware store to check on the rocking chair he had finished only the evening before. Luke had asked him to deliver it as soon as possible but, with so many people crowded into the house to meet the newest member of the Starns family, John thought it best to hold the delivery until the following day.

"On the other hand," he muttered to

himself as he ran a soft cloth over the finish to remove any remaining sawdust, "no time like the present." He grinned as he realized delivering the chair later that very evening would be the perfect opportunity to spend a little time alone with Liddy. Luke would be with Greta and the baby, the other children would surely be in bed and all the rest of the company would have returned to their homes. It would just be Liddy and him — alone.

He looked down at the sawdust that had formed a fine covering down the front of his trousers. He should go to his rooms and make himself more presentable. Before his partner had married, George would take his lady a gift like flowers or candy. But the Amish did not believe in such things, and what could John possibly bring Liddy, anyway?

Your heart.

And suddenly he fully grasped the mistake he had made in leaving. Liddy had tried repeatedly to tell him that material goods did not matter to her. She had always believed and assured him that all they needed was each other and God would take care of the rest. Now he understood she'd been saying that the only thing that mattered to her was that he loved her.

But John knew that love could not last on an empty stomach. He had seen families fall apart — good, solid families where there had once been bonds of love that had seemed unbreakable. When hard times came even those bonds weakened and unraveled. And his bonds to Liddy had come unraveled, as well. Hard times had had little to do with it. It had been her stubborn refusal to trust in him that had been their undoing.

Okay, that wasn't exactly true. But maybe now that her livelihood was in jeopardy, she would come to some understanding of why he had gone away. Maybe now he could convince her that work — money — was important. Of course, there was always work to be had. He had heard her tell Greta that she could no doubt find a position cleaning houses in Sarasota, an idea that caused him to cringe. The very idea of his Liddy on her hands and knees scrubbing floors for some wealthy family in Sarasota was unimaginable. He had to come up with some viable way to show her he could earn a living that would be enough for both of them to live on.

"First things first," he said as he reached for the brush his aunt kept on the tool rack and whisked the dust from his trousers. "First step is to ease her fears about whether or not you've changed. Once you've earned her trust, then you can worry about how you're going to earn a living."

He placed the brush back on its hook, then wrapped the rocking chair in an old clean blanket. His purpose was not only to protect the finish from any lingering raindrops but also to hide it from Greta should she look out the window of the upstairs bedroom and see him coming up the street.

Not likely, he thought as he recalled the cries of the newborn filling the house. Liddy — his Liddy — had delivered that baby girl all by herself. He grinned as he remembered the way her eyes had glittered with pure triumph as she held that baby. He could only imagine how beautiful she would be holding their child.

Lydia had finally gotten the other children settled for the night and all of the friends and neighbors had left. The house was quiet as she sat by her sister's bedside. Luke had gone to see Dr. Benson to his car. The doctor had stopped by unexpectedly "just to be sure everything is all right."

Dr. Benson had assured her, "I'm just here for the extra innings," using a baseball phrase that Luke had had to explain to her. "Mother and daughter are doing just fine, thanks to you, young lady."

Lydia had blushed at that. No one had called her either young or a lady in a very long time. It was the kind of meaningless flattery outsiders doled out on a regular basis. Lydia had bowed her head to acknowledge the compliment but said nothing. Still, she found that she liked the gray-haired doctor. He reminded her of her father, and his willingness to come whenever someone in Celery Fields called had endeared him to the entire community.

"Get some rest," he had advised. "All of you. That daughter of yours strikes me as one determined to have her way." He actually winked at Greta. "Seems to me she might be a lot like her mother."

Greta smiled, her features revealing nothing of the trauma she had been through earlier that day. Years earlier Dr. Benson had been called for the delivery of both Greta and Lydia and in that moment he reminded Lydia even more of their beloved father. How she missed him. She couldn't help wondering what he would say about John's return.

Her father had always been wary of John. "That boy has his head in the clouds," he would tell her. "Be careful, Liddy, that he doesn't lead you astray." It had been the only topic of contention between them. After John left, Lydia had consoled herself in the stronger bond she and her father developed as he turned his attention toward worrying about Greta and her capricious nature.

Greta was sleeping by the time Lydia heard Luke close the front door and climb the stairs. But she realized he was not alone and, when she turned toward the door, she saw John entering the room carrying a large blanket-wrapped object. She could just see the graceful curve of the rocker peeking out from beneath the covering. Luke grinned and signaled for her to remain quiet while he silently directed the placement of the chair next to the crib. He moved their mother's rocking chair into the hall.

John removed the blanket and then adjusted the position of the chair. He touched his handiwork with such reverence that Lydia believed he was reluctant to part with it. Then he stood for a long moment looking down at the sleeping newborn in the crib. She saw him swipe the back of one hand across his cheek before he turned around, grinned at Luke and tiptoed out of the room.

"I'll just see him out," Lydia whispered, but Luke had already taken her place next to Greta's bedside. He was holding his wife's hand as he watched her sleep.

John was downstairs and reaching for the doorknob. "The chair will serve them well," she said softly. It was as close as people of their faith ever came to handing out a compliment.

"Maybe one day," he said as he watched her descend the stairs, "I can make such a chair for you — for us and our child."

"Perhaps," she whispered as she reached the foot of the stairs and walked without hesitation into his embrace. She could not have said whether it was the emotional drama of the day or simply that the dark silent house made her bold. What she did know without a single doubt was that with John's arms embracing her and his strong heartbeat thudding in her ear, which was pressed to his chest, she was home.

After a moment John took her hand and led her out to the porch where he sat down in the swing with her curled against his side. She was asleep in less than a minute as he kept a steady pace rocking the swing like a cradle.

The mist of the humid dawn curled around them as the reality that Lydia had spent the entire night sleeping next to John roused her. She leaped up from the swing, her hands flying to her prayer covering to check that it was still there. "John, wake up," she whispered, glancing around to see if any of the neighbors were out and about yet. "You have to go."

He blinked and then grinned as he stretched out his arms and legs and yawned loudly.

"Shh," she hissed. "You'll wake the entire town."

"I doubt that," he said in his normal voice. "My guess is that most people in town are already awake and going about their morning chores." He grinned up at her and showed no sign at all of leaving as he stretched his long arms along the back of the swing and set it in motion. "How did you sleep?"

She ignored the question as she retrieved the hat that had fallen off sometime during the night and handed it to him. "Go," she ordered. "Now."

"Going," he said as he stood up and accepted the hat. And then his expression sobered as he cupped her cheek with the palm of one hand. "But I'll be back this evening and the one after that and the one after that until the month you need has come and gone, Liddy."

The man was impossible.

Impossibly handsome.

Impossibly stubborn.

Impossibly charming.

Long after he had gone Lydia stood on the porch, her hand on her cheek holding on to the warmth of his hand caressing her. As she heard the sounds of Greta's family stirring and headed inside to start breakfast, she realized that she was smiling.

Her high spirits stayed with her throughout the day as she went about the business of caring for Greta, the baby and the other children. She prepared meals and carried a tray up to Greta, who was dressed and sat rocking her newborn. She washed and hung out the sheets and other linens used in the birthing all the while keeping an eye on the children playing in the yard. Pleasant brought sweets and three pies from the bakery and told Lydia that Jeremiah was churning up a fresh batch of strawberry ice cream as a special treat for Greta. She also reported that she had stopped by the school and she assured Lydia that Bettina had everything under control.

Later that evening, after they had finished supper and Luke had taken the children upstairs to sit with their mother and new sister before going to bed, Hilda Yoder's youngest daughter stopped by with a basket of food and detailed instructions for Lydia to follow in caring for Greta and the baby. Hilda did not approve of calling for help from outsiders and her daughter made it clear that Hilda was adamant that there should be no need for Dr. Benson or his noisy vehicle to disturb them further. Her aversion to relying on outsiders for anything was the sole reason that the town's only telephone was located at the hardware when it more logically should have been at the dry-goods store that already housed the post office. And yet it had not escaped anyone's notice that when tourists vacationing in Sarasota found their way to Celery Fields it was Hilda who welcomed them into her shop.

"That's just good business," she had protested when Pleasant commented on the double standard one day after watching Hilda fuss over a trio of *Englisch* women who had made multiple purchases. Hilda had glanced at Lydia then and added, "Perhaps if enough tourists visit and buy from us we can afford to keep the school going."

Now as she completed her final chore for the day, scrubbing the kitchen floor, this particular train of thought was not helping to sustain Lydia's good mood. She paused in her scrubbing and considered whether or not she might truly make a home and future with John, one that would give her the same sense of purpose and security she had always felt in teaching. *God's will be done,* she reminded herself sternly. And she attacked the floor more vigorously with the brush and soapy water.

"You'll rub that wood to splinters if you keep scrubbing so hard," John said with a hint of laughter.

She had not heard him enter the kitchen. She resisted the urge to drop everything and walk into the welcome haven of his embrace. Instead, she exchanged the scrub brush for a rag soaked in clear water and wiped up the soapy residue from the floor. "You are late, John Amman," she said.

"Ah, you missed me. This is progress and we're only on the second day of our month of decision." He was grinning as he relieved her of the rag, dropped it into the bucket and then offered her his hand to help her to her feet. "Haven't you done enough for one day, Liddy?" he asked as he studied her features.

"Work does not wait for sleep," she said, quoting one of Pleasant's maxims as she picked up the pail of soapy water and headed outside to dump it. The pure joy she felt at being in his presence was overwhelming. She needed to take this more slowly. He had left her once, after all, and she could not convince herself that he would not be struck by wanderlust yet again.

"Dr. Benson is on his way over," John said as he leaned against the door frame and watched her wash out the soapy bucket and set it in its place. "I saw him when I was in Sarasota making a delivery for my uncle."

Lydia shot him a look. "Is he worried that Greta might . . . will there be problems?"

"He didn't say, but he also did not seem particularly worried. I think he just likes seeing the babies he helps bring into this world."

Just then they both heard the rumble of a motorcar coming closer.

"I should put the kettle on," Lydia murmured as she stepped past John and started preparing a tea tray.

"I'll get the door," John offered as he headed down the hall as if they were a married couple preparing to welcome a guest to their home. It was a feeling that Lydia felt was surely not proper, but it was also one that brought the smile back to her face. She barely noticed she was humming as she sliced the loaf of banana bread that Gert had sent earlier with John.

After the doctor had checked on Greta and the baby, he joined Luke, John and Lydia at the kitchen table. "Right as rain they are," he assured Luke, then turned his attention to John. "I was admiring that rocking chair, young man. Greta tells me you made it."

"Yah."

"It's a fine piece of carpentry. My wife has been after me to buy her a cabinet for displaying her china and knickknacks. Do you do that sort of thing?"

"I have work at the hardware and Jeremiah Troyer has asked me to build some tables for his ice-cream shop."

"No hurry. Her birthday's in summer. I just thought I could surprise her." Dr. Benson glanced at Luke and grinned. "Women do like surprises, right, Luke?" He finished the last of his tea and stood up. "Think about it, John. You have a gift and I know a number of people in my community who would pay top dollar for that rocking chair. If the rest of your work is that fine, you'd have more orders than you could fill in no time once word got around."

Lydia could practically see the wheels turning in John's mind. This was the opportunity he'd been hoping for and, while she did not especially like the idea of John doing his business primarily with outsiders, the other side of that coin was that if he had enough work here he would not be tempted to go elsewhere.

"You could perhaps draw up a sketch for Dr. Benson to consider," she said quietly.

"Good idea," the doctor boomed as he donned his fedora and picked up his medical bag. "I'll get you some measurements. My wife has already picked out the exact place in our dining room where she wants the cabinet to sit." He chuckled. "Come to think of it, the only surprise in all of this would be if I didn't do something about getting that cabinet for her — and that wouldn't be good." Luke walked him down the hall to the front door while Lydia cleared the dishes.

"It could be our future, Liddy," John said quietly as he remained at the kitchen table and picked at the crumbs of the banana bread.

"You've always wanted a business of your own," she replied.

"Uncle Roger would be relieved if I could start making my own way without having to rely on him."

"A few tables for Jeremiah and a cabinet

206

for the doctor are not a business, John," she warned, worried suddenly that he was setting himself up for disappointment. "Perhaps your uncle would keep you on — just until . . ."

"I know this will take time." He stood up and carried the plate to her for washing. He leaned in close to her ear and whispered, "But I've got almost a whole month before you say you'll marry me — plenty of time to get this business going." He kissed her on the cheek. "You will say yes," he added.

As Luke walked back into the kitchen and cleared his throat, Lydia realized that this had not been a question. "You are sometimes too sure of yourself, John Amman," she said as she brushed past him to wipe the table.

"Ah, Liddy, have a little faith."

If Lydia had thought a month was ample time to decide her future, she had not counted on the way the days — and especially the evenings she sat with John on Greta's front porch — seemed to race by. They laughed a lot together, recalling the adventures they had shared as teenagers.

"Remember that time we went to the beach?" he asked one evening, chuckling and shaking his head.

And although there had been many trips to the beach to wade in the Gulf of Mexico and look for her favorite olive and moon shells, Lydia knew exactly which time he was recalling. "I had never seen you so nervous before."

"Well, I had never before borrowed a boat without actual permission although I did know the fisherman who owned it. Remember on our way over we saw the police patrolling the waters?"

Lydia giggled. "I thought you were going to faint when they came so close to us. And then they just waved and went on about their business."

"And then it was your turn to be nervous when the waves they left in their wake rocked that little rowboat to the point of practically tipping it over." He put his arm around her shoulder. "You clung to the sides so fiercely that your knuckles turned as white as the clouds above us."

"And you rowed all the faster. By the time we reached the islands you were breathing as if you had just run a footrace and, oh, the blisters you had." She ran her thumb over his callused palm then rested her head against his shoulder as they let the motion of the swing and the whispers of the night breeze in the palm trees lull them into silence.

"Let's go to the beach, Liddy," he said.

"Now?"

"Tomorrow. It's Saturday and we can ride our bicycles over the causeway and take a picnic. It will be like before."

Oh, how she wanted to believe that such a thing could be true, but the truth was that in all the years that had passed they had both changed — the world had changed. "I don't know, John. Isn't it dangerous trying to relive old memories?"

"Maybe. On the other hand, I thought we had decided to spend this month trying to build some new memories."

"I do love the beach," she admitted. "But you have to work and . . ."

"We'll go after the hardware closes for the day. We can watch the sunset together."

"It sounds nice," she admitted. "You wouldn't say anything to Gert, would you? I mean everyone knows about your visits in the evenings, but riding off together on our bikes in broad daylight . . ."

John sighed. "You leave whenever you think best and I'll meet you at the start of the causeway. No one need know, not that it matters to me one way or another."

"But it should matter, John Amman. Of

course, others know, or at least have their suspicions, but they also respect that our seeing each other is meant to be a private matter and . . ."

"Then how come I feel like shouting it out to every person passing by?" He took her hands. "I promised to do things your way, Liddy, and if that means going separately to the beach, that is the way of it. Just promise me that we will come back together."

"Well, of course," she said primly, and then she smiled mischievously. "By then it will be dark."

The following afternoon Lydia had only been at the foot of the causeway for ten minutes before she saw John pedaling toward her. The sight of him took her breath away. His broad shoulders hunched over the handlebars of the black bicycle, his long legs pumping furiously as if to cover the distance separating them as quickly as possible. And the smile that said, more than any words, how seeing her made him as happy as it did her.

"Ready?" he asked as he slowed his bike and balanced it with one foot on the ground while she mounted hers.

"Ready," she agreed happily. "I'll race you

to the circle!" she shouted as she took off.

"Not fair!" John called back. "You have a head start."

She laughed and pedaled all the harder, determined to outdistance him. She thought she was well ahead of him, but when she reached the circle of shops and restaurants that stood at the entrance to Lido Key and the road that led north to Longboat Key, she saw that he had deliberately lingered just behind her until they reached the circle. Once there he grinned and shot past her then eased his speed down to coasting, waiting for her to catch up.

"Beat you," he teased as, side by side, they dodged traffic on the circle until they came to the road that turned off and led to the beach on Lido Key.

"Maybe I let you win," she challenged.

He laughed at that. "Not likely." They both knew that as a girl Lydia had been very competitive and she usually won once she set her mind to something. They rode along the path that followed the beach until they reached an area shaded by a small cluster of cypress trees. "Looks like a good place for a picnic."

She leaned her bike against a tree and removed the sheet she had packed for them to sit on. While John spread it on the ground, anchoring the edges with stones, she unpacked the sandwiches, oranges, cookies and thermos of tea that she had brought for their supper. John had devoured two whole ham sandwiches before she had finished a half. She found herself thinking about what it would be like to prepare food for him every day. What would he want for breakfast? Would they, like most families in Celery Fields, take their main meal at midday, or had he come to prefer the ways of the *Englisch,* having his main meal in the evening?

As he ate he stared out toward the Gulf, his eyes watching the waves rush at the beach, break and retreat. She tried to imagine what he was thinking and took his silence and his attention to a distant horizon as evidence that he still longed for unexplored shores.

She was surprised when he said, "You know, ever since I got back to Celery Fields I have felt such a sense of homecoming. I don't think I was ever in my life so reluctant to leave a place — to leave friends and family. To leave you especially."

Then why did you? She wanted so badly to ask. But she would not risk spoiling the moment. "It is your home, John. It has been since the day your family first moved here when you were, what? Eight?"

"Nine." He chuckled. "It seemed to me like we must be moving to the ends of the earth. The trip was long and then when we got here everything seemed very different from what we had known in Pennsylvania." He cut his eyes her way and then immediately back to the water. "Then I met you and I was glad we came."

She felt heat rise to her cheeks. "You exaggerate. As I recall, you were not at all sure about me in those early days. Especially not when I bested you at dodgeball in the schoolyard."

He shrugged. "I let you win then." He stuffed the last of the cookies into his mouth. "Made up for it today, though," he teased. He stood, brushed the crumbs from his shirt and trousers and held out his hand to her. "Walk with me, Liddy. The sun will set soon."

They gathered the wax paper wrappings of their picnic and John carried them to a trash barrel while Lydia folded the sheet and replaced it and the thermos in the basket of her bicycle. Then she fell into step with him as they walked hand in hand across the wide expanse of the beach, nearly deserted now as the last of the tourists packed up their belongings and headed away.

Close to the edge of the water they removed their shoes and set them well away from the rising tide, marking the spot they would return to once their walk was done. They stepped into the clear water that had gone calm now, the waves barely breaking over their bare feet, then headed north to where they knew the beach would curve and bend. There they stood on a point looking across a pass that separated Lido Key from Longboat.

Occasionally Lydia would stop and retrieve a shell, show it to John and then return it to the water.

"Keep one to remember," he said after she had repeated this process half-a-dozen times.

"You find one for me to keep."

CHAPTER ELEVEN

The shadows lengthened as the sun turned to a fiery orange low on the horizon. As they walked along, they were both focused on the water.

"Let's stop here and watch the last of it," John said, and gently turned her attention to the sun half-gone already. He stood behind her and wrapped his arms around her as they watched in silence. "Here," he said, handing her a perfect but tiny Florida conch shell that was the exact color that the sun had been. "To remember."

She turned to face him and cradled his cheek with her hand. She removed his hat and ran her fingers through his thick hair.

"Next week it will be a month, Liddy." His voice was raspy with emotion.

"I know." And although she knew he wanted his answer, she also knew that she could trust him not to press her.

She could trust him.

Not only had John shown no recent signs of wanderlust, he seemed perfectly satisfied to give her the time she might need. He was content. He worked every day at the hardware store and in the evenings and on Saturdays he worked at establishing his carpentry business. He had even gone so far as to make needed repairs and renovations for members of the congregation at no charge. He had especially endeared himself to those women in Celery Fields who were widowed and perhaps reluctant to become too dependent on their neighbors, although that was the Amish way of things. John had a way of just showing up as if he had simply been passing by and noticed a loose hurricane shutter or a wall with some rotted boards. He would assure the women that they were the ones helping him to make amends for his past.

Everyone in town knew that he was courting Lydia, but it was not their habit to speak of such matters. Courtship was private and that was a good thing as far as Lydia was concerned. For if things did not work out for them she could be sure that others would not speak of it — at least openly.

But things were working out. These days she could hardly get through an hour without some thought of John that brought a smile to her lips. He was wonderful with Luke and Greta's children, and sometimes he even came by the school during classes on some pretext or another. Her students looked forward to these impromptu visits. Even Pleasant seemed to be working hard to accept the idea that John was back to stay and that he intended to marry Lydia if she would have him.

If she would have him.

It was up to her. In so many ways it had always been up to her. "John," she said now as she wrapped her arms around him and rested her cheek against his chest. "Is there a reason that we need to wait out the entire month?"

She actually felt his heart beat a little faster. "I cannot think of one."

"Neither can I," she whispered, and stood on tiptoe to kiss his cheek.

He placed his finger under her chin, holding her uplifted face to the minuscule amount of dusky light left, trying to see her face. "Do not tease me, Liddy."

"Do you still wish to marry me?"

"You know that it is all I have ever —"

She pressed her fingers to his lips to silence him. She would not allow him to lie. There had been all those years when he was away and thought only of his life in that world beyond Celery Fields, a life that had not included her. "Then you should see the deacon so he can meet with my family, and the bishop can make the announcement at services week after next."

"You are certain?"

"I am," she assured him, and she brushed his hair back from his forehead. "We have wasted far too many years, John Amman. I will not waste another day."

He pulled her tight against him, his lips brushing her ear. "I love you, Liddy. I have always loved you. We are going to have a good life together. I promise you that."

"As God wills it," she added, with a silent prayer of thanksgiving that God had brought John home to her.

John hardly slept that night so anxious was he to call on Levi Harnischer, the deacon of their congregation, after services the following day. His uncle was not especially pleased that he wanted to take an hour off first thing on a day when he had orders to fill and customers to serve, but his aunt intervened.

"Really, Roger Hadwell, the boy has been working tirelessly for weeks now. Would you deny him one hour?" Gert demanded.

"An hour — no more," Roger instructed, wagging his finger at John.

And so the planning for his wedding with Liddy was set in motion. Once he had met with Levi, he knew that later that evening Levi would go to Luke and Greta's house to meet with Liddy and her family, making sure marriage was what Liddy wanted and her family approved. Levi would then go to Bishop Troyer's house to let him know that the planned nuptials should be made public.

After returning from Levi's and making sure he went straight to work unloading supplies and restocking shelves, John glanced at the calendar that his aunt kept hanging behind the counter. It was the fifteenth of March. Ten days hence the community would gather for the biweekly service, after which Bishop Troyer would make the announcement. By the middle of April he and Liddy would be married.

But as he stacked lumber in the shed behind the store, he overheard his uncle talking with Jeremiah Troyer.

". . . no choice," Roger said. "I mean if it has to be, perhaps now is the best time. We're coming to the end of the term and, with Lydia and John planning their wedding, maybe this is God's will."

John tightened his grip on a board and felt a splinter prick his palm. He bristled at the idea that it might be God's will to take away the one thing that Lydia loved almost as much as he believed she loved him. What about the fact that God had blessed Liddy with a gift for teaching? What about the remaining children of school age who would not have the privilege of learning from her? What about . . .

"Perhaps Lydia could offer private lessons in her home for the time being," Jeremiah suggested. "After all, these hard times will not last indefinitely. In time the community will start to grow again and we can reopen the school."

John felt a whisper of hope. With their wedding only weeks away, the one thing John wanted more than anything was to assure Liddy's happiness. She would be saddened by the closing of the school, but Jeremiah had offered a possible solution at least for the short term. Private lessons. In spite of his earlier reservations, it was an idea worth considering. There was certainly plenty of room to set up the front room of Liddy's house — soon to be their home — for such lessons. And Liddy was such a practical woman. He had no doubt that she, like Roger and Jeremiah, would take the closing of the schoolhouse where she had spent so many years simply as God's will.

In the meantime he felt a real urgency to

work doubly hard on building his business. For without Liddy's stipend as the community's teacher they would struggle to make ends meet on the small wages his uncle could afford. And if they should be blessed with children the financial burden would grow.

With all of these responsibilities dogging him through the rest of the day John could hardly wait to finish his work. He would not be expected to call on Liddy that evening, because Levi would go to Luke's house after dark to maintain the privacy of the matter. So, as soon as possible after bidding his aunt and uncle a good evening, John took a large piece of the wrapping paper his aunt used for purchases and rolled it up. Then he spent the rest of the evening making signs to post in Sarasota advertising his furniture-making business. And before dawn he rode into town and put up signs on every public bulletin board that he could find and still make it back to Celery Fields before the hardware store opened for the day.

To his delight and surprise he didn't have to wait long for his first order. That very afternoon Dr. Benson walked into the store and asked to speak with him. John knew the unusual request aroused Gert's curiosity, but to her credit she called him and then left him alone with the doctor to talk business.

"I'd like to order that cabinet we spoke about for my wife," Dr. Benson said. "I showed her the sketch you made and she said it was exactly the thing. Name your price."

John's heart was beating so hard he thought surely the doctor must hear it. He knew it was important to give a price that would cover materials and still leave a decent profit. Yet, it was also important that he not price his skill so high it would discourage other orders.

When he hesitated, Dr. Benson named a figure that was higher than John had been considering. "If you think that's fair," John managed.

The doctor laughed. "If you knew what they're charging for these things in the stores you'd know it's a bargain." He stuck out his hand. "Do we have a deal, then?"

John shook Dr. Benson's hand and grinned. "We do."

"Remember now. I need the thing finished and delivered on her birthday — June the first." He tipped his hat to Gert, who had lingered in the back of the store and left.

"You are doing business with the *Englisch* now?" she asked.

"I need to earn a living."

"You have a job here." She tapped her pencil on the counter. "Your uncle will not —"

"This is work that I do after hours."

"Using your uncle's tools," she reminded him.

"And how am I ever to have the money I need to buy tools of my own, Tante Gert? How am I to build a secure future and start a family?"

Her scowl softened. "Oh, Johnny, is it never enough for you?" He understood that her use of his childhood name was deliberate. She intended to remind him of mistakes brought on by his decision to go out into the world to seek a future instead of building one with his own kind in Celery Fields.

"It's not the same," he said, and was surprised to see tears well in his aunt's eyes.

"I hope not, Johnny. We would hate to lose you twice."

The bell above the door jangled and she hastily wiped her eyes on the hem of her apron before calling out, "Be right with you." She turned then and walked to the back of the store, leaving John to serve the customer.

That evening Lydia waited eagerly for Levi's

visit. At supper she had told Luke and Greta that she would be moving back to her house at the end of the week. Greta and the baby were thriving and the other children had settled into the new routine of having a newborn in the house. They no longer needed Lydia to help manage her sister's household.

"I must make plans for the closing of the school," she told them.

"That's not been decided," Greta protested.

"I am speaking of the end of the term, Greta," she corrected. "But the truth of the matter is the elders are leaning toward a permanent closing for the time being, and that will require a great deal of work, as well."

"How can you be so calm about this?" Greta asked her later as the two of them washed the dishes after supper while Luke read the older children a story. "I do not see why the school can't remain open," she fumed. "In time. . . ."

"But until such time, Greta, it is the practical solution."

Still, Lydia was concerned about losing the income that her stipend provided. But surely with John's wages they could make do. After all, they would have a roof over their heads and it was Florida, where the growing season gave ample opportunity for raising a variety of fruits and vegetables in the garden that lay between the house and the livery. Their needs were simple. Of course, if they were blessed with children . . .

Knowing that Levi would not come until well after dark, Lydia walked down to her father's house, that she and John would share once they married. She wandered through the rooms, smiling as she mentally arranged the furnishings to suit their new life. This small bedroom had once been a nursery for her and Greta, then it had been Greta's sewing room and most recently the place where Lydia prepared her lessons and graded her students' work. "By this time next year perhaps it will again be a nursery," she said aloud, testing the sound of the words against a vision of the room furnished with a brand-new crib and rocking chair made by John for their baby.

She pressed her palms over her flat stomach and closed her eyes as she considered all the changes that would surely come once she and John were married. "May it be Your will that they are happy changes," she whispered.

"Liddy!"

John's voice echoed through the house, filling Lydia's heart with such joy that she could not help but hurry back down the hall to greet him. "I am here," she called out.

His eyes glittered with excitement and she was sure that he had brought good news, perhaps about the school. Perhaps, it would not have to be closed, after all. Perhaps . . .

"I have been given a commission," he said. "Dr. Benson has officially ordered a china cabinet for his wife's birthday. And he will pay handsomely for it."

"John, that's wonderful news."

"It's more than wonderful, Liddy. With the money he is paying me we can manage a proper wedding trip, and with his influence there are sure to be more orders. Things are getting better all across the country and people are once again looking for ways to spend their money."

"Englischers," she said. She wanted to share in his excitement, but the idea that he might once again be drawn to building a business based on the patronage of outsiders gave her pause.

"People in Sarasota, yes. It's always been a town that attracted people of wealth. They come down for the weather, to escape the cold, and many of them stay on. Or if they don't they build winter homes here —

homes that need furnishing." A little of his initial excitement had faded. "I'm not leaving, if that's got you worried," he added, and this time she heard the hurt in his tone.

She laid her hand on his wrist. "I am sorry, John. It is good news."

"For both of us," he said, his eyes holding hers.

"For both of us," she repeated, because that seemed to be the assurance he needed. But instead of the smile of relief that she had expected, he frowned. "What else?"

"I overheard my uncle talking to Jeremiah Troyer," he said, and he did not have to say the rest aloud.

"It's decided, then," she whispered, and looked down at the floor, suddenly aware that her shoes needed a good polishing.

John pulled her into his arms and rocked with her from side to side. "We will be fine," he said huskily. "I will make things good for us. Don't worry. I will provide for you."

She raised her face to his. "We will do it together, John. With God's help." She saw the slight frown that marred his handsome features. "We have each weathered hard times before, John, and now we will have each other to lean upon when challenges come."

The frown was conquered by his smile. "I

love you, Lydia Goodloe."

She rested her cheek against his chest, taking comfort from the hard strength of him. Surely God would not have reunited them if a match between them was not to prosper and thrive. Still, for all her happiness at having John back in her life, she could not quell the dull pain of disappointment that the school would close and her role as teacher was coming to an end.

"Jeremiah suggested to my uncle that perhaps after the school is closed you might offer private lessons here. You could use the front room. The extra money could be a blessing when we have children of our own."

Lydia stepped back from him. "I could never charge our neighbors and friends for lessons. Of course, I will teach any child but I will take no money for doing it."

"Why not? You are offering a service in the same way Luke offers his services to shoe horses or repair machinery. Besides, you are already being paid for that work."

"Luke is in business. What I am paid comes from a general fund for services that benefit the entire community. Yes, everyone contributes to that but no one is asked to pay individually." She saw that her answer did not satisfy him and once again realized that in the world where he had spent much of his adult life the very idea that a person might simply give away something that could bring a fee was not likely. "John, these are the children of our neighbors, my sisters. How can I ask them to pay?"

There was a beat of silence between them and then John smiled uneasily. "Then we will make do. I will work at the hardware and build furniture and in time . . ."

She hugged him. "It will all work out, John. I am certain of it." But it was only a half-truth. Liddy wasn't sure at all, mostly because she could see that John was not convinced.

He kissed her forehead and grinned. "Enough talk of finances," he announced. "I believe that we have a wedding in need of planning."

"So we do," she agreed, happy to have the discussion of how they would make their way behind them. "Will you want to live here, John, in my father's house?" She had really never thought they would do otherwise, but their discussion of money had reminded her of the many times her father had expressed objections to her spending time with John.

"It is your house now, Liddy, and if it suits you then it suits me, as well. Or we can start fresh somewhere else."

"I want to be close to Greta," she replied.

"Then this is the place." He gave her a hug and then stepped back. "I have to get to work on that china cabinet," he said. "Will you come to the hardware store after Levi leaves and keep me company?"

"I will," she promised as they walked together through the kitchen to the back door. "I'll bring some of that strudel Greta makes that you like so much. We can have a picnic on the loading dock."

"You aren't worried about someone seeing us?"

"Let them look," she said with a recklessness that was completely out of character for her. She felt giddy with her love for John, and for once in her adult life she was going to permit herself to enjoy that feeling.

After John left, Lydia walked back to her sister's house at the end of town. In her absence Pleasant and Jeremiah had arrived, bringing Bettina along in case the baby started to fuss while the family met with the deacon. It seemed as good a time as any to prepare Bettina for the news of the school's closing that would soon be spread throughout the community.

"But they can't," Bettina protested. "I had thought that after you and John Amman married . . ." She blushed scarlet, realizing her mistake in mentioning a courtship and marriage that were not yet properly announced.

"You had thought that one day you might become the teacher." Lydia finished the thought for her. "I would not leave my position, Bettina."

"But if you and John Amman married and had children . . ."

"We would still need my income and, besides, we have known for some time, Bettina, that the school's future was precarious at best."

"But I had planned . . . Caleb and I had . . ." She stopped speaking again, this time shoving her fist against her lips as if to stem any further admissions.

It was well-known that Caleb Harnischer was intent on marrying Bettina one day. In so many ways the young couple reminded Lydia of herself and John when they were that age. So filled with plans for the future they were. And, just as with John and Lydia, it did not occur to this young couple that God might have other plans for their lives. She could only hope that neither of them would make a decision as John had that would separate them for eight long years.

"It will all work out," she promised Bettina. "You must simply trust that God will send you in the right direction even as he is guiding the elders regarding the school. Besides, it is not forever. In time the population will grow again and there will be children in need of schooling and the school will be reopened."

"But I have heard that they plan to tear it down and use the land for other purposes," Bettina protested,

Lydia had heard the same thing. "Then when the time comes the elders will build another school."

Bettina made a face. "But by then . . ."

"Shh. God will show us the way. We may not always see His path clearly, but in the end . . ."

Bettina's face brightened. "Just like He did for you and John Amman, you mean."

"That's right. Just like that."

But as she watched Bettina climb the stairs to care for the crying baby, she could not help worrying about Caleb and her niece. They might face a great deal of heartache before they found their way together, if that was God's intent for them at all.

Outside she heard the crunch of buggy wheels on crushed shell and the muffled snort of a horse. Levi had come at last. It was time to put aside any worries she had about the school and give all of her attention to the happy task of planning her wedding.

CHAPTER TWELVE

As the days passed leading up to Sunday services and the bishop's announcement of their wedding, nothing could dampen Lydia's good mood. Not the closing of the school — the news public now. Not even her previous concerns about John taking orders from outsiders. For if Lydia had suffered doubts about John attracting *Englisch* customers, such doubts were soon put to rest as word spread of his gift for making fine furniture. Besides, as Greta repeatedly reminded her, Luke served many in the Sarasota community with no ill effects. Thanks to Luke, John now had half-a-dozen small orders in addition to the china cabinet for the doctor's wife.

Even his uncle, as well as Hilda Yoder, came around to seeing the benefit of John's growing business. Hardly a customer who came to place an order with John left town without purchasing something from the hardware store or crossing the street to browse the wares of the dry-goods store. And if Lydia had worried that Josef Bontrager might not like the fact that John was in competition with him, she needn't have. One Sunday after services, as they all enjoyed the communal meal, Josef had approached John.

"I saw the cabinet you are building for Dr. Benson's wife," he said. "It reminded me that I have a supply of wood in my barn that I have no use for. I need the room that it's taking up, so if it is something you could use . . ."

John was on his feet immediately. "I'll stop by and have a look at it, but I would pay you . . ."

Josef held up his hands. "You would be doing me a favor, John Amman. Managing my land holdings and farm takes all my time these days. I am out of practice with crafting furniture and it would be good to see the wood put to some use."

"I'll come tomorrow evening if that suits," John said.

"That'll do nicely," Josef replied, and walked back to the table where his wife and her parents sat.

"So looks like you're to be the resident woodworker," Luke said after Josef left.

John grinned. "Life is *sehr gut*," he said. "I'll have to think about a place to store the lumber, though."

"You can use the stables for now," Luke offered. "Not that much call for livery services these days. There's plenty of room."

Lydia didn't know when she had felt so certain that God's plan was playing out exactly as He had intended. How could she ever have doubted it? It was true that most of the orders were for small things — caning a chair seat, building a small side table or a simple bookcase. But over time John's business would grow. Times were clearly getting better. They might struggle in the beginning, especially after the school closed, but for the first time since John's return she realized that she was clear of any doubt that he might leave again. He had found his place in Celery Fields.

With the joy of a future she had only dared dream of in her heart, she scrubbed the iron skillet. Just after breakfast John had gone to make a delivery with Roger and after that he would go to Sarasota to call on a prospective customer. Lydia intended to finish scouring the skillet before settling in to prepare the lessons she would teach the following day. A knock at the front door interrupted her work.

"Coming," she called out as she set the pan aside. Using her apron, she wiped her hands, reddened now by the hot water, and made her way down the hall. She could not imagine who of her neighbors might be calling at this time of day. Besides, anyone she knew would surely have come to the kitchen door.

A stranger waited patiently on her front porch, *Englisch* by his dress. He was a short, stocky man who looked, given his tan linen suit and soft straw hat, as if he had done well in the world. He carried a walking stick and was looking around when Lydia reached the door. "May I help you?"

His smile showed brilliantly white teeth set off by the ruddy color of his skin. This was a man who had spent a good deal of time in the sun but not necessarily doing hard work. She could not help but notice that his hands, folded on top of the walking stick, featured clean fingernails polished to a high sheen. Behind him she saw a motor-car parked in front of the house and a uniformed driver waiting next to it.

"Good day, ma'am," he said, removing his hat in the gesture of respect for women common to outsiders. "I wonder if you might help me. My name is George Stevens and I am looking for an old friend of mine

— John Amman?"

Lydia felt a wave of panic sweep through her. George Stevens had been John's business partner and whenever John spoke of the man it was always with admiration, even a certain nostalgia. *Not now,* Lydia silently prayed. *Not when he's finally come back to me.*

"I apologize for disturbing you at home," George Stevens hastened to add. "We — my driver and I — tried several of the businesses, but they all seemed to have closed for the day. A boy sent me to the apartment above the livery, but also said if I didn't find him there I should try coming here."

"John Amman is not here." Lydia forced out the words.

The stranger frowned as he glanced back toward the town and the setting sun. "I was certain that he told me . . . this is the town of Celery Fields, is it not?"

She should not be explaining anything to this man — she should not even be speaking with him. She was relieved to see Luke coming up the path. "May I help you?" he asked politely as he positioned himself between the stranger and the still-closed screen door.

George Stevens repeated his question. But it was clear that he was less sure of himself

238

when facing Luke. It was as if he realized for the first time that he had left his world behind and was now standing in the midst of theirs. "I . . . John Amman and I were friends and business partners at one time. Unfortunately, the economy ended the business, but we parted as good friends and I had hoped . . ." The man was babbling to fill up the silence that Luke and Lydia greeted him with. It was an *Englisch* habit that Lydia had always found especially annoying.

"John Amman will be in town tomorrow — at the hardware store," Luke said. "We will let him know that you were here. *Guten abend.*" And with that he stepped inside the house and closed the inner door. He handed Lydia a basket. "Greta said you needed these things for the wedding supper."

"*Yah.* It could have waited until tomorrow, but I'm glad you came."

"Would you like me to stay until we're sure he's gone?"

Outside, the motor of the car rumbled to life. "I think it is all fine now," Lydia replied.

"*Gut.* Then I will go." He opened the door and stepped onto the porch, looking down the street to where the car was making a turn that would take George Stevens away from Celery Fields.

"But, Luke, what if . . ." Lydia's hands started to shake and she felt the sting of tears filling her eyes.

Luke grasped her concern at once. "He's not going to leave you a second time, Liddy," Luke said softly. "No man could be so dumb."

"But . . ."

"Do you not trust him, Liddy?"

And there was the crux of it. She was certain of her love for John and of his for her. But John had once been drawn to that other world. Look where he was at this very moment, sitting with some *Englischer* hoping to get an order for a clock or piece of his furniture. Oh, why could he not be satisfied to wait for orders from his friends and neighbors in Celery Fields?

"It's not the same as before, Liddy," Luke said as if reading her thoughts. "All of us trade from time to time with them. I could not have made it these last two years without their business. But my place is here with my own people, and so is John's."

She took some comfort from Luke's words. "You do know that were you ever to decide otherwise Greta would come after you," she said, and smiled up at him.

He grinned. "*Yah.* She keeps me in line, your sister." Then his expression sobered.

240

"You will tell John that his friend stopped by."

Lydia bristled. "Of course. I would not keep it from him."

"Then you will have your answer," Luke said softly as he turned and headed for home.

John was just leaving his meeting with two men preparing to open a new restaurant on Main Street in downtown Sarasota. In his hand he held the order for the tables where patrons would be served. He had turned down their request for him to also build a bar. John was certain Lydia would draw the line at him making anything remotely associated with the sale of spirits. He already was concerned that she would object to his accepting the order to build the tables.

The men had acquired the chairs they wanted and it was from the simple design of those chairs that they wanted John to design the two dozen tables. He could not wait to tell Liddy. With an order of this size he could afford to cut back his hours at the hardware store, giving him more time to work on his carpentry orders. His uncle would no doubt grumble something about him being unappreciative. But that would pass the moment John reminded him that

241

fewer hours also meant less wages.

He was crossing the main street, bustling even at this hour with traffic and people, when he had to jump out of the way of a long sleek Packard automobile coming toward him. The car braked and stopped just as John made it safely to the other side of the street. From the corner of his eye he saw a man get out.

"John Amman? Is that you?"

John turned and broke into a grin as he saw his friend and former business partner coming toward him. A wave of nostalgia for all the times, good and bad, that he had shared with his friend swept through John and propelled him forward. He walked straight into George's bear hug.

"Look at you," George said as he held John at arm's length and took in the straw hat, shirt with no buttons, collar or cuffs, and homespun trousers held up by black suspenders. "I hardly recognized you."

"What are you doing here?" John asked, suddenly a little self-conscious to be standing in the middle of a busy sidewalk talking to someone who was not Amish.

"I came to find you," George replied. "Come have something to eat with me at the hotel. I'm staying there and word has it that they serve a fine shrimp dinner. It'll be like old times."

Only it wouldn't — couldn't. John was not the man he had been when he and George had worked together. "I can't," he said. "It is not our way."

George blinked and studied him as if trying to decide whether or not John was teasing him. Back east they had often played practical jokes on each other. "I want to talk to you, John. There's a new business opportunity that's come my way."

John indicated a park bench in front of a business that had closed for the night. "We can sit here and talk," he said.

George motioned to his driver to leave without him and sat down next to John. He glanced up and down the street. "Things seem to be prospering here," he said.

"Times are better," John agreed. "How are Bonnie and the children?"

"They are fine." A moment of awkward silence passed. "I met your Lydia," George said.

"How? Where?"

"I went to Celery Fields and asked for you and eventually ended up at the house behind the livery. She's lovely, John."

"We're to be married in two weeks."

"Congratulations! That's wonderful news."

The sun had set and before long it would be dark. The streets that had been so busy just minutes earlier were more deserted now. He should be getting back to Celery Fields, back to Liddy, but he was curious. George had come west to see him. "What is this business opportunity you have?"

"How much do you folks keep up with world news, John?"

You folks? There had been a time when George would not have thought to make such a distinction. "We hear some things," John hedged. Once he had been very aware of all that was happening in the outside world. George had talked of nothing else.

"There's every possibility that war is coming to Europe," George continued. "Several of the countries that allied themselves with the wrong side in the Great War now seem to think they got the short end of the stick in the peace. There's a lot of unrest and political upheaval, especially in Germany."

"I do not understand what this has to do with your business opportunity."

"It has everything to do with it. The American government mostly wants to stay out of things, but on the other hand, they are concerned about our allies — England, France . . ."

John did not understand where this was

heading, but he could see that George was very excited. "Go on," he encouraged, hoping that his friend would soon come to the point.

"I — *we* if you want in — have been offered a government contract to build parts for submarines. They want us to reopen the factory and retool it for the work. The government will pay for everything — refurbishing the factory, raw materials, everything. In less than a month you'd recoup the losses you took when the market crashed, John."

"This is a good opportunity for you," John said.

"For us," George corrected. "The government won't just hand over the money. They're going to need proof that we can do this. Without you to design the parts, there's no chance of getting the contract. I can't do it without you, John."

"I know nothing of submarines."

"You are a design wizard," George said. "We have to figure out how to make the parts so that they can be mass-produced. That's where you come in."

"I am to be married," John reminded him.

"Bring her east."

John fought a smile. It was all so easy for George. It had been that way when they

245

worked together. For him obstacles simply did not exist, or if they did they were merely challenges to be overcome. "Our home is here with our own people," he reminded his friend.

George frowned. "Did I mention what the government is offering to pay us, John?" He named a figure that was more money than John had ever dreamed of earning. "With that kind of money you could work with me for a couple of years and then retire for good."

With that kind of money I could assure the future for Liddy and our children. For Gert and Roger Hadwell.

"Talk to your Liddy about this, John. She seems to me to be a levelheaded young woman, one who would see the advantages for both of you." George stood up and extended his hand to John.

John also stood and accepted his friend's handshake. "I will discuss it," he promised.

"I need your answer by tomorrow, John. The government doesn't wait."

John nodded.

"We'd have to get started right away."

"Before the wedding?"

George chuckled. "Not that soon. Get yourself hitched, my friend. But I'll need you out east by the end of the month at the latest."

All the way back to Celery Fields, John thought about the offer George had made him. It was true that in their business before, John's role had been one of figuring things out — how best to design a piece of furniture so that it not only served its purpose but also looked good alone and with the other furnishings in the room.

But this was different. This was designing parts, like for a clock. Like for a missile or bomb. The thought gave him pause. No one in Celery Fields would approve of him building anything connected with war. The Amish were a peace-loving people. They did not take part in war or anything to do with it. He snapped the reins, urging the team of horses into a trot. He needed to talk to Liddy. She would know what to do.

"You cannot seriously be considering this," Liddy said after he explained everything to her. Her voice came out in little gasps as she struggled to catch her breath and force out the words. Her head was pounding and her heart was racing as she fought to suppress the image of her world falling apart yet again.

"It is not for the war, Liddy. George says

that the Americans are trying to maintain the peace. All they want to do is protect the shoreline and the best way to do that apparently is with submarines."

"Those ships are instruments of war, John." Surely, it was the excitement of seeing his friend after all these months. Surely, it was the fact that it was now nearly eleven o'clock and he was exhausted after his long day. He was not thinking clearly.

"They are also instruments for keeping the peace. Why can't you understand that I would do this for us, for our future? It would not be forever, Liddy. I am not leaving you. George says —"

"I do not care what George says," she said through gritted teeth. "This man is not of our faith, and he knows nothing of our ways."

"He has been a good friend to me."

"And for that I am grateful, but John, can you not see that I am afraid?"

"And can you not see that all I want is to make sure you never have anything to fear ever again?"

"You cannot control what happens to us, John. If it be God's will that —"

"Why then might you not consider that *this* is God's will, that the sudden appearance of my former business partner is part of God's plan for us?"

"Or perhaps George Stevens with his fancy motorcar and his driver and his expensive clothes is nothing more than temptation, John Amman, a test to see if you have conquered your wanderlust once and for all and will never again be tempted by the outside world."

The light of excitement that had lit his eyes — indeed, his entire face — from the moment he'd come to tell her the news dimmed. "Will you never have trust in me, Liddy?"

"Oh, John, I love you so very much and . . ."

"But you do not trust me, Liddy."

"I . . ." She struggled to find the words. "You can understand that I have doubts. You were away for eight years, John, and while it's true that you have returned to us — to me — you cannot deny the pull of that outside world still works within you."

"They are not our enemy, Liddy."

"I know, but they are also not of our ways."

"And in our ways, is it not the duty of the man to provide for his wife and children? To make sure they have shelter and food and the children have a future?"

"This is true, but . . ."

"This is all I am trying to do, Liddy. We are getting a later start on our life together than most. We do not have the years younger couples have to build a business and a future. Our need is now."

"We have shelter and food enough. You have work and in time . . ."

He stood up and started to pace. He turned once as if to say something more and then paced again. Lydia sat in her chair, hands folded in her lap, and waited.

"There is another side to this, Liddy. George Stevens is my friend. He has told me that if I turn this down he will not be awarded the contract. The government wants to begin at once."

"There must be others who can do what he wishes you to do in this project."

"No doubt. But finding that man would take time that George doesn't have. He has also suffered great financial losses these last years and . . ."

Lydia could not suppress a laugh. "Yet he arrived here in a shiny motorcar with a driver," she reminded him.

John shrugged. "That's George. He has a habit of spending before he earns. He thinks it is important to make the good impression. I expect he is deeply in debt for his trouble."

"Then all the more reason not to become involved in his plan," Lydia argued. "He is not to be trusted."

"His father hired me when no one else would. George made me an equal partner in that business. He is my friend."

Would it truly come to this? That she would have to demand that he choose her or his friend? "I am so very tired, John, and not thinking clearly. Can we not discuss this tomorrow?"

"George needs my answer tomorrow," he replied as he stood at the window staring into the darkness.

Lydia let out a sigh of resignation. "Then do what you must," she said quietly, all the while silently praying that he would choose her this time.

Instead, he picked up his hat and walked to the door. "I would like your blessing, Liddy, and your trust that I am doing this for us as much as for George."

So he was going away again. "I cannot . . ." she began, and her voice broke as the sobs she'd been holding back spilled out. "Please just go," she managed when he started to cross the room to her. She looked up at him. "Go," she whispered.

His lips hardened into a thin line and he turned away and stalked to the door. "I'm

251

going, then, and this time I won't bother to write, Liddy," he said as he left.

When Lydia woke the following morning after most of the night spent pacing the floor, fighting the desire to run across the yard that separated them and up to John's apartment, Greta was in the kitchen frying bacon.

"What are you doing here?" Lydia croaked, her throat raw from crying most of the night.

"I came to find out what is going on. I mean it is perfectly understandable that as you and John approach your wedding day one or both of you will get a case of nerves but this business is ridiculous. Luke says that John has packed up and left with that man. How could you let this happen yet again, Liddy?" She scooped up two strips of the bacon and plopped them onto a plate that she set in front of Lydia. "Eat," she commanded as she pulled out a chair opposite Lydia and sat down.

"I did not let this happen this time nor the time before," Lydia protested. "John is a grown man and . . ."

"A man who loves you," Greta reminded her.

"Then why did he leave?" Lydia said

quietly as the tears once again leaked down her cheeks.

Greta grasped her sister's hand and squeezed it. "Oh, Liddy, he wants to make a good life for you. The wages Roger Hadwell pays him wouldn't be enough to support John alone if Luke hadn't bartered the living space for John maintaining the stables."

"He has orders for his furniture."

"And in time there will be more orders, enough to build a proper business, but that will all take time, Liddy, and Luke says that with the school closing and the loss of your stipend . . ."

"I can get other work," Lydia protested.

"Doing what? There are no jobs in Celery Fields. Are you truly going to go out into the Sarasota community and clean houses?"

"It's honorable work."

"It is, but I seem to recall that you were the one who was concerned about John taking orders for his furniture business from outsiders. How could you work for them?"

Greta's occasional burst of logic could be maddening. She had a point, of course. "Still . . ." Lydia began searching for some counterargument. "The point is that John keeps returning to their world and I am afraid . . ."

"Ah, finally we get to the root of it. You are afraid of losing him. Well, look around, Liddy. He's already gone. Now, the question is what will you do about it?"

"He has made his choice."

"And who placed him in the position of having to choose?" Greta rolled her eyes. "The way he explained the whole thing to Luke when he came by late last night, his friend needs his help. Would you have him ignore that?"

"No, but . . ."

Greta continued as if Liddy had not spoken. "What would Luke have done when his business burned to the ground if friends and neighbors from both Celery Fields and Sarasota had not stepped up to help him rebuild? It's what we do, Liddy, and if you needed some reassurance that John has indeed returned to his roots, this should surely be it."

"Now you are truly making no sense," Lydia fumed as she picked at a strip of bacon. "John has chosen, all right. He has chosen the outside world."

"No. He has chosen to help his friend. He will come back once that is done just like Luke's customers from Sarasota went back to their lives after helping him after the fire."

This time I will not write.

John's parting words rang in her ears. He hadn't written last time, either, so why say such a thing? "It's over," she said wearily as she carried her dishes to the sink. She stood there for a long moment and looked across the yard to John's rooms. There was no difference that she could see, but in her heart she felt his absence as surely as if there had been some physical sign that he had left. "Where are the children?" she asked.

"Bettina is watching them." Greta got up and began wiping the kitchen table and clearing away the skillet she'd used for the bacon. "Pleasant will need to be told," she said.

"I expect that Gertrude Hadwell has already let her know, along with Hilda Yoder and others." It would be some time before the gossips in the community stopped talking about this. "I am sorry for Gert," she added wistfully. "She has gotten so used to having John back again."

"I am not worried about Gertrude Hadwell, Liddy. I am worried about you — to have your heart broken once is bad enough, but to repeat that experience?" She actually shuddered. "I can't begin to imagine what . . ."

"I will be fine, Greta."

But would she? She had lost her livelihood, work she truly loved and now John had left her for a second time. Would she ever be fine again?

CHAPTER THIRTEEN

It had been a long time since John had ridden in a motorcar, especially one as fine as George Stevens's Packard. His Amish faith allowed him to ride in such a vehicle when necessary as long as he neither operated nor owned the car. He had to wonder if the elders would consider this trip "necessary." He ran his palm over the soft cloth seat, marveling at the space available for a third person to sit comfortably between George and him.

George had dozed off almost as soon as his driver had pulled away from the Sarasota hotel. He had asked no questions when John had showed up at his suite and said that he was ready to accept his former partner's offer. John suspected that George was just relieved to hear his decision and didn't want to risk jinxing it by asking too many questions. All through breakfast George had talked about his wife, Bonnie. But not once had he asked about Lydia.

John studied the folders of papers George had handed him at breakfast. His education had stopped after eight years, as did formal learning for all Amish boys, but in the years he'd spent working with George and other *Englischers* his reading and understanding of the written word had increased significantly. Still, the government contract and the specifications for submarine parts that George expected him to design made little sense to him. Not for the first time he wished Liddy were riding in the car with him.

He laid the papers on the seat next to George and pinched the bridge of his nose as he squinted his eyes closed and then opened them again to stare out the open window. Florida was flatland dotted with orchards of citrus trees, fields planted with vegetables, swamps, horse farms and small towns. The recent drought had turned the landscape a greenish-brown and the fronds of the tall, slender coconut palms drooped toward the ground as if willing the water to rise up and satisfy their thirst. He watched an egret fly next to the car, keeping pace with it for a bit before veering off to land in a ditch. He saw a flock of roseate spoonbills fly across the sky in the distance, their pink bodies reminding him of the sunset that he had watched with Liddy at the bay.

Liddy. Beautiful. Stubborn. Impossible.

Why couldn't he make her understand that everything he did, every decision he made, was for one purpose only? Her happiness was everything to him. After returning to Celery Fields and learning that he still had a chance to make things right with her, to win her heart this time forever, how many nights had he paced the small confines of his rooms above the stables thinking of how best to build a life with her?

He frowned.

And why did he need to prove himself to her over and over again? After all, she had been the one to put community ahead of their happiness. And he had come to accept that decision, so why was it so difficult for her to accept that he was doing this partly because George needed his help? She had refused even to consider the possibility that George Stevens might have been sent to them, a blessing in disguise. She was always talking about how God would provide. Well, to John's way of thinking, a person had to be open to such messages and opportunities. Annoyed by thoughts of Liddy's obstinacy, he set his lips in a tight, hard line, folded his arms across his chest and closed his eyes.

But sleep did not come. Instead, his mind reeled with memories of Liddy's laughter, her smile, her touch, her kiss. Not even George's snoring or the thud of the car's tires on the uneven road could block out the sweetness of those times that he and Liddy had shared recently. He felt his features relax into a smile as he recalled her story of Greta's plans for their wedding.

"You would think she was planning her own nuptials," Liddy had said with a shake of her head after describing the menu for the wedding supper that Greta had suggested. "I keep trying to tell her that we need everything plain, the way it should be, but she seems determined to find a way to turn the entire event into some kind of community celebration."

"Well, isn't it?" he asked, suddenly unsure whether or not Liddy truly loved him or simply saw this as her last chance to marry.

"Oh, John, of course it is. But we have waited for so long and all that truly matters is that we will finally be together. A wedding is an event, a celebration. But it is the marriage that I am looking forward to — the years we are going to share together with God's blessing."

And after that he'd entertained no more doubts.

Until now.

"Are you hungry, John?"

John opened his eyes and found George watching him, a puzzled expression on his face.

"Do you want to stop?" he replied, not wanting to be any trouble.

George chuckled. "You haven't changed a bit, my friend. Still answering a question with another question." He leaned forward. "Henry, next diner you see let's pull in."

Over lunch George explained the project in a way that set John on the path to understanding the task before them. He realized that the work was exactly as George had described it, like building the workings of a clock. As they ate John made some detailed sketches on a napkin and showed them to George.

His partner grinned. "That's the ticket," he said. "I see what you've done. Just in changing the angle of that piece, it will eliminate the necessity of this connector and . . ." He released a low, satisfied whistle. "If we get this order done early, there's every possibility that the government will give us another project and then another and before you know it, my friend, we will be right back where we were before."

John forced a smile. *"Yah."*

But the truth was that he didn't wanted to be back where he was with George and their business. What he really wanted was to be back with Liddy.

After John left, Lydia found that she could not stand being in the house alone. Over the weeks that had passed since she had accepted John's proposal she had spent most of her time imagining them living there together. She had even started to make small changes in preparation for John moving in after the wedding. The chair she knew he favored had replaced the one her father had used in the front room. She had taken down the hat her father used to wear from the peg by the back door where it had hung since his death a few years earlier. Now the peg was empty. The house seemed to be waiting for John's arrival.

"An arrival that will never happen," she muttered as she shook out the small rag rug she had placed on the floor by the bed they would have shared.

"You are talking to yourself, Lydia." Her half sister, Pleasant, frowned with concern as she crossed the yard.

Lydia gave Pleasant a weak smile. "So I

am. Come in. I just squeezed some fresh juice from the oranges you brought me yesterday."

Pleasant sat at the table in the chair that Lydia had imagined John using for their shared meals. Lydia could feel Pleasant watching her closely. "You look tired," she said when Lydia set two glasses of juice and a plate of ginger cookies on the table.

Lydia shrugged. "There's a lot to be done to finish the school year and then prepare the building to be permanently closed."

They sipped their juice in silence. "You haven't heard from John?"

He'd been gone for ten days. "I don't expect I will. After all his parting words were that this time he would not write." She gave a bitter bark of a laugh. "As if somehow this time were any different than . . ."

To her shock she began to cry and because this was Pleasant, ever practical and stoic, rather than the more excitable Greta, Lydia gave in to the tears she had held inside for days now.

Pleasant waited for the storm of tears to pass, acknowledging the outburst only by passing Lydia a napkin to use for wiping her eyes and blowing her nose. It was their way to not make a fuss. The two of them had always enjoyed this special bond.

"In time I suppose . . ." Lydia began but did not finish the thought as she took a sip of her juice.

Pleasant tapped her fingers nervously on the tabletop. "I have something I must tell you, Liddy," she said softly. "Jeremiah says that I should have told you long ago, but that is the way he is."

"Has something happened with one of the children?" Lydia felt ashamed that she had been so focused on her own misery that she might have overlooked something that would be a concern for Pleasant.

"This has nothing to do with my family, Lydia," Pleasant replied brusquely. "We are speaking of you — and John."

With a weary sigh, Lydia started to rise from her chair to refill their glasses. "It is over, Pleasant. I would expect Greta would continue to live in blind hope, but surely not you, as well."

"Sit down, Liddy." She waited until Lydia was facing her across the table. "When John went away before — all those years ago — he did write to you."

"He didn't, Pleasant. Are you trying to say that I have forgotten?"

"I am saying that you never knew. Our *dat* asked Hilda Yoder to make sure anything that looked as if it might have come from

John be first given to him. There were letters, Lydia, several of them."

"But why . . . ?"

"He did not wish to see you hurt and he was afraid."

"Of what? John is . . ."

"He was not afraid of John. He was afraid of losing you. He was afraid that you would follow John and be lost to us forever."

"But I wrote John, as well, and . . ."

"Those letters were never sent."

Lydia felt a tightening of her chest that she recognized as fury at Hilda Yoder for her part in this. But when she lifted her gaze to meet her half sister's eyes, that fury was directed at Pleasant. "You knew and said nothing?"

"I am not pleased with my actions, Lydia. It was a time in my life when I suffered from the sin of envy. You and Greta held such a special place in our father's heart. You represented your mother to him and he had loved her so very much and grieved for her untimely death. Perhaps if I had known Jeremiah then, I might have —"

"What happened to the letters?" Lydia felt a twinge of hope that perhaps somehow they had been saved.

"He burned them, both yours and John's."

"And John never knew? Would not Gertrude have known or John's mother?"

"No one knew but Hilda, *Dat* and me."

"I thought that he had abandoned me — all those years, Pleasant . . . lost."

This time when the tears began Pleasant did not sit by and wait. She knelt next to Lydia and wrapped her arms around her. "I know. I am truly sorry for my part in all of this, Liddy. I wish I could make amends. Jeremiah said that I could by telling you the truth, but now I see I have only upset you further."

"He thinks I don't care, Pleasant. For eight long years he thought I had turned from him, and still he came back."

"He loves you in spite of the fact that he believes you turned away from him. He has always loved you, Lydia, as you have always loved him — as you love him now. There may yet be time to salvage this. Write to him at once. I will post the letter myself and this time there will be no question that it is sent."

"It's been almost two weeks since he left," Lydia moaned. "What if . . ."

"You will have no answers if you do not try, Liddy." Pleasant led Lydia to the front room and the small desk in the corner. "Write to him. I will clean up in the kitchen."

"But what can I say that will change anything?"

Pleasant cupped Lydia's cheek. "Tell him what I told you. Tell him you love him. Ask him to come home to you."

Lydia sat at the desk for nearly half an hour, the words pouring onto the page before her. Finally she could write no more. She folded the thin pages and placed them in an envelope and sealed it. "We have no address," she said, carrying the letter to the kitchen, where Pleasant sat waiting patiently at the table.

Pleasant smiled. "That man, George Stevens, stayed at the hotel in Sarasota. Jeremiah was able to get his address. We will send the letter in his care and it is sure to reach John."

Lydia watched Pleasant head back to town, to the ice-cream shop her husband owned, and a few minutes later she saw Pleasant and Jeremiah in their buggy headed for Sarasota. She closed her eyes and sent up a silent prayer that the words she had written would bring John back to her.

A week passed with no word. And then half of another week.

Finally, one evening after he returned from Sarasota and the ice-packing business he ran there, Jeremiah walked slowly up to

her house and handed her an envelope —
her envelope, her handwriting. She turned
it over in her hands and saw that the seal
had not been broken. The letter had been
returned to her unread.

She had her answer.

At the biweekly services that Sunday, Lydia
once again endured the barely concealed
glances of pity and sympathy cast her way.
By now everyone had heard the story. John
was gone — again. And this time not a
single person in the community believed he
would come back, not even Lydia. And yet
in the still-dark hours before dawn as she
had stood looking out toward the windows
of the rooms above the stable, she felt
something in her heart that she could only
describe as hope.

Foolish, foolish woman, she thought as she
bowed her head for the first prayer of the
morning. She prayed for understanding, for
God to reveal His purpose for her life. The
school would be closed in another week and
John was gone. What was she supposed to
do?

She barely heard the first sermon so
focused was she on thoughts of John. Was
he happy? Was he well? She prayed that both
were true. But oh, how she missed him —

his smile and his laughter. Missed his hand holding hers, his arm around her as they sat on her porch swing planning their future.

Every day that he'd been gone she told herself that in time the pain would lessen. In time the memories would not sting so much. In time . . .

But the truth was that her every waking moment was spent thinking about John. If only she had known about the letters her father had intercepted and burned. Those letters were proof that John had kept his promise. Pleasant had told her that they had come for months after he left — one a day at first and then, later, one a week, and finally they had stopped.

And suddenly she knew her purpose. Her eyes flew open as the decision came to her. This time she would be the one to go and find John. And even if there was no chance of rekindling their love a third time at least he would know the truth as she now did. He deserved that. Yes, as soon as school was closed, she would pack up her things and take the train east. She would leave notes of explanation for Greta and Pleasant, but she would not let anyone know of her plan.

And then?

She closed her eyes and clasped her hands together. She was certain that God had brought John back into her life for some purpose. Perhaps that purpose was only to lead both of them to an understanding of the past that had caused each of them pain and kept them from moving forward in their lives. Now she was certain that God was leading her to John to explain what neither of them had known. And would God be gracious and bless them with a reunion that brought John home to Celery Fields, home to her?

One step at a time.

The remainder of the three-hour service went by in a flash, so preoccupied was Lydia with crafting her plan for leaving to find John. She had the address for George Stevens. He had seemed a kind man. She thought that if she went to him first he would help her arrange a meeting with John. Yes, that was the best idea.

She rose with the rest of the congregation for the closing hymn. And by the time she and the other women had gathered in the kitchen to lay out the meal, she felt a new lightness of spirit.

John's first time back inside the large, rambling factory where he and George had built their earlier fortunes brought back a flood of memories, some pleasant and some incredibly painful. There had been the day that the workers they'd hired had completed the first large order of grandfather clocks to be shipped to a chain of department stores in New York. George had declared the day a holiday and given each employee a cash bonus.

Then there had been the day when he and George had called the remaining employees that they had not already had to let go onto the floor of the factory. Behind the dozen or so men the machinery stood silent and unused. Everyone knew what was coming. They were closing the factory for good. It was Christmas Eve and George had bought each of the men the makings for a turkey and ham Christmas dinner to take home to their families. It was the best he could offer and John remembered how, after the last man was gone and the doors of the factory closed behind them for the final time, George had cried like a small boy.

But when John walked into the factory after the drive across the state, he was surprised to see some of their former employees already at work cleaning and oiling machinery and painting walls — walls they were also lining with patriotic posters. They greeted him with smiles that spoke of trust and optimism and John's heart was filled with a determination to make this work, if not for him, then for these men and their families.

Refusing George's offer of a room at his parents' mansion, John chose instead to set up a cot in the factory office, citing the need to be near the work when ideas for design changes came to him in the night. He did not admit even to himself that the nights were when he did most of his work. At least if he could force himself to focus on the designs and patterns for the pieces the factory would produce, he could get through the night without constantly thinking of Liddy.

Or so he thought.

The truth was that thoughts of her haunted him day and night. He tried to remind himself that he had been in this position before, that in time the memories and the pain of them would lessen. In time he would fill his days and nights with work and the joy of seeing the business that he and George had built together thrive once again. But every time he walked out onto the factory floor to try modeling one of the parts they would be producing his thoughts went back to Celery Fields. The stables that Luke had told him he could use for his woodworking. The smell of fresh-cut wood mingling with the smoky fire of Luke's blacksmithing. The rocking chair he had made for Greta and the china cabinet he had built for Dr. Benson's wife.

And there had been the orders from Luke's customers — orders he had stayed up all night before leaving to finish. He thought about the kitchen table and chair set he had started making for Liddy as a wedding gift. Those pieces sat unfinished at the back of Luke's stables. Remembering the smoothness of the tabletop John ran his hand absently over one of the worktables in the factory and was stung by a sliver of metal filing that nicked his palm. They would work in metal now, the machinery having already been retooled. They would not build clocks, cabinets, tables or rocking chairs. The assignment was for small parts that would have to fit perfectly with other parts being made in other factories. Parts for submarines that would silently patrol the waters offshore.

In Liddy's eyes the work he was doing would be used in instruments of war and, as she had reminded him, their faith was rooted in peace and forgiveness. It was hard not to face the fact that war would come, if not to the shores of America then surely to Europe. He could tell himself anything he liked, but he knew in his heart that Liddy was right. And as each day passed he watched his designs and patterns turned into actual parts that the men on the factory floor produced. His certainty that agreeing to George's plan had been a mistake hardened into a lump of solid regret that lodged in the very center of his chest.

There was no doubt that he could make enough money to secure a future for himself. The government contract had provided separate funding for the creation of the designs and patterns that could be easily transferred to other factories making the same parts in other places. After John had been back only two weeks George had presented him with a check. "With the gratitude of the United States government," he had said.

But John had refused to take the money. Liddy was right. Any way he looked at it, the factory was running on what George called "war time" whenever he reminded the employees of the urgency of meeting production numbers on time.

Then one night George came to the factory late. John assumed that he had come to be sure the night shift was running smoothly as he often did when they were approaching a delivery deadline. Only this time George came straight to the office and he was carrying a large new toolbox. The men from the third shift crowded into the doorway behind him. For once the machinery behind them that ran round the clock was silent.

"You won't take the money. I get that — sort of. But without the work you did to make the patterns, John, we would all be unemployed. So, the men and I decided to get you a present to show our appreciation. This has nothing to do with the government, you understand. Just a bunch of once-out-of-work guys wanting to say 'thanks.' "

He placed the toolbox on the desk. When John just stared, he said, "Well, open it." Behind George the men pressed forward, their excitement palpable in the small office.

John unhooked the locks and raised the lid. The box was completely outfitted with a set of woodworking tools — hammers, chisels, handsaws, clamps — everything anyone would need to build furniture by hand.

"One day," George said softly, "you'll go home again to Celery Fields and we want you to have a good start on that shop you're going to open."

"I don't know what to say," John whispered as he lifted a tack hammer from the toolbox to admire it, feel the fit of his fingers around the grip.

One of the men broke the uncomfortable silence that fell over the room by starting up a chorus of "For He's a Jolly Good Fellow" and the others joined in. When the song ended George was grinning broadly as he wrapped his arm around John's shoulders. "We might be a bunch of outsiders, John Amman, but every man here is your friend." Then he turned to those crowded into the office and with a good-natured sternness shooed them all back to work.

After the others had left George closed the office door and sat down at the desk watching John go through the toolbox, admiring each implement.

"Go home, John," George said softly. "Go home to your furniture building and your lady. I don't think you've slept more than two or three hours a night since you got here. It's pretty obvious to me that it hasn't been the work here keeping you up at night. You miss her — you miss the whole place. Go home, my friend."

"What if there's nothing to go back for?"

"You think she won't forgive you? She did once before, didn't she?"

John shrugged. "That was different. We were young and . . ."

George stood up and put on his fedora as he pulled an envelope from the inside pocket of his suit jacket. "Go home to your people, John. Your work here is done, and once this war comes and goes I'm going to be calling on you for some of those furniture designs we used to make before the bottom dropped out." He placed the envelope on the desk next to the toolbox. "This is a check, John. It's from me not the government. I'm buying you out."

"But . . ."

"I know what you're going to say but we went into this together, and you may not have invested money, but you deserve something for the designs you developed. I'm buying the rights to those."

John thought about all the times that Liddy had reminded him that God would show him the way. And all of a sudden his path seemed clearer than it had been at any time in his life. He grinned at his friend and extended his hand. "Thank you, George."

"I expect to be invited to the wedding," George said as he left the office and closed the door behind him.

John stood at the desk long after George and the others had left as he once again examined each tool in the box. They were of the finest quality, especially the wood-carving chisels and knives. He could do excellent work with these replicas of the tools he had once bought with the money he and George had made in their first venture. In those days, as apparently he continued to do now, George had spent his money on clothes and dining out at fine restaurants. He had even bought himself a diamond ring for his little finger. But John had had no such wants. For him the luxury of a handcrafted tool intended for crafting wood into usable objects was enough.

As he replaced each item in its designated space in the large metal box, he realized that what George had given him was far more precious than the simple hand tools. He picked up the envelope, opened it and found inside crisp new bills totaling more cash than he had ever held before and a one-way railway ticket to Sarasota. *Go home,* his friend had advised him.

For perhaps the first time in his life, it was advice that John fully intended to heed.

Lydia was counting down until the last day of school and the next, when she would finish packing up the supplies and books and maps she used for teaching and move them to her house. The morning after that she would board the train for St. Augustine and even if John refused to see her she would tell his friend, George Stevens, the story of the intercepted letters and plead with him to act as an intermediary between John and her.

From the moment she had devised her plan she had thought of little else. Fortunately Greta and Pleasant assumed she was simply mourning John's departure and the loss of her job. The two of them were constant in their suggestions for what she might do now that she would have no responsibilities for teaching the children. Luke had come by one day to invite her to move in with them if she chose. "Or, if you won't accept our help, then Jeremiah and I will provide you with a monthly stipend to replace your lost wages so you can continue living in this house."

She had thanked them and begged for time to attend to her remaining duties before she made any decision about her life going forward. And then she sat up late into the night working out the details of her journey to find John and bring him home. She studied the train schedule, set aside the money she would need for the ticket, packed some spare clothing in the basket she normally used for carrying her books to and from the schoolhouse. That way if anyone saw her, they would not think anything of it.

As anxious as she was to go to John, she had a duty to the community. The school was closing and her students and their families deserved the best she could offer them. But at night she sat at her desk, writing letter after letter trying to find the words that might explain how her late father had duped both of them. She tore up every single letter. From the little she had seen of George Stevens she had no doubt that he would find words far more persuasive than hers could ever be for bringing John home.

But then George Stevens might not agree that Celery Fields was the best place for John. After all, the man had a business venture that was dependent on John's skills as a draftsman and designer. What if he decided to sabotage her efforts to reunite with John? What if he laughed at her?

Lydia gritted her teeth. Well, God would show her the way. She felt more strongly than ever before in her life that God was guiding her steps. Never in her life would she have even considered leaving Celery Fields for so much as a day, much less for the week or more that it might take to find

John and persuade him to forgive her. Such reckless actions were more Greta's style. And yet here Lydia sat, night after night, plotting and planning every little detail of her adventure.

It occurred to her that she might be feeling what John had felt when he had left that first time. Like her, he had set a purpose for his journey. Like her, he had been certain of his cause. Like her, he must have had moments when he questioned the wisdom of his actions. And, like her, he had cast all doubts aside and moved forward. She would tell him all of that and more once she found him. She would tell him how she now realized that it had been her own fears that had prevented her from seeing his true purpose.

She shook off all such thoughts. There was only one thing she needed to tell him and make him understand: that she loved him, and if only he would give her one more chance she would show him how happy a life they could build together.

In just two days she would say goodbye to her students for the last time. The day after that she would pack up her supplies and close the school for good. And the day after that?

She would set out in search of the only man she had ever loved.

CHAPTER FOURTEEN

George insisted on driving John to the train station and seeing him off. "I have a confession to make," he said as the two of them stood on the platform, the train hissing and belching next to them while men loaded the freight and passenger luggage.

John had noticed how quiet his friend had been on the ride to the station. He had assumed George was struggling with the reality that John was leaving. "Look, George, let's not . . ."

"There was a letter," George blurted. "From her. From your Lydia."

John thought he must have heard wrong. The noise from the train and shouts between the men loading it had surely distorted George's words.

"It came after you'd been here for a couple of weeks. We were in the midst of everything by then and the pressure to get the designs completed and the patterns developed — Well, I just didn't want you to have any distractions."

"Distractions?" John felt his grip tighten on the toolbox that he fully intended to keep by his side for the entire journey. "Lydia is not a distraction, George. She is . . ."

George looked away, his cheeks blotched with red. "I know. I'm sorry. I assumed that she would write again and by then . . ." He turned back to face John. "Besides, when we left Sarasota you were so hurt that I figured you wanted nothing more to do with her. As you told me, it wasn't the first time that she had —"

"The letter," John interrupted. "Give it to me."

"I don't have it."

"You destroyed a letter meant for me?"

"I sent it back unopened."

A dozen scenarios danced through John's brain as he tried to imagine what Liddy must have thought when her letter was returned. In his heart he knew that there was only one true reaction she could have had. She would have thought he had refused her letter and was cutting all ties to her, this time for good.

"I'm so sorry, John. I don't know what I was thinking. I've never met anyone like your Lydia and I thought that in time you

284

would meet someone else. But then as the days passed I realized how miserable you were and I knew I had done the wrong thing. That's why I encouraged you to go home. That's why . . ."

"But you made sure you had gotten what you needed from me first," John said, fighting to keep his temper in check. He set down the toolbox and fished out the envelope that held the cash and his train ticket. "You would buy my forgiveness, George?"

George pressed the envelope into John's hands. "The money is yours, John. You would not take payment for your designs and patterns and so per your wishes I divided that money among our employees. But this is payment for your part of the factory building and machinery. We owned that together. I am simply buying you out."

"And the tools?"

George looked down at the box between them. "Yes, that part was guilt. I hoped to make it up to you by giving you a stake to start your business. But the men insisted on being part of it when they learned that their bonus money had come from you. They wanted to show their appreciation."

"I did not give the money to be handed it back in another form," John argued as the conductor moved along the platform making his first call for passengers to board the train. "I cannot accept . . ."

"The men are innocents in this, John. Do not reject their gratitude out of some false sense of pride or hurt."

"All aboard!" the conductor shouted for a second time. All around them people were saying their farewells and heading for the entrances to the passenger cars.

"I am asking you to forgive me," George said. "I do not deserve it and I fully understand that I may well have ruined any chance you might have had to make things right with Lydia. I've never had someone in my life that I cared about so deeply, much less anyone who cared about me beyond what I could buy her. But then I realized that what you had with Lydia was the kind of love we all search for in this life. I just hope I didn't realize that too late."

John stared at his friend, a myriad of emotions throbbing in his veins. He felt anger and pity and regret and, oddly, hope. "Maybe it's not too late," he said as he picked up the tool chest and handed it up to the porter. "Goodbye, George," he called as he stood on the landing between cars and waved to his friend.

"Write to me," George shouted back as he ran alongside the train.

John laughed at the irony of George's words. Letters sent and returned. Letters sent and never answered. As far as John was concerned, letters were a poor way of saying what a man needed to say. This time he intended to talk to Liddy in person. This time there would be no more room for misunderstanding.

And if she rejects you?

"Then God's will be done," he murmured as he found his seat and the porter slid the heavy toolbox onto the floor next to him.

On the last day of classes the children were almost beside themselves with excitement. Lydia knew that for them this was just the same as other years when they would be off school for a few months and then return. Only Bettina and one or two of the good students seemed to realize that the school would be closing for good.

"Do you want me to help you pack up everything tomorrow?" Bettina asked at the end of the day as the children enjoyed the picnic that Lydia and some of the other women had prepared for them.

Lydia smiled and patted the girl's hand. "You are kind to offer but I would prefer to do it alone. There are many memories here and I need to savor them a bit before I close that door one last time."

"Do you think the elders will truly tear it down and sell the land?"

"That is for them to decide." She saw a tear trickle down Bettina's cheek. "Come now, this is not a day for sadness. Look at the children, how happy they are."

"I had so wanted to teach . . ."

"And if it be God's will, one day I have no doubt that you will lead a classroom full of children, Bettina. But it won't be in this building. You must accept that."

Bettina nodded and dabbed at her eyes with the hem of her apron. "What will you do now?"

Lydia's heart swelled with the excitement that had lodged there now for days, but she could hardly reveal her plan. "Oh, I will be fine, Bettina. You mustn't concern yourself about me." She stood up and clapped her hands loudly, her signal for the children to make a circle and join hands. "Let us all give thanks," she said once their chatter had settled into a low murmur of whispers and giggles.

And as every head bowed, Lydia silently prayed that she would have the courage to follow through on her plan to travel east and find John. And she dared to add a plea that God would soften John's heart and make him receptive to her gesture of reconciliation.

The following day she arrived at the school early. It was a hot, humid day and her first job was to open all of the windows and block open the double doors hoping to capture as much of a breeze as possible. Next she packed up her books in the cartons that Roger Hadwell had left for her and loaded them onto the cart waiting just outside the door. Luke would come by at the end of the day and move the cart up to her house where Bettina and her sweetheart, Caleb, would help unload it.

At first Lydia had protested the elders' decision that she should take everything that was usable from the building. "You have earned it, Lydia," Jeremiah told her. "By the time we can reopen a school the maps and such will surely be outdated. And, besides, if you plan to offer private lessons you need something with which to teach."

It was simply assumed by most people in town that once she had closed up the school Lydia would set up her house for private lessons, not that anyone in Celery Fields had the money for such a thing. It was further assumed that either she would continue living in her father's house alone or that more likely, in the absence of an income, she would move in with either Greta or Pleasant. The women in town had it all planned out for her and Lydia had been annoyed more than once over the past few weeks at their assumptions.

The truth was that as her plan had developed she had rediscovered the impetuous girl she had once been, the girl John had fallen in love with. More than once she had almost blurted out her intentions during a conversation with Greta. Her sister had developed a habit of looking at her with pity, and it seemed nothing Lydia said or did would convince Greta that she was not yet defeated when it came to John Amman.

She smiled at the thought of him. She did a lot of that these days, imagining his surprise when she simply appeared one day at the factory he owned with George Stevens. She had debated whether or not to write to George and let him know she was coming but, from what John had told her about his friend and business partner, she was not sure the man could be trusted to keep a secret.

No, better to simply go there. The train would arrive midday, so there was plenty of time for her to seek directions and make her way from the railway station to the factory. She refused to even consider the horrid thought that had awakened her one stormy night — the idea that John might have found someone else.

Once the books had been packed and she had loaded the rest of the supplies onto the cart, she began the process of cleaning the single room. How she had loved being here. It had been her refuge in those weeks and months that passed with no word from John after he left that first time. And in the years that followed it had given her a purpose for rising each day. The children needed her.

The shadows lengthened into late afternoon, and she climbed to the top of a ladder so that she could use the broom wrapped with a dust rag to sweep away any cobwebs that might be lingering in the corners. As she stretched to reach the high peak of the beamed ceiling she heard someone enter the foyer where normally the children would leave their coats. "I'll be right there," she called out, assuming it was Luke coming to deliver the loaded cart up to her house.

"I had not thought it would be necessary to do so thorough a cleaning if the school is to be closed." The voice was familiar but not that of her brother-in-law. She grasped the top of the ladder as the broom fell from her hands and clattered onto the floor.

Below her, John Amman was walking around the now-barren room, running his hand over the wide sill of a window and then standing before the chalkboard that she had washed earlier. He picked up a piece of chalk from the tray and lightly tossed it in the air, catching it each time as he continued to stare at the board.

"You came back," she said, and realized that her voice was no stronger than a whisper, so unsure was she that weariness had not created a mirage before her.

If this were a vision then it was one she savored. Unlike the time before, when she had discovered him kneeling next to the woodstove feeding kindling into the fire, he was not a bedraggled man. This time he was dressed plain but everything about him was pristine — from his white shirt tucked into black trousers supported by wide suspenders to his black straw wide-brimmed hat resting on top of his golden hair. Only his shoes showed any signs of the dust of travel.

He used the chalk to begin sketching on the board and, as Lydia descended the ladders and moved closer, she saw that he was drawing a floor plan for the building where they stood. "I have just washed that board," she said, reverting to her usual habit of reprimanding him whenever she was unsure of what to say to this man.

He shrugged and kept drawing. "I had thought perhaps to place a counter here with a desk there where we might take orders and manage the accounts. That way when customers first come through the door, they will be welcomed." He sketched in the counter and desk leaving most of the rest of the space open. "We will need to add a door here and a loading dock." He added these two features to the back wall of the plan.

"John, the building is not yours to change," she said softly.

He glanced at her, cocked one eyebrow and gave her half a smile before turning back to his sketch. "I think we'll keep the chalkboard. I like having it available to work out measurements and such."

"John, what . . ."

"And the building is mine to do with as I please — I just bought it."

"I . . . you . . . how . . ."

The smile tugged at his cheeks, fighting to break free as he continued his study of the sketch. "I paid the money the elders thought was fair and we shook hands and I am now here. Come to think of it, it is good that you have done such a thorough job of cleaning, although why you insisted on doing the job alone is beyond me. Nevertheless, it gives us a clean slate for planning the renovations."

"What renovations? What are you talking about, John Amman?" She placed her hands on her hips as she stepped around him so that she stood between him and the chalkboard.

"This building will house my furniture-building and carpentry business, Liddy. It's near enough to my uncle's hardware and the rest of the businesses in town to draw customers. Tourists, I suspect, will make up the bulk of the business. Those *Englischers* do have an appetite for our simple ways. Not that they would ever change their ways, but they enjoy pretending. We can build a business on that."

"What about the factory and the government contract and George Stevens?"

"George bought me out and that gave me the money to buy this place. It's taken me nearly a decade, Liddy, but it's all I ever wanted. And now . . ." His voice trailed off as he studied her as if truly seeing her for the first time. "The question is, Liddy, do you want what I want?"

He sounded almost wistful. She would have expected him to be angry or dismissive given the fact that he had returned her letter unopened. "I want you to find peace," she said, uncertain of what he was asking her. "If building furniture for outsiders is the path to that, then I am pleased for you."

He reached around her and replaced the chalk in the tray, then dusted his hands off by rubbing them together. "I did not know about your letter, Liddy," he said quietly. "Surely you know that I would have answered you."

"I knew nothing of the sort." She moved away from him, busying herself by wiping a thin film of dust from the desk she had used all the years of her teaching. "And if you did not know of it, if you did not refuse to accept it, then how do you know of it now?"

He told her about George's admission at the train station. "I don't think I have ever come so close to striking another man as I did when he told me what he had done."

She saw him clench and unclench his fingers.

"I do not think, John, that you and I should trust the habit of communicating by letter," she said softly. "After you left — this time — Pleasant told me some startling news. My father destroyed your letters to me and mine to you. He was afraid that I would follow you, that he would lose me as your family had lost you."

"They did not lose me," John protested. "I always intended to return. But we had no future, Liddy. How was I supposed to provide for you and our children?"

"You had work on your father's farm," she reminded him.

"I was never a farmer, Liddy."

"That was not for you to decide. Only God can guide the path we will take."

"And do you not see God's hand in all of this?" He waved his hand to encompass the bare schoolroom. "Do you know how I have prayed constantly for God to show me His way?"

"As have I," she replied defensively.

"And yet here we stand. Why would God keep finding ways to reunite us if we are not meant to be together?"

"You must not question or test or bend His plan to fit what you want, John."

John removed his hat and set it on the desk, then ran his fingers through his hair, drawing it back from his face — a face she now realized reflected hours without sleep and the weariness of all that they had been through separately and together. "Will you marry me or not, Lydia Goodloe?"

The words that she would have hoped to hear uttered sweetly and softly came out as if he had reached the end of his patience.

She bristled at his tone.

"I wouldn't wish to upset your plans," she replied and turned away.

John caught her forearm and held on. "Just yes or no, Liddy."

"How do I know that you won't decide that God has called you into the outside world yet again?"

"Because my purpose in leaving — both then and recently — was the same. To find a way that we might build our future together. I have secured that for us now."

"And what about George Stevens and his plans? How do I know that one fine day he won't show up at our door wanting you to join him in yet another business venture?"

John closed his eyes, his lips working in exasperation. "How many times do I have to explain myself, woman?"

She felt her heart soften at that. After all, because of her father's actions she was every bit as much at fault for the lost years they had endured as he was. "I suppose you will have to start over — go to Levi Harnischer and seek his approval and then call on my sisters and . . ."

Slowly John opened his eyes and looked at her. Doubt and hope flickered across his handsome features. "Do not tease me, Liddy," he pleaded. "Give me your answer."

She cupped her hand around his cheek. "*Yah,* I will marry you, John Amman."

With a victorious yelp of joy, John picked Lydia up and spun around the room with her. He stopped just as Luke Starns stepped inside the school.

"Here we go again," Luke muttered as he retraced his steps and started pushing the loaded cart up the path to Lydia's house.

Lydia giggled and rested her forehead against John's. He was still holding her so that her feet did not touch the floor. Somehow she doubted that even after years with this incredible man she would ever again feel as if she were standing on firm ground. The feeling gave her such a rush of joy that she threw back her head and laughed.

John grinned up at her. "Why are you laughing?"

"Because I have never been happier."

"Just wait," he said, and sealed the unspoken promise with his kiss.

John certainly understood what Liddy meant when she said she had never been happier. The pure joy that seemed to flow through his body in the place of normal breathing was remarkable. How could he ever have thought that going away and leaving her was the answer? He had been a fool and he saw now that because she never received or even know of his letters, and her own to him had also been destroyed, they had not had a chance to work things out. Oddly he understood her father's actions, his need to protect Liddy from hurt and perhaps harm if she had chosen to follow him into that world of outsiders. If she had been his daughter he knew he would have done the same.

But he had not allowed for such possibilities then. He had, instead, permitted his hurt and disappointment to dictate his actions. Making the money he needed to start a proper business had become less about getting the stake he needed and more about proving to Liddy that he could be a huge success. He had seen the way his partner lived and he had recalled the way that Levi Harnischer had once lived in such luxury when he owned the circus. Once he and Liddy had taken their bikes all the way to the place where Levi's former mansion was set on the shores of Sarasota Bay. The house had been huge and beautiful.

But he recalled now that Liddy's only comment as she stood next to him staring at the house with its stained-glass windows and tower that soared three whole stories into the blue sky was, "It must take days to clean that place properly."

Still, John could not get the image of such wealth out of his mind. He told himself that it wasn't some grand mansion he wanted for Liddy, but he did want what that mansion represented — security and a future. What he had refused to remember was the story well-known in Celery Fields of how truly miserable Levi had been in those days and how deeply happy he was now that he had turned his back on all of that and married Hannah. He had not sold his worldly goods for money. The story was that he had given everything away to his former employees. He had returned to the people of his youth empty-handed, needing nothing more than Hannah's love.

And now that Liddy had agreed to marry him John was determined to follow the example that Levi had set. He would take whatever time necessary to build a business that would support her and the children he hoped they would have. Twice he had left her, with his only thought being gathering enough money to set them up for the future. Twice she had taken him back. He would not risk testing her a third time.

Later that evening, when Levi Harnischer came to call on Lydia and her family — this time at Lydia's house, Pleasant seemed more than a little reluctant to give the proposed union her blessing. "He has left you twice already," she reminded Lydia as the two of them stood in the kitchen preparing glasses of sweet tea while Greta waited in the front room with Levi.

"But now we understand why," Lydia protested. "The letters that our *dat* destroyed without either my knowledge or John's and more recently the letter that George Stevens returned without even so much as showing it to John. You were the one who encouraged me to write to explain everything."

"This is not about letters, Lydia." She held up her hand to stop further protest. "Hear me out, for I have given this a great deal of thought. This is about the fact that John left in the first place. Against everything his family and the elders taught him, against the very foundation of the faith in which we were raised he went out into the world — and stayed there."

"*Yah,* but he had his reasons. He thought that he was doing what God was leading him to do."

Pleasant shook her head. "That might be forgivable for a lad of seventeen, but what I cannot ignore is the fact that John is a grown man now and still he left you again."

"He did not leave *me,*" Lydia argued, although deep inside she could find little fault with Pleasant's reasoning.

"Nor did he stay when you asked him — no, when you *pleaded* with him to do so," Pleasant said softly. She placed her hand on Lydia's and then picked up the tray and carried it into the front room. "My concern is for you. I do not wish to see you hurt."

Lydia stood for a long moment staring out the window. It was a moonless night and she could only just make out the silhouette of the livery and a single lamp set in the upstairs window where she knew John was watching for Levi's buggy to leave their house. After that he would wait until he saw Greta and Pleasant leave, as well, and then he would come to her. He would expect that nothing would have changed, that her sisters would have given their blessing, that Levi would be on his way to let the bishop know to announce their planned union the following Sunday at services.

But if Pleasant had doubts . . .

"Lydia Goodloe, I wonder if I might speak with you privately." Levi stood at the door of the kitchen. "I have asked your sisters to wait for us in the front room."

Lydia indicated a kitchen chair for him to

sit and pulled out one for herself. "Pleasant is not . . ."

Levi held up one hand. "Please hear me out."

Lydia nodded and folded her hands in her lap.

"You know, Lydia, there was a time when I was also drawn into the outside world, where I remained for years. I, too, thought that I would find happiness there. And, like John, I was wrong."

Lydia smiled. The tale of Levi and his wife, Hannah, was well-known in Celery Fields. Levi had run away from his family as a boy and eventually became the owner of one of the most successful circus companies in all the land. Years later Caleb, Hannah's son from her first marriage to Pleasant's brother, had also run away to join Levi's circus. Hannah had been beside herself and she, along with Pleasant and Lydia's father, had boarded the circus train with Levi to go bring the boy home again. Along the way Levi had fallen in love with Hannah. More to the point, he had realized that all the financial success and material wealth he might gain in that outside world could never satisfy him the way the plain and simple ways that Hannah brought back to his life did. Eventually he had renounced his former lifestyle, sold his company to his business partner and come to Celery Fields seeking Hannah.

"Your story is different from John's," Lydia reminded him. "You ran away as a boy. John had already joined the church when he left."

Levi chuckled. "Some would say that I had the longest *Rumspringa* ever."

Lydia could not help but smile. The very idea that a successful businessman could be seen as enjoying the time set aside for Amish teens to test their wings before joining the church and renouncing all things connected with the world of the *Englisch* was ridiculous. "Still, John made his choice."

Levi nodded. "That he did and it seems to me that in both cases his choice was his desire to do what he thought best for you, for the two of you to build a future."

"He tells himself that now, Levi, but the first time he left . . ."

"He has paid for that, Lydia. He has sought and been granted forgiveness."

"And this time?"

He took a swallow of his orangeade. "Times are changing, Lydia, and if we are to remain strong in our beliefs and practices we must face the fact that we will be tested many times over."

"So, you are agreeing with Pleasant? You believe that this is a test for me?"

"I believe that you must look into your heart and open yourself to God's will. If you truly are convinced that marrying John is the path God wants you to follow then take it. As for Pleasant . . ." He smiled as he stood up and carried his now-empty glass to the sink. "As I recall she made her own journey, one no easier than the one you face now. It seems to me that it has turned out well. Now come, your sisters are waiting."

Lydia followed Levi back to the front room, dimly lit by the single lamp on the table by the window. Both Greta and Pleasant looked up expectantly.

"Well?" Pleasant asked.

"Here is what I propose," Levi said, taking the chair that Lydia had placed by the window with the idea that in time it would be John's place. "We will spend some time now in silent prayer, each searching our hearts for God's guidance. We will not dwell on what we as individuals might think best but open our hearts to receive His will."

Greta nodded and sat upright with hands folded, prepared to bow her head in prayer.

"And then?" Pleasant pressed.

"Then we will all accept the will of God when Lydia Goodloe gives us her answer as to whether or not she wishes to marry John Amman."

Lydia met Pleasant's gaze and saw her half sister purse her lips as if about to protest. But then she nodded and took her seat.

"Let us pray," Levi said softly, and a silence settled over the room, interrupted only by the steady ticking of the clock on the fireplace mantel.

CHAPTER FIFTEEN

John kept a watch for Levi's buggy to leave but the time stretched from minutes to over an hour and he was still there. What could be taking so long? It wasn't as if Pleasant and Greta didn't know what was coming. Was Levi expressing doubts of his own, perhaps making Liddy think twice before agreeing to marry him? Pointing out that she would not wish to do something rash simply to fill the hole left in her life by the closing of the school?

These were all things that John had certainly considered. The idea that Liddy still wanted to marry him after all that he had put her through was sometimes a mystery to him. But in spite of everything she had accepted his proposal — again. Almost from the moment she had learned that he had bought the schoolhouse and its land and planned to open his business there she had enthusiastically joined him in planning the space, in planning the future they would share.

"We could perhaps add a porch to the front of the building," she had suggested. "A place to display your rocking chairs. The tourists will be drawn to those, I'm sure. Perhaps you could even design a smaller version for children."

"I can see that you are going to have me working round the clock," he had teased. Now as he stood on the loading dock of the hardware store after closing up for the day he wondered if perhaps Liddy was having doubts.

He could hardly blame her and yet when, on the night that he'd returned, they had sat on her porch talking until the sun streaked the eastern sky, he had thought she had accepted his reasoning for leaving a second time.

"I cannot deny that everything seems to have worked out," she had told him, and he had ignored the hesitancy in her voice.

But what if she had had second doubts through the day while he had been at work at the hardware store and she had been occupied sorting the materials that she had taken to her house from the school? What if instead of dwelling on the future, she had spent her time reliving the eight long years when she'd had no word from him?

The familiar creak of Liddy's front screen door brought his attention back to the moment. He saw Levi standing on the porch and Liddy was there with him. Their voices were muffled, but he did not need to hear their words to know that something was missing. At a time when their voices should have been filled with the joy of a happy event, there was no lightness in either their tone nor their posture. Liddy stood rigidly on the porch, her arms folded into her apron as she watched Levi walk to his buggy.

"You are certain?" he called before taking up the reins.

"Yah."

Levi drove away and Liddy continued to stand on the porch watching him go. After a moment Greta and Pleasant joined her. The three women talked in low tones and then Pleasant walked away and Greta hurried after her, catching up to her on the path that led into town. Greta seemed to be making some point, her hands fluttering around the way they did when she talked. Pleasant strode along looking neither left nor right and seeming to have nothing to say.

John turned his attention back to the porch and saw that Liddy had gone back inside the house. His heart thudded with apprehension. Something was not right here. Without bothering to take off his work apron, he jumped down from the loading dock. After only a few steps his pace quickened to a run. *Please,* he prayed as he covered the distance between the store and the house. *Not now.*

The front door was closed and the house was dark when he reached it, but he was undeterred. He hammered on the wood with his fist. "Liddy?"

The house was silent.

"I know you're in there," he said more softly, pressing his face close to the door. "Please, Liddy, open the door."

After what seemed like forever he saw the knob turn.

"The door is not locked," she said, her voice heavy with weariness as she opened the door and then walked away from him toward the kitchen.

He saw that a single lamp burned in the back of the house. Some of the dishes she had used for serving Levi and the others were soaking in the dishpan while the rest had been washed and set to drain on the side counter. He followed her to the kitchen and pulled out a chair at the table while she returned to her chore.

"What happened, Liddy?"

Her shoulders lifted and then collapsed in defeat. "It's Pleasant," she said softly, her hands pausing mid-motion as if she had momentarily forgotten what she was doing. "She has had a change of heart concerning . . . us."

"I am not marrying Pleasant," John replied. And when Lydia said nothing, he added, "The question is, am I to marry *you*?"

She let the dish slide into the soapy water as she turned to him, her eyes wide with surprise. "Oh, John, yes. We will marry. It's just that I had hoped for ours to be such a happy day."

He went to her and wrapped his arms around her. "And it will be — the happiest of days in our life together so far," he promised. "Pleasant will come around." He did not need to ask what Liddy's half sister's doubts might be. After all, Pleasant had known all along about the destroyed letters and never said a word. "You do not need her permission, Liddy."

"It is not her permission I was seeking. I want her blessing. She is family as much as Greta is, and you and I are not in a position to take such ties lightly, John Amman."

She turned back to her washing up.

John picked up a dish towel and began

drying the glasses and plates, setting each carefully on the open shelves that ran along one wall. He rummaged around in his brain for words that might offer comfort but decided against trying to make things better when he might make them worse.

"That was unkind of me," Liddy murmured as she placed the last glass on the counter and then wrung the soapy water from the dishrag before turning to wipe the table. "I am sorry, John."

"Perhaps if I spoke to Pleasant, gave her the chance to state her concerns, maybe I could put her doubts to rest," John said, choosing his words carefully.

Liddy took the towel from him and dried the last of the dishes. "No. Greta has tried that. I have tried that, as has Levi."

"Levi is on our side, then?"

"Oh, John, there are no sides in this. It is not some schoolyard game we are playing. Pleasant is concerned and that concern comes from her love for me. She wants only the best."

"But Levi . . ."

She told him then about the silent prayer that Levi had counseled and how when it was done Levi had asked each of the three sisters if she approved the union. He had begun with Greta, as the youngest, and her endorsement had been enthusiastic. Then he had asked Lydia.

"I love this man with all my heart," she told him she had said quietly. "I believe God would not have brought him back to Celery Fields not once but twice were it not His divine will that we should spend our lives together from this time forward."

Liddy bowed her head as she recalled the evening's events.

"And Pleasant?" John coaxed.

"She was silent for some time, opening her lips as if about to speak and then closing them again."

"And when she finally did speak?"

A shudder ran through Lydia's shoulders. "She said that she was afraid for me, for us. She said that only time would tell what the future might bring. She spoke of her marriage to Merle Obermeier, how unhappy they had made each other."

"You told me that Pleasant and Merle did not love each other," John reminded her. "That he married her for the sake of his children and she married him because . . ."

"She thought it would be her only opportunity. Her fear for me is that I am making this decision for that same reason."

"I have no children in need of a mother, Liddy," John said as he took her hands in his. "Not yet, anyway," he added with a hesitant grin.

"Oh, John, we will make a good life, won't we?" she asked, tightening her grip on his fingers. "I mean Pleasant is right that we cannot know what the future may bring, but I so firmly believe that our being together is God's will."

John let his smile broaden into a grin. "And everyone knows, when you have made up your mind as to God's purpose in your life, nothing and no one can change it."

Liddy met his smile with one of her own. "That's almost exactly what Pleasant said. So when Levi asked if she had intentions of disputing the union, she said that she did not. But John, she is wary."

"With good cause given her history — and ours. Time will put her fears to rest, Liddy. You will see. By this time next year she will understand that we have made the right decision."

He saw in her eyes that she wanted to believe him and he prayed that it would not take an entire year for him to prove to Pleasant that everything he had ever done, good decision or bad, had been for one reason: his love for Lydia Goodloe.

Pleasant made no further comment on the

proposed marriage, but over the next several days Lydia was well aware that her half sister could not put aside her doubts and concerns. So on Saturday she was thinking of going to the bakery to speak with Pleasant and to try to persuade her to be happy for them. She was pacing the kitchen floor putting together the points she thought most likely to sway Pleasant when she saw Hannah Harnischer coming up the back porch steps.

"Lydia?" she called as she shaded her eyes and peered in through the screened door.

"This is a surprise, Hannah," Lydia said as she welcomed the woman inside. Hannah had been married to Pleasant's brother — Lydia and Greta's half brother — and years after he died she had met and married Levi. The story of their romance had been quite the talk of the town at one time, as no doubt John and Lydia were the objects of much speculation these days. In spite of the fact that she and Hannah were not especially close, Lydia felt a kinship to this woman.

"I have some sweet tea, freshly made," Lydia offered.

"Just a glass of cold water."

Lydia got two glasses from the shelf and pumped water into the dry sink to fill them

315

while Hannah took a seat at the kitchen table. She accepted the water and nodded toward the door where Lydia's shopping basket sat. "Were you on your way out?"

"I was going to the bakery, but that can wait. I am glad you have come, Hannah."

Hannah's smile was kind but concerned. "Pleasant tells me that she has concerns about your proposed union with John Amman."

Over the years Hannah and Pleasant had become close friends, as were their husbands. The two couples and their children spent lots of time together. Lately Greta and her family often joined that circle of friends and family. They always invited Lydia to partake in the meal or outing they had planned, but she felt like the person she was — the spinster aunt tagging along.

"She has said that she will not protest the union," Lydia said quietly. "Has she changed her mind?"

Hannah set down her glass and held up her hands. "Oh, no, Lydia. She simply wants you to be happy and she knows the future is in God's hands."

"Then why . . ."

"Why have I come?" Hannah smiled. "I have come because we brides of Celery Fields must stand together. I have come

316

because I think you have doubts of your own, as each of us did in those days before we married. I have come, Lydia, to do whatever I can to assist you in making your wedding a happy time that has been far too long coming in your life."

Lydia's eyes welled with tears and she reached across the table and clasped Hannah's hand. "You are too kind," she whispered.

To her surprise Hannah laughed. "Not at all. Levi says that I am an incurable romantic who simply cannot stand it if two people I care deeply about are not completely 'over the moon' — that's what he calls it. An expression that lingers from his days as a circus man."

Lydia giggled and felt much of the worry and anxiety she'd carried since meeting with her sisters and Levi melt away. "Oh, Hannah, will it be like this always? This feeling that you could actually fly because your heart is so light and at the same time so full?"

"Heavens no. There will surely be days when you will wonder if you haven't made the biggest mistake of your life," Hannah assured her. "Unfortunately, men do not seem to lose any of their headstrong ways simply because they have married. It will take time and patience, but you have both in abundance so there is no reason to believe that things will not go well for you and John. That's what I told Pleasant."

"And did she believe you?"

This time Hannah's reassuring smile was slower to come. "She'll come around, Lydia." She stood and took her glass to the sink. "Now then, have you made your dress yet?"

"I am not much of a seamstress," Lydia admitted.

"Well, fortunately, Pleasant is. Now let's go shopping for the fabric she'll need and . . ."

"I cannot ask Pleasant to make a dress for my wedding."

Hannah handed Lydia the bonnet hanging on a peg by the back door. "Of course you can."

They stopped first at the bakery where Bettina was helping out now that the school was closed. "Bettina can manage," Hannah said, overriding Pleasant's protest that she could not be expected to simply close up shop for the day. "And it's not like you to exaggerate. Half an hour for choosing some fabric — no more. Now come along."

Lydia was fascinated to see Pleasant remove her apron and take down her bonnet without further protest. "I suppose you have decided on a color already," she grumbled as the three of them walked to Yoder's Dry Goods.

"I hadn't really given it much thought," Lydia admitted.

"Well, as this is the second time you have decided on marrying John Amman, what color had you planned on wearing before?"

"Blue," Lydia replied with a smile as she remembered how John had once compared the color of her eyes to a summer sky.

"Blue will do," Pleasant declared. "I had feared you might be inclined toward something . . . less proper."

Hannah smothered a giggle.

"What?" Pleasant snapped as they entered the shop.

"Forgive me, Pleasant, but I was just imagining our Lydia here all dressed in pink or bright purple for the occasion."

Pleasant frowned and then looked away and Lydia feared she was about to lose her temper with the two of them. But then she heard Pleasant's well-known laugh. It was a laugh that bubbled up from somewhere deep inside her on the rare occasions when something struck her as funny. And once it began, Lydia and most everyone else in town knew that it would take time for Pleasant to regain control. There was nothing to do but join in.

So as the three of them approached Hilda Yoder at the counter they were hard-pressed to get out the words they needed to tell the shopkeeper what they wanted. "Fabric," Pleasant finally managed. "Blue . . ."

"Or did we decide on the purple?" Hannah whispered mischievously, and the three of them broke into fresh gales of giggles like three schoolgirls out on a lark.

Hilda frowned and took down three bolts of fabric in shades of blue. "This just came in," she said, tapping the thickest of the bolts.

Pleasant pushed it aside in favor of the bolt with the least amount of yardage left. "This one if there is enough," she said, and began unfurling the fabric and measuring the yardage by extending it length by length from her nose to her outstretched fingertips. "That should so it," she announced. "And we will need fabric for a prayer *kapp,* as well."

"I already have . . ." Lydia began fingering one of the white ties of the covering she wore beneath her bonnet. But under Pleasant's gaze she abandoned any protest. "Yes, a *kapp* and an apron," she added, winning

320

Pleasant's approving glance for the first time in days.

It was tradition that the clothing a woman wore for her wedding was the clothing she would be buried in at the end of her life. It was not different in the sense of being made of special fabric or with lace trim. At her wedding Lydia would look little different from every other woman there. But she would always know that this dress and apron were unique and she would always know that she had chosen the fabric for the outfit in the company of her beloved half sister, a woman who had been more of a mother to her than any other.

Hilda prepared to wrap their selections in brown paper and tie the package with string. "Is there anything else? Thread? Needles?"

"That will do," Pleasant replied. "I will send Jeremiah in to pay."

"Oh, no," Lydia began, but Pleasant's look told her that this was as close as her half sister was going to come to openly giving her blessing to the marriage. She would buy the material for Lydia's dress as their father would surely have done had he been still living. *"Dienki."*

"I'll come by after I close up for the day to take your measure," Pleasant said, studying Lydia's tall thin frame as if truly seeing her for the first time. "You've lost weight."

It was Hannah who laughed. "Well, I shouldn't wonder. The poor woman has been through a great deal these last several weeks with the closing of the school and . . . everything else."

Pleasant's eyes softened as she studied Lydia for a long moment. "*Yah,* there has been too much of that. Hannah, why don't you come tonight, as well, and I will ask Greta. We have a wedding to plan and a dress to make." And with that she turned from them and went back to the bakery.

"So we do," Hannah said softly as she squeezed Lydia's hand and winked at her.

On the Monday morning after Bishop Troyer had announced the plan for John and Lydia to marry, John woke well before dawn. Today was the day he would begin renovations on the former schoolhouse. His plan was to spend at least three hours there in the mornings before going to work at the hardware and then return in the evenings to work for several more hours before retiring for the night. If he could keep to this schedule he was fairly certain he would be able to have his business ready to open the day after the wedding, which would take place in just ten days.

He dressed in the predawn darkness, drank a cup of black coffee and packed up some cold biscuits and sausage he'd prepared the night before. The air was already heavy with humidity as he made his way to the schoolhouse. He wondered if he would ever stop thinking of the building as a school. Liddy had suggested that he call his business something like The Old Schoolhouse Clock Shop. It had a nice ring to it and he did plan to make clocks his primary ware in these early days. He was still thinking about the name and envisioning the sign he would eventually mount above the double front doors when he reached the school and found the double doors standing wide-open. He heard the buzz of male voices inside the building.

"Hello?" he called out.

Luke Starns, Jeremiah Troyer and Levi Harnischer all turned to greet him. Then he saw Liddy pouring mugs of coffee and passing one to each man. "You're late, John Amman," she called out in the voice he was sure had struck fear into the hearts of her students.

But then she turned to him and her smile was as radiant as the morning sun just beginning to make its way through the tall thin windows. "Surprise."

"What's all this?" he asked as he moved into the room and took the coffee she handed him.

"This is what neighbors do for neighbors," Luke said. "I know you've spent some time out there in the world, John, but surely you have not forgotten all our ways."

From outside John heard others arriving and soon the building was filled with men talking and drinking their coffee as they studied the chalkboard and John's plans for converting the schoolhouse to his business. "Let's get started," his uncle announced. "If you three men will come with me we can start bringing over the lumber and supplies I've been storing at the hardware."

Roger Hadwell paused next to John. "It's a good plan you have, John. I think we can have you up and in business by the end of the week." John understood that this was his uncle's way of giving his blessing.

As the others went about their assigned tasks, John saw Liddy watching him from across the room. "You knew?" he asked as he moved next to her.

"I suspected," she corrected. "Greta's boys let something slip when I was there the other day." She picked up the tray of used coffee mugs. "I'll just wash these and bring them back with a fresh pot of coffee. Cover those cinnamon rolls that Pleasant sent over so the flies don't get to them," she instructed, nodding toward a tea towel draped over a sawhorse.

"Liddy?"

She turned and smiled and he knew that for the rest of his life he would ask for nothing more than the blessing of awaking every day to this face, these lovely eyes bathing him with their trust and their devotion. "I love you."

Her hands shook slightly, rattling the cups on the tray, but she met his gaze without hesitation. "I know," she assured him. "I think I have always known. That's why I waited."

EPILOGUE

Five years later . . .

"Liddy!"

Lydia wiped her hands on a towel and walked out to the back porch. She had noticed early in their marriage that whenever John called out for her to come to him there was an urgency in his voice. Early on she had gone running to him every time, especially after the children started coming. Her heart would pound within her chest as she imagined all sorts of mishaps. Their son, Joshua, perhaps bleeding from some cut. Their daughter, Rose, almost certainly nursing some bruises from a fall. But then she would see them and John would look at her, smiling as he pointed to the blossom of an orchid that he and the children had planted for her in a tree, or at a butterfly that had come to rest on Rose's finger.

Now she rested one hand on the mound of her pregnancy as she shaded her eyes against the bright noonday sun with the other. In the yard outside their barn she saw Joshua sitting astride their horse, his short, chubby legs dangling to either side as his laughter rang out across the yard. John was holding the reins as he led the animal in a large circle.

"My turn," Rose shouted. "My turn now," she demanded sounding very much like her aunt Greta had at that age.

"Be careful," Lydia shouted as she watched John lift Rose onto the huge animal so that she was sitting in front of her brother.

Joshua wrapped his arms around Rose as she shrieked her delight. "Faster, *Daadi.*"

Her cries brought John's aunt and uncle out onto the loading dock of the hardware store and Lydia saw Gert press her fist to her mouth in alarm. "John Amman, those children are far too young . . ." she shouted.

"Never too young, Tante Gert," John called back, but Lydia saw him glance her way and knew that if she told him to stop, he would.

"Come wash up," she said instead as she turned to go back inside. But suddenly she was seized by a familiar pain in her back and she reached for the door to steady herself until it passed.

"Liddy!" John's voice seemed to come from far way but this time there could be no doubt of the edge of panic.

Don't leave the children astride that horse, she mentally instructed even as she gritted her teeth and willed the pain to subside. "I'm all right," she managed to call out to him.

"You are not all right," he fumed, reaching her side and leading her to one of the rocking chairs he'd built for them. "I'm going for the doctor."

"You will do no such thing, John Amman. Now, get those children down off that horse and . . ."

"Luke is tending to them. Said something about taking them for ice cream."

"It's too close to suppertime and . . ." She looked up at him with surprise as she felt her water break.

Please, no, she prayed. She was not due for weeks.

Dr. Benson had warned them that having another baby would be dangerous. Both Joshua and Rose had been difficult births for Lydia. "You are thirty-five years old, Lydia Amman," Dr. Benson had warned.

"Many women in our community have children late in life," she had replied. "If it be God's will that John and I should be blessed with more . . ."

Dr. Benson had sighed heavily. "Just take time to heal, all right?"

Lydia had not wanted to explain to him that whether she would have another child or not — and when — was in God's hands. But it did seem as if God had heeded the doctor's warning, because it had been three years before Lydia had become pregnant again. By that time she had almost given up and John had assured her that two healthy children were blessing enough. Still, she had not missed the look of pure joy he had given her when she had announced that he might want to get started on a set of bunk beds for either Joshua or Rose's small bedrooms.

"Of course," she had mused, "if the twins are one of each . . ."

"Twins?" he had exclaimed hardly able to believe what he was hearing.

"So, Dr. Benson seems to believe."

The one thing that John had insisted on from her first pregnancy was that the doctor should manage everything. "I will not have Hilda Yoder catching our babies," he declared. "Something could go wrong and I will take no chances on your health or the child's."

To Lydia's surprise Hilda had been in complete agreement with John's decree.

"Times are changing, Lydia," she had said when Lydia tried to explain John's wishes without hurting the older woman's feelings. "And you are not so young anymore yourself. John is being very wise."

"Maybe you should call Dr. Benson . . ." Lydia said to John.

He turned back toward the hardware store and shouted, "Call for the doctor, Tante Gert. The twins are coming."

It thrilled Lydia to hear the tone of pure unadulterated joy with which he delivered this news. "Well, you don't have to tell the entire town," she teased, and started to rise from the chair.

"Just sit there," he ordered as he knelt next to her. He dipped the towel she'd wiped her hands with into the bucket of water they kept on the back porch for washing up and wiped her forehead. "Where is that doctor?" he muttered after no more than five minutes had passed.

"He'll be here," Lydia assured him and took hold of his hand, forcing his attention to her face. "John, I know it's before my time, but I am sure that God knows best. Pray with me until the doctor arrives." It warmed her heart knowing how John had settled into the strength of their faith following their marriage. Together they had built a home and were raising a family and they were doing both with the support and bond that they had found together in their congregation and community.

He folded the towel and laid it across her forehead and then took both of her hands in his and bowed his head.

John had prayed often in his life. Early on his prayers had been selfish pleas for something he wanted or felt he needed. In those earlier years when he had left Celery Fields he had prayed for God to make Liddy come to her senses and understand that everything he was doing was for her, for them. But since marrying Liddy his prayers had all focused on the well-being of Liddy and the children.

And he believed with all his heart that God had heard his prayers. Over the past five years his business had blossomed and enough new families had moved to the area that the elders had announced plans to build and open a new school. Bettina would be the teacher, since Liddy's time was taken up with their children and managing their household as well as taking orders and keeping the books for his business. Their son, Joshua, would be in the first class to occupy the new building, one that John had worked side by side with their neighbors to build.

So God had blessed them many times over, so much so that when Liddy warned him that hard times were bound to come again, he had assured her that they could weather any storm as long as they were together. But hard times came in many disguises, he realized as he held on to Liddy's hands. It was too soon for the babies to come and the doctor had warned them both of the danger of another pregnancy at her age.

Please, God, we need her — the children and I. Please let the twins be all right and protect Liddy.

He opened his eyes, first checking on Liddy, who sat with her eyes closed and the sweetest smile on her face. Then he turned his gaze toward the lane that passed their house, willing the sound of the doctor's automobile even as he saw his aunt crossing the space between the hardware store and their house at a run. "He's coming," she called out. "He's on his way."

In the moment John realized that what had seemed like hours had in fact only been a matter of minutes since he'd first seen Liddy grab for the door frame and grimace in pain. "Her water . . ." he said when Gert stepped onto the porch and knelt beside him.

"It's only a little," Lydia told Gert.

But Gert — having never had children of her own — tended toward hysteria in times like this. "Roger Amman!" she shouted. "Leave the store and come now."

In seconds John saw his uncle running toward the house.

"Let's get her inside out of this hot sun," Gert ordered as she held open the screen door and waited for the two men to help Liddy inside.

"I can walk on my own," Lydia protested.

By the time they reached the bedroom Gert had already prepared the bed for the birthing by lining the mattress with newspapers and padding. "Lay her down here."

"Truly, you are all getting ahead of yourselves," Lydia fumed.

The sound of a car outside had them turning toward the open window. "That'll be the doctor," Roger muttered, and headed back through the house to meet him.

As the doctor came through the front door, Pleasant and Greta came through the back and suddenly the bedroom that John had always thought spacious was so filled with people that he had no choice but to stand in the doorway trying to see his wife.

"Liddy, I'm here," he said, and the others turned to him.

"Come," Pleasant urged, making a place for him as they crowded around the bed. "She needs your strength, John Amman. She needs to know you are here with her."

"I would never leave her," John replied, annoyed at the implication that there was cause for Liddy to doubt his devotion.

Pleasant placed her hand gently on his forearm, forcing him to look at her. She smiled. "I know that, John. There was a time when I doubted that you. . . ." She sniffed loudly and pursed her lips. "I was wrong."

It was as close as Pleasant Troyer would ever come to an outright apology and John understood that. He patted her hand and then turned his attention back to his wife.

"This is ridiculous," she said, ignoring her family and addressing the doctor.

"Tell me about the pain," he said. "When did it begin?"

"Twenty minutes ago and there's been nothing since," she reported. "Now . . ." She started to raise herself up from the bed, but Dr. Benson gently pushed her back.

"Lie still please. We have work to do here and then you can go do whatever you seem to be in such a worry to take care of."

John was not at all sure that he liked the

doctor's brusque tone, but it seemed to work. Liddy fell back onto the pillows and almost immediately she grimaced and half sat up as a fresh pain grabbed her. John glanced at the doctor.

"Now Herr Amman, you know well enough how this goes. She's going to have some pain. You can either hold her hand and offer her comfort or wait out there," he told John as he indicated the hallway outside the bedroom.

"I will not leave her," John said. "Tell me what is needed and let me help."

Dr. Benson glanced at Pleasant, who nodded. "Very well, position yourself behind her there so that she is partially sitting up and leaning against you. If you start to feel queasy you will need to fight against that. The only person whose comfort matters right now is your wife's and once we begin you cannot leave her. Understood?"

"This is not my first time doing this," John grumbled as he positioned himself at the head of the bed and pulled Lydia against him. "I'm not going anywhere," he added in a tone that defied anyone to dispute him. Then he leaned close to Liddy's ear and repeated his promise. "Ever again." He smoothed back her hair after Greta took away her prayer covering and handed him a cloth that she had dipped in cold water. Recalling the births of their two older children, he prepared himself for a long siege of Liddy fighting gripping pain followed by long periods of her collapsed in exhaustion against him. It had taken nearly twelve hours to bring Joshua into this world and seven for Rose.

He tightened his embrace on Lydia as she cried out and the doctor ordered her to push. In what seemed only a matter of a few seconds the doctor handed Pleasant a bundle that John realized was their child.

"A boy," Pleasant told him, her face wreathed in smiles as the doctor cut the cord and she handed the child to Greta for washing.

"And here comes the other one," Dr. Benson announced.

The second child was a girl and once freed of the umbilical cord that had wrapped itself around her neck, she let the world know with her cries that she had fought her way into a world that she clearly intended to take by storm. Once again Pleasant handed the child to Greta and turned back to assist the doctor.

Lydia could not recall a time when she had felt quite so filled with joy — or quite so exhausted. She closed her eyes.

"Liddy," John whispered.

"She'll need her rest," Lydia heard the doctor say as he completed his work.

"I'll be fine," Lydia insisted, forcing her eyes open and holding out her arms to receive her babies.

Dr. Benson handed Pleasant a vial of pills and gave her instructions for administering them. "I'll stop by later tonight," he said.

Lydia barely heard him as she and John cradled the newest members of their family. "They're so very small," John murmured.

"They'll be bigger soon enough," Pleasant advised as she and Greta continued to clear away the refuse from the birthing.

"Do you . . . did you and Lydia choose names?" Greta asked as she bent down for a closer look at the red-faced infants.

"Noah and Ruth," Lydia and John said in unison, and then they both laughed.

Pleasant laid out a fresh nightgown for Lydia, her take-charge demeanor reminding them all that the world did not stop even for the birthing of twins. "Go get yourself cleaned up and have something to eat, John," she ordered. "Gert has made some supper for you. Greta and I will take care of things here while you and Luke tend to the chores and keep Joshua and Rose occupied."

"You won't leave her," John cautioned.

"Not for an instant," Pleasant promised.

"John Amman, there is work to be done and children to be fed," Lydia instructed. "Now go."

Gently John handed baby Noah to Greta and eased himself from behind Liddy. He walked to the door and then turned around and walked back to her, grinning. "You'd think at a time like this you might be the one to take orders not give them," he teased as he kissed her temple.

Lydia could not seem to open her eyes although she tried to do so. She could hear the low murmur of John's voice from somewhere very close to her and yet he seemed so very far away.

She felt a damp breeze pass over her and realized that somewhere a window was open. She could smell lemons mingling with the telltale scent of baby oil.

The babies!

She was very tired and so much wanted to sink back into the sleep that called to her. But her children needed her — her four precious children. John was hopeless when it came to managing the children. They would be spoiled rotten in no time if he were left to tend to them. Look how he had spoiled Joshua and Rose already. The man could refuse them nothing and those children knew it. She felt a smile play over her parched lips. On the other hand they were good children, caring of each other and their many cousins and friends. So what if John gave in to their pleas for one more story at bedtime or one more slice of cake because they had indeed finished eating all their vegetables?

She forced her eyes open and waited for the hazy image of him to clear. He was sitting in the rocking chair he'd clearly brought inside from the porch. "Well, hello there. It's about time you came back to us. Were you planning to sleep through the first year of our babies' lives?"

"I have always been right here and you know it." She was upset with herself for having left all the work to others. "You are the one who left, not once but twice."

He smiled and sat on the bed next to her. "Are you never going to let that go, Lydia Amman?"

"Probably not," she said as she reached up and cupped his cheek. "Otherwise, you might just forget how miserable you were without me."

"And were you not just as miserable without me?"

She stroked his face, smoothed back his hair and then placed her fingertips against his lips. "I thought that I might die from that misery," she said.

"Then it is good that God saw fit to lead us back to each other every time," John murmured as he leaned in to kiss her.

"The babies? I mean it was early and . . ."

"Noah and Ruth are fine, Liddy. Doc Benson was here while you were sleeping and has pronounced them hale and hearty."

"Bring them to me."

"You're sure you don't need more rest?"

"Oh, John, what I need is my family — you and the children."

"All right, but if you tire . . . I'm going," he promised when she presented him with the expression she had perfected in all her years of teaching to get her students to follow her instructions.

He was gone only a minute and then back, a baby cradled in each powerful arm and their two older children peeking at her shyly from next to him. Behind him Pleasant and Greta peered in, their faces wreathed in smiles.

Before she could say a word, all of them were crowded around the bed. John handed her a bundle. "Your son Noah," he said, even as the bundle still in his arms started to writhe and fuss. "And this," he said, pulling back the covers from the second baby's face, "is your daughter Ruth, and I fear that she is going to be very much like her mother."

"God willing," Lydia murmured as she held out her free arm to receive her daughter. They were perfect, she saw as she examined them. And as Joshua and Rose scrambled onto the bed and took up places on either side of her, Lydia met John's gaze.

He looked a good deal like the man she had found kneeling next to the stove at the schoolhouse that morning. His clothing was just as rumpled and his hair was as tousled as it had been that day. But this time his unkempt appearance was not because he had been away from her for eight long years. It was because he had been — and with God's blessing would be right there at her side — for years to come.

Dear Reader,

And so we come to the fourth and final "bride" in our Amish Brides of Celery Fields series. Lydia has played a part in most of the other three stories so it was time for her to have her happy ending. She almost misses it — not once but twice! I hope you love Lydia's story as much as I loved helping her find her way to true love. And I hope if you haven't already read them, you will return to the fictional Florida village of Celery Fields to read the stories of Hannah (*HANNAH'S JOURNEY,*) Pleasant (*FAMILY BLESSINGS*) and Greta (*A GROOM FOR GRETA.*)

It has been my joy to create this wonderful family of women and this inspiring community of Celery Fields. Please stop by my website at www.booksbyanna.com or write me the old-fashioned way at P.O. Box 161, Thiensville, WI 53092 to let me know which "bride's story" was your favorite!

All best wishes to you!

Anna Schmidt

QUESTIONS FOR DISCUSSION

1. God's will be done is a recurrent theme throughout this story. Name some examples.

2. In what ways was Lydia's life changed by John's leaving when they were both younger?

3. In what ways might it have been different and how would that have affected his return?

4. How does John's reason for leaving the second time differ from his going the first time?

5. Both Lydia and John are people of strong faith, but how do their beliefs differ?

6. How did John attempt to prove his love

for Lydia throughout the story?

7. How did Lydia learn to trust in John's love for her?

8. Have you been in any relationship (romantic, friendship, etc.) where trust or the lack of it became an issue? If so, how did you resolve that?

9. How did John really feel about "outsiders"?

10. The Amish faith is rooted in forgiveness. Give examples of ways that were illustrated throughout the story among the people of Celery Fields.

11. What do you think it means to truly forgive another person?

12. Talk about a time when you had to forgive or were forgiven.

ABOUT THE AUTHOR

Anna Schmidt is an award-winning author of more than twenty-five works of historical and contemporary fiction. She is a two-time finalist for a coveted RITA® Award from Romance Writers of America, as well as a four-time finalist for an *RT Book Reviews* Reviewer's Choice Award. Her most recent *RT Book Reviews* Reviewer's Choice nomination was for her 2008 Love Inspired Historical novel, *Seaside Cinderella,* which is the first of a series of four historical novels set on the romantic island of Nantucket. Critics have called Anna "a natural writer, spinning tales reminiscent of old favorites like *Miracle on 34th Street.*" Her characters have been called "realistic" and "endearing" and one reviewer raved, "I love Anna Schmidt's style of writing!"

The employees of Thorndike Press hope you have enjoyed this Large Print book. All our Thorndike, Wheeler, and Kennebec Large Print titles are designed for easy reading, and all our books are made to last. Other Thorndike Press Large Print books are available at your library, through selected bookstores, or directly from us.

For information about titles, please call:
  (800) 223-1244

or visit our Web site at:
  http://gale.cengage.com/thorndike

To share your comments, please write:
  Publisher
  Thorndike Press
  10 Water St., Suite 310
  Waterville, ME 04901